Bluegrass

Blush

By Carolyn Bond

To Jan!
Enjoy
Carolyn Bond

ISBN-13: 978-1539075394
Printed by Createspace Independent Publishing.

Carolyn Bond would love to hear from you if you enjoyed this book. Follow her web page at www.carolynbondwriter.com or email her at carolynbondwriter@yahoo.com.

Acknowledgements

I would like to thank my husband and children for the time away from them that it took to write this. I appreciate you supporting my writing so very much. It means the world to me.

I thank my very good friend of so many years, Kari Williams, Attorney At Law, who owns an elder law firm in Frankfort, Kentucky and let me ask her all sorts of crazy questions.

Thank you to my good friend and writer, Joan Graves, who cheers me on like I'm a rock star. Every writer needs a friend like you. You are awesome. Many thanks to Nancy Griffin for her editorial services. Veronica Brown, Dawn Chapman, and Brandie Pagel, your input and encouragement are invaluable to me. I would like to thank the staff and guides at Mammoth Cave National Park for upholding a tradition of discovery and love of nature.

And last, but certainly not least, to the readers who enjoy my work. You keep me always day dreaming for new ways to touch your heart.

Table of Contents

Chapter One

Events happen that change us. One turning of fate changes the rest of our life. Maybe we can see it coming and we brace ourselves. Sometimes it happens so fast, we just get pulled into another timeline like the current of an undertow.

Everleigh settled into the cab clutching her purse with one hand and tugging her polyester knit top down to smooth it over her abdomen with the other hand. The vinyl seat's polished sheen from the thousands of passengers reflected the dull gray light of the rainy day. Without conscious thought, she tucked her shoulder-length, straight, dishwater brown hair behind her right ear and began to fidget with her right earlobe. Leaving Bluegrass airport, she peered out the rain-speckled window and looked forward to a hot bath at the inn in Versailles. Her legs ached from being crammed into the middle seat on the two-hour flight from Charleston.

Gentle hills of green grass and black board fences wavered through the blotches of water on the glass. She had never been to the Bluegrass. She'd been to a conference in Louisville once, but this was another world. Anticipation knotted her stomach and a small smile curled her lips as she reveled in the one great part of her job: she got to travel often. She liked getting away to places where no one knew her. As a business consultant for disability law compliance, she was highly sought after. That almost made up for the pain of not being highly sought after as a woman. At 35, her plans for marriage and a family were passing her by.

She wondered why she ended up in this body and other people got other bodies. It seemed so random. She had never felt especially attached to her body. She mostly felt like just a soul stuck in that particular skin peeking out through eyes that served as windows like windows of this taxi. Her soul was no more defined by her body than her Honda Civic at home defined her. She wished people could know the real her inside her skin and not judge her by the body that carried her soul around. She never could get past people's perception of her as a frumpy wallflower. That's what she saw when she looked in the mirror.

She sighed quietly and pushed back the pain in her heart. The driver's eyes darted into the rear-view mirror and back to the road.

"The Versailles Inn is a nice place. You gonna get to sightsee much?"

Focusing her thoughts to the question, "Oh, no. Probably not. I'm just here on business."

Eyes in the mirror glanced at her again, pausing. And then, "That's a shame. There's nowhere like the Bluegrass in the world."

"I'm sure there isn't." She smiled politely and turned back to the rain-streaked window trying to make out the landscape.

He's just making conversation. I don't want him to think I'm being forward.

Her gut tensed as she contemplated what she would do if he wanted to go out or something.

He is nice looking, but surely he isn't interested in me. Oh, Lord. Just try to look out the window and hopefully he won't say anything else.

The rest of the short ride from the airport to Versailles was quiet. She tried to look like she was thinking of something and hopefully he wouldn't say anything to her again. The cab turned down a short street off Main Street and pulled up to a charming white inn with a large porch. The cabbie jumped out, opened her door and carried her bag up the walk through the drizzling rain. As he approached, a middle-aged man with a beard and a welcoming smile opened the door.

Everleigh opened her purse and dug out the fare and a generous tip before gathering herself to get out. She ducked her head and trotted up the sidewalk to the porch upsetting puddles as she went.

"Good evening, madam! Welcome to the Versailles Inn."

"Thank you," she smiled her friendliest smile as she stepped across the threshold.

"Is there anything else I can do for you, ma'am?" said the cabbie.

"Oh," she turned to him and blushed slightly giving away her attraction, "um, no. Here is the fare. Thank you very much." She darted her eyes down to his hand to give him the money and then glanced back at him quickly before looking down again.

"Anytime. Call us again if you'd like to tour some sights. Ask for Jim and I'll be right over." Everleigh almost let herself think he winked at her, but surely not. She was a middle-aged dowdy overweight woman. She must be fooling herself. She couldn't imagine what any man would see in her.

"Th-Thank you, Jim." She smiled and turned to the inn keeper. "Do I need to register?"

Jim nodded his head in their direction and headed out the door.

"Yes, madam, right over here at the desk."

The inn keeper checked her in and gave her a room key. He picked up her bag and told her to follow him up to her room. The small inn only had ten rooms upstairs over a restaurant and lounge. The chatter of conversation and clinking of glasses and silverware carried up the stately wood staircase.

"If you need anything, Ms. Anderson, just press the intercom right here on the wall." He pointed to a metal plate with holes across it and a black button. Then turned and went into the hallway.

"Thank you very much." She smiled appreciatively and gently closed the door behind her.

***

The light in her room gave a peaceful soft glow to the bed covered in a white spread. An antique walnut dresser with a gracefully curving mirror above it perfectly matched the timeless atmosphere of the room. Red linen curtains beckoned her to the window where a white sheer curtain let her peek out at the world like a ghost hiding from the light of day. She watched a couple walk up the side walk and disappear beneath her. The hearty aroma of southern cooking wafted under her door and she remembered reading the Inn was a popular place for locals to dine. Her legs ached and she needed a cleansing soak in a warm tub.

Through a sturdy wood door beside the bed, she spotted a porcelain sink. She wondered if the feeling of the room was extended to the restroom, too, and made her way to the door. Pushing it open, she turned up a satisfied smile as she saw the antique claw foot tub with a metal shower ring above and a white cotton curtain pulled around it. She sat on the edge and felt the cold metal through her slacks as she leaned to turn the white four-lobed knob for hot water. A gentle gush poured out and spilled into the tub. A hot bath was just what she needed to wash away the grimy feel of traveling and let her mind rest from being so close to other people cramped in an airplane. Her anxiety was creeping up in her chest like a caged animal ready to bust loose. She set the rubber stopper in the drain and left to get her toiletries out of her bag.

Her mind drifted to fantasies of times past when at her age, a woman would be the matron of a bustling home full of nearly grown children and content to be the head of her domain. Such different times from now. Now she worked long hours all around the country. She spent very little time in her tiny apartment that overlooked Charleston harbor.

She pulled her top over her head and slipped off her slacks, and undergarments, leaving them draped over the bed. Catching a glimpse of herself naked in the dresser mirror, she grimaced and looked away. Her overweight figure was a source of loathing and the result of consoling herself with food to compensate for her loneliness. It was a vicious cycle.

She opened her toiletry bag and pawed around for the little round bar of lavender soap her mother had given her for her birthday. She loved sweet smelling soaps in pretty paper wrappers. Her mother would search high and low to find imported soaps to surprise her. This one came from a town in the France. A woman that owned a shop had given it to her mom as a gift. She held it to her nose and breathed in the scent. A delicate sweet scent of an ancient flowered garden stopped all thoughts in her head. It tickled her nose with the crisp clean scent of lavender. Closing her eyes, she could get lost in it.

In the bathroom, she slipped into the water as vapors of steam curled around her legs. She lowered herself down holding on to the solid sides of the tub and the warm water engulfed her body. She reclined back until her shoulders touched the cold metal of the tub. Wincing at the chill, she slid down a little further until the water crested her collar bones. Steam floated like fog giving the small room a veiled feel where she felt safe to relax. She reached out to a small stand next to the tub and picked up the soap still in the wrapper. She carefully opened the paper and laid it back on the stand. Then she reached for a soft white washcloth and laid it around the soap.

Submerging the washcloth and soap, she watched as tiny bubbles escaped and a curling wisp of cream soap floated into the water. She rubbed the washcloth and soap together and the hypnotizing scent of the soap was caught up in the steam rising from the water. She lathered up the washcloth until a frothy soft foam covered it and placed the soap onto the paper on the stand. Taking her time to enjoy the moment, she slowly ran the washcloth down her right arm leaving a trail of glistening warm skin. She did the same on the other arm and then washed behind her neck. The lavender scent was intoxicatingly strong. She wasn't sure she had ever used a soap that had such a concentrated infusion. She would have to tell her mom to get more from wherever she found it.

She pulled the washcloth around the back of her neck and laid her head back against the high end of the tub, closing her eyes. After a time, she blinked open her eyes, unsure if she might have dozed off for a while. Feeling completely relaxed and like a new person, she stood up to wash the rest of her body in the now, tepid water.

As she grasped the sides, she realized the tub was now just a short metal basin which she recalled from a trip to a museum would have been a hip basin. She noticed she felt stronger, or was it lighter, as she pulled herself up. She looked down at her legs and gasped. Her legs were thin and toned. She clutched her belly and felt a tiny waist. Smoothing her hands over her hips, she stifled a shriek. Stretching and twisting to see herself, she felt her alien body. It made no sense. Looking backward down the length of pale white sculpted thigh and calf, her mouth dropped open as she rotated her foot on a tiny ankle. She surely had to be 50 pounds lighter.

She was no longer in the bathroom of her room. There was no door. It was an alcove behind a large screen. Panic seized her.

Bursting from the basin, she sloshed water up the sides and all over the floor to get over to the mirror which now was over a small bureau. Standing on an oil cloth, the woman that faced her had a look of utter shock. Her hands flew up to her delicate ivory cheeks. Long flaxen blond hair was pulled up into a massive bun on the top of her head with moist tendrils caressing her neck. Her full bosom made her blush deep red, she instinctively covered herself with her arm.

What on earth?

She turned backwards and twisted around to see the shapely back end of a woman who couldn't be over 20 years old.

"That is some soap!" she breathed.

Chapter Two

Everleigh stumbled backwards and caught herself, caught the body of this stranger, on the edge of a chair next to an oval little tub and sat to think. The tub looked like an old fashioned clothes washing tub with handles. On the little bureau sat a wash basin and pitcher.

How could this be?

She stretched out her arm and turned it over.

Am I dreaming?

She could feel the cold of the tub against her leg. She could smell the aroma of dinner downstairs. The steam of the bath water clung to her face. If this was a dream, it was awfully realistic, but it was impossible.

What happened to her body? Whose body is this? Where am I?

Without any notion of what was happening or how long it would last, she looked for a towel and saw only a piece of linen that was on the bureau and dried off and wrapped it around her, tucking in the corner between her breasts. She sucked in a gleeful breath at the site of actually covering all of her when it was wrapped around her. For a good many years, only a beach towel came close to wrapping all the way around her and even then she had to hold the bottom corner closed.

"I hope this woman isn't in my body right now or she'll freak out," she chuckled out loud.

Everleigh reached up and felt her hair for pins. She found three pins strategically tucked into the bun.

"How in the world did she get all this hair to stay up with just three pins?"

Undoing them, waist-length silky waves fell around her. Everleigh gasped. Her arms fell to her sides and she stared into the mirror. If ever she had imagined beauty in the form of a woman, it was the person she saw. The person in the reflection who moved when she did. Turned when she did. This wasn't just ordinary; this body that now wrapped around her soul was perfection. She puckered her lips into a pout and stared. Intrigued by sultry pink lips, she furrowed her brow and even that expression could make a man clamor to please her to bring that delicate smile back.

She raised her arms and looked at her proportions of bust, waist and hips on the petite frame that looked barely over five feet and she was scandalously gorgeous. She wrapped her hands around her waist and her fingers touched, yet her bosom blossomed into perfect firm orbs that would smother a babe.

Eager to try out this body in the lounge, she set her mind to quickly dressing and seeing how much attention she could get hiding under this skin. All her fears of rejection evaporated with the bath water on her damp hips. She dropped the linen and pulled the door open. Two steps later she stopped dead in her tracks. The clothes on the bed were not the slacks and stretchy shirt she'd worn earlier. Instead, a high necked silk gown, wool stockings, chemise, corset and corset cover and some odd-looking wire contraption with straps were draped across the white bedspread.

Caught dumbstruck, she glanced around the

room to see what else was different. She saw a steamer trunk in the corner near two pair of shoes. One pair of black granny boots and a pair of satin slippers. Scanning the rest of the room she noted the deep green velvet curtains.

Weren't those red before?

She tiptoed to the window and, hiding behind a panel of velvet, peeked outside through the gap in the sheers. Her breath caught in her throat as she watched a stage coach pulled by two horses trot down the cobblestoned Main Street with a driver holding the reins. A driver who looked like he fell out of a western movie. A man and woman walked up the sidewalk toward the inn. The woman scanned the front of the inn and her eyes fell on Everleigh's window. Everleigh jerked back behind the green curtain. Something wasn't right. How had the town changed like that? Why were those people dressed like they were in an old time photo? She glanced at the clothes on the bed again.

Her head started to swim and she felt dizzy. The edges of the room started to go black as she moved hand over hand to sit on the bed. She clasped her hands to her heart and felt her chest not moving.

Breathe, Everleigh. Breathe!

She inhaled deeply and felt better immediately. In an effort to keep from fainting, she began panting. She wasn't even sure how to put on these clothes. She picked up the corset and remembered a movie with a servant cinching strings on the back of a corset while the woman gasped for air. She grimaced and dropped the corset. Picking up the chemise, she was surprised to feel the satiny finish of the cotton material.

"Wow. This woman must have been rich!"

She pulled the delicate shirt-like lingerie over her head and shifted her shoulders to feel the luxurious softness on her back. An item that resembled a pair of shorts with a draw string lay under where the chemise was. She picked them up and stepped into them, tying the string to hold them on. She assumed the corset was next.

"How on earth can I get this on by myself?"

Examining it closely, she saw that the corset appeared to have crossed laces in the front rather than the back. The laces were loosely open just enough for her to get it over her head and pull over her chest. Like lacing a pair of roller skates, she started at the bottom and began tightening the laces. She had them as tight as she could get them and tied the ends in a bow.

She picked up the corset cover and looked it over. It had beautiful embroidered flowers around the edges. She slipped it over her head and pulled it down over the corset.

She had no idea what the wire strappy contraption was. Apparently it was like a section of a hoop skirt. She ignored it and moved on to the gown. Although Everleigh had been in a sorority in college and had attended several balls in fabulous dresses, none of those dresses could compare to this one. It felt like something Princess Kate of England would wear. The blue silk fell across the bed like a waterfall of fabric, shimmering like it was alive. The color was midnight blue with white lace on the ends of the sleeves and around the neckline. Lace that, Everleigh was certain, had been hand crocheted with a tiny crochet needle, not by any machine. She pulled it over her head and it fell around her hips like a glove. The tiny buttons up the back were going to be a problem. Wiggling this way and that, she managed to get the low buttons and the high buttons done. The buttons in the middle were impossible.

How do people dress themselves like this?

She was assuming that somehow she not only had a different body, but somehow she must be in another time. She was not sure what year it was, but it had to have been sometime in the 19th century.

A knock at the door startled her. She looked at herself to see if she was presentable and decided she seemed covered well enough.

"Who's there?"

"It's me ma'am, Angela. I just came to see if you needed any help with your gown."

"Oh!" Everleigh felt a surge of relief. "Yes, yes, I do. Please come in."

A young girl in a plain black dress opened the door and curtsied with a bob and then closed the door.

"I tried to do what I could but I'm afraid I couldn't get all my buttons."

"Certainly ma'am. I'd be happy to help you." She furrowed her brow at the wired strappy thing.

Everleigh stood and turned her back to the girl who apparently was a maid with the inn. She tugged a bit at the dress and then said, "Ma'am, uh, I might need to tighten your laces a bit more. I'm not sure I can get the buttons unless I do. And, are you not going to put your bustle on?"

"Oh. Yes, could you help me with it?"

Before Everleigh could say anymore, the maid was undoing all the buttons and pulled the dress up for Everleigh to duck out of. She laid the gown on the bed. She opened the white tape of the bustle and sat it on the floor. It collapsed into a flat one-dimensional set of wires. Taking the cue, Everleigh stepped into the center. The maid pulled it up to her waist and loosely secured the white tape belt. Two poofs of wire were unfolded behind her. One out from her back side and the other closer to the floor.

The maid went to work on the laces tugging with great strength. Everleigh gasped a little to breathe. The maid stopped and looked at Everleigh and pursed her lips. Everleigh got the distinct feeling Angela thought she was fat. Angela was very slight of form, most likely due to not having enough food. Everleigh couldn't imagine anyone thinking this hottie body was flawed, but sure enough, she sensed a mild disapproving air from the girl.

"Ma'am, you'll have to blow out and hold your breath for me to get it all the way."

Everleigh looked at her considering if she might pass out if she did that. Then using her "tight jeans" method, she inhaled, blew out all her breath, and sucked her belly in holding her breath. Then she nodded at the maid. Angela set to work as fast as she could pulling in the laces. Everleigh's lungs began to burn and just when she thought she might pass out, the maid said she was finished.

Everleigh let go of her breath and then panicked when the crushing corset wouldn't allow her lungs to expand. The maid gave her a quizzical look as Everleigh started to pant shallow breaths.

"Did-you-*pant*-tighten them too-*pant*-much?"

Furrowing her brow, "No, ma'am. I can loosen them if that's what you're accustomed to, but I'm not sure your gown will button."

By now Everleigh was figuring out how to breathe very shallow breaths rather than pant.

"Maybe I just need to rest. I think I'll-*pant*-lie down a while."

"I should help you put on your stockings and shoes. You'll never get them on by yourself now."

"Oh. Uh. Yes. I suppose that's true." Everleigh was sure she could not bend over now. She wasn't sure how she would be able to sit. Maybe she could just lean against walls.

She held onto the bar across the footboard of the bed with one hand, held up her gown with the other hand and raised one leg at a time while Angela pulled the stockings up to her thighs and put her shoes on her. The shoes were narrow but remarkably comfortable as though made for her feet.

"Now then, ma'am, if you'll sit at the vanity, I'll do your hair."

"My hair?" Everleigh reflexively reached up and ran a section of hair through her hand.

"Why yes, ma'am." Angela looked bemused again. ""Are you feeling quite well, Miss Everleigh?"

"Uh, yes. I'm sorry." She shook her head. Then she realized Angela had called her Everleigh. Apparently whose ever body this was happened to be named Everleigh also. "I- I just, I suppose it's the strange bed or something that has me thrown off."

"Thrown? Thrown off? Have you been injured?"

"No, no, I just mean I must be tired."

Angela sighed a breath of relief. "Certainly, ma'am. That's to be expected. Now just sit here and I'll put your hair up and then you can refresh yourself a minute."

"Right. Okay."

Everleigh managed to perch on the edge of the dainty stool while continuing to take long shallow breaths. Angela pulled a horsehair brush through her hair until it lay in smooth silky waves. Then with the ease of a practiced hand, she twisted the long locks up into a graceful swoop and pinned it in a secure bun with just three pins. Everleigh realized that Angela must have been the one to do her hair before.

"You are really good at that!"

Angela's mouth turned up a demure smile. "Thank you, kindly, ma'am." She pinned a navy blue straw hat that curved around gracefully to the back of Everleigh's head.

"If you have no further need of my assistance, I shall return at bedtime to help you prepare for bed." Angela then stood waiting.

"Oh, no. I am fine now. Thank you!" Angela bobbed a curtsy again and disappeared out the door without a sound.

Everleigh was dumbfounded. Without the maid's help, there was no way she could have gotten dressed. Did all women in whatever time this was need help just putting on their clothes? Then she remembered that Angela's dress was plain and loose. She didn't wear a corset or a gown.

Awe struck her. She apparently was of a lady's class. The maid called her ma'am. But, the maid was not in that class. The very clothes they wore distinguished them from one class or another. In her time, wealthy and poor women could wear the same style clothes, albeit differing quality.

Her time. This was not her time. Her mother was not here. She knew no one. Not that she had many friends and certainly no "significant other", but her mother felt so far away. Would she be able to get back? Would this end?

She glanced toward the screen and remembered the soap. She was sure somehow it was the soap. She needed to keep it. She would play around here for a while and explore and then take another bath with the soap and go back. Surely it would work.

She stood and hobbled tiny steps back to the tub. The soap lay on top of the paper just as she left it. She wrapped the paper around it and folded it over the sides. Where could she put it? She needed to keep it close and safe. As far as she knew, this was the only way home. She lifted her skirt and slipped it into the top of her wool stocking. She let the skirt fall and smoothed it down.

She caught sight of herself in the mirror and straightened with confidence. She was breathtaking. Without even a smudge of makeup, she was a mythical goddess. Her sunshine-colored hair waved around her face in a graceful feminine swoop. Her long eyelashes were slightly darker than her hair and made a thick outline of her royal blue eyes. Flawless translucent skin covered cheekbones any model would die for. The slightest hint of natural pink blushed her cheeks. A perfect pouty bow of rose lips demanded attention but when she licked them, the effect was multiplied if that was possible.

Her gaze settled down on her figure which, to a modern woman, looked cartoonish. Her ample bosom was accentuated by the deep V design that plunged to an inhumanly tiny waist of the gown. The gown flared in a poof over her hips before falling in a cascade of silk. She turned backward to twist and see the back but wasn't able to make such a maneuver. Picking up a silver hand mirror, she turned again and peered at her double reflection to see a gathered row of white ruffles across her rear where it extended out before cascading into an elegant sweep. The gown was expressly designed to accentuate every uniquely feminine detail of her body to the extreme. Compared to her usual dowdy clothes, even a mini skirt and tube top would have seemed less suggestive. She wondered if the men of this time were disappointed when they finally saw a nude woman on their wedding night and found out she didn't have a tiny waist or that much junk in her trunk.

The only reason why she didn't feel like hiding in a closet was the fact that the body now housing her soul rocked this outfit. She felt like she'd traded in her practical Civic for a 1968 Corvette. With the confidence that only a mature woman can own, she threw her shoulders back, lifted her chin and summoned every flirtatious gesture she could remember and headed to the door.

At the end of the hallway, she slowly descended the stairs to the lobby.

"Ah! Miss Addison! You will be dining with my wife Suzanne and her sister Faith. They are awaiting your arrival," said a man who must have been the inn keeper for this time. He held out his arm and waited.

Everleigh was taken aback but accepted his arm and let him lead her to a table near a window. Two ladies about her age, in her time, sat chatting quietly. They looked up when the inn keeper approached. The lady on the left wore a yellow silk gown in a similar style to hers. She had blond hair pulled up in the same hairstyle. Everleigh wondered if Angela had done her hair, too. The other lady had brown hair that was fixed with braids under an elegant hat. Her gown was dark green. Both ladies looked Everleigh up and down and with a look of approval, smiled sweetly.

"My dear Suzanne, Faith. May I present Miss Everleigh Addison?"

Everleigh wasn't sure whether she should curtsy or shake hands or neither. So she just blurted out, "So pleased to meet you both!" and smiled.

The inn keeper pulled out a chair for her and she tried to sit down. The bustle took up half the seat. With an awkward second attempt, she managed to get the hoops over her back end to fold together vertically. It made the gown jaunt upwards but she wasn't sure what else to do.

"Thank you, dear Edward." Suzanne gave him a look like he better not look too long at Everleigh if he knew what was good for him. Edward turned his eyes to the side and excused himself.

Everleigh, my dear, it's so good to make your acquaintance. I'm so sorry to hear of your family's tragedy." Suzanne pursed her lips in a perfunctory look of sympathy.

"Oh," Everleigh had no idea what she was talking about. "I see, thank you. That's kind of you to say."

Faith spoke up, "How are you holding up. *Tsk! Tsk!* You're so young to go through so much. I must say, though, you certainly look well." She smiled as though that were the understatement of the year.

"Yes, I am trying to manage." Everleigh offered. "What are you ladies having for dinner? Maybe I'll have the same thing."

Suzanne answered, "We are having hot browns. Have you ever had it? It's a Kentucky dish."

Everleigh remembered once having a hot brown at a conference in Louisville.

"Yes, I have. That would be great."

"Yes, it is a large portion, but not too great, I assure you."

Everleigh paused and then realized her miscommunication. She would have to try harder to not use modern lingo.

"I'm sure it will be delicious!" Everleigh said."

The ladies then smiled reassured.

The footman brought a tea service for three, poured the tea, and asked for their selection for an entrée.

After he left, Faith asked, "Everleigh, my dear, have you heard from your aunt? Did she leave a message for you?"

Everleigh was stumped. She had no idea who her aunt was or why she would leave a message. She had to be careful or they would think she had suffered a head injury or something equally debilitating. Certainly time travel and possession of a body wouldn't go over well as an excuse.

"Ah, no. No, I don't think I have received any messages."

"Faith, she did only arrive this afternoon," Suzanne offered.

"Hm. True. You know, Everleigh, I have not talked to your aunt in years. She lives so far from town. I'm sure you wouldn't know having never been here. How long has it been since you saw her?"

"It's hard for me to say really. A long time I suppose."

"And your poor parents, did they suffer long with the flu?" said Faith.

"Ah, no, you know, just a few weeks," that seemed a safe answer.

"And now you are left alone. How did you manage to travel alone? Was it frightful? I can't imagine."

"Er, I suppose. I mostly stayed to myself."

"I can only imagine," said Suzanne. "At least you are here now. Did Angela help you? Do call on her whenever you need the assistance of a lady's maid."

"Oh, yes. She was a great help. Thank you, I will." Faith and Suzanne chatted to each other about the perils of traveling alone and Everleigh took the opportunity to look around at the other guests. The small dining room had about eight tables with white tablecloths and silver, china and crystal. All the tables were occupied with couples or men dining together. She studied their outfits and gestures. Everyone was so formal and polite, speaking about only light topics and in hushed tones. Everyone's posture was ramrod straight. Everleigh unconsciously straightened her back to imitate them.

Boy, times sure have changed.

She felt the hairs on her neck prickle as though she were being watched and very discreetly lowered her eyes and stole a glance over her left shoulder. Her heart thudded to a stop and her mouth parted slightly in shock at the man sitting at a table not six feet away. He was alone, holding a goblet, and he was staring transfixed at Everleigh. All the hairs on her head then prickled in an ecstatic instinctive response. As though her whole body betrayed her, reacting to the electricity in the air between them, her face blushed and she blinked repeatedly in the struggle to gain her composure yet not wanting to look away.

The man seemed too tall for the table with his lanky legs folded under it, he was leaning back in his chair with all the confidence of a town sheriff. A glass in one hand and the other arm resting on the table. As her gaze followed his body up, she noticed the perfectly pressed white shirt and commanding black jacket. His collar folded up to hug a muscular neck that begged to have arms around it. Finally, with all the resolve she could muster to look in his eyes, fighting the conflicting urge to at once dive under the table and never look away for the rest of her life, she fell into a pool of heaven as her eyes met his. Green eyes framed in a handsome face with a strong jaw line, wide cheekbones, and dark black eyebrows. When the intensity of his gaze nearly crushed her, she let her vision wander to his wavy dark hair that came over his collar and nearly touched his shoulders. Everleigh had not only never seen a man so ridiculously desirable, but she had certainly never had one look at her the way he was. He was in no way taking liberties with his gaze, but yet his eyes spoke volumes saying he could love her for eternity.

Just about the time she nearly melted into her chair, she heard Suzanne say, "Everleigh dear, where did you say you are from?"

With a wrenching effort, she tore her gaze

away from the stranger and turned back to Suzanne.

"What? I'm sorry. What did you say" she breathlessly managed to say.

"I asked where you were from. Edward told me but I don't recall exactly."

"Oh, I'm from Charleston," she mumbled before realizing she had no idea where the Everleigh of this time had been from.

Faith lifted her chin, closed her eyes and took on a dreamlike expression, "Oh, I just love Charleston! Couldn't you just die living there?" Then Faith caught herself as she realized the insensitivity of that statement considering Everleigh's recent loss. "Oh Everleigh, I am *so* sorry. I didn't mean to be insensitive. Please forgive me."

Everleigh had to think a minute about what she was talking about and then offered, "Oh no, Faith. I understand what you meant. Yes, Charleston is a unique town. I have truly enjoyed living there."

Faith sighed a relieved breath that she had not caused Everleigh anymore distress.

"So," Faith continued, "will you be living here with your aunt from now on? You'll miss the big city now, won't you?"

It was beginning to pull together now for Everleigh. Apparently her parents had died from the flu and she had come here to Kentucky to live with her aunt. She remembered reading about women not living alone in these times unless they were a widow. Certainly as a young unmarried woman, she would need to live with a relative. She wondered when this aunt would show up and how would she recognize her.

"Everleigh? Are you sad, dear? I'm so sorry to

keep saying the wrong thing." Faith began to pull at her napkin in dismay. Apparently causing distress was an etiquette faux pas.

Again, boy have times changed. These people would be horrified if they saw Facebook, but I bet they would look at it all the same.

"Oh, no! I'm alright. I was just thinking about my home in Charleston but I am excited to learn about Versailles. Can you tell me about the history?"

Faith and Suzanne's faces lit up now with jubilant smiles. Everleigh then realized how odd and yet delightful it would be to meet a twenty year old that actually cared about the history of a town. No wonder they were impressed.

"Oh, Everleigh dear, what a keen intellect you must have!" Suzanne gushed. "Let me tell you about my family's history here."

Suzanne explained in great detail about the founding of the town and when her family arrived and opened this inn. It was getting to the point where, even for her 35 year old patient attention span, she was beginning tune her out. She really wanted to sneak another peak at the handsome man behind her, but she didn't want to look rude by not paying attention to Suzanne.

With all the calculation of a southern belle, she dropped her napkin to the left of her chair. She bent to pick it up, sucking in her breath and stole a glance. About the time she noticed the table behind her was empty and her heart dropped, the server ran toward her with his brows knotted in distress.

"Madam, please! I'll get that," and he snatched up the offending napkin before her fingers could find it.

Everleigh sat back up, partly confused about the server and partly feeling like a deflated balloon because the man was gone, when she was abruptly cut short by the stunned expressions of her dinner companions. Apparently she had made a manners faux pas herself. Somewhere in the back of her mind she recalled her mother saying you never pick up a napkin that falls on the floor.

"Oh, pardon me! What was I thinking? I'm sorry but I must be too tired to think straight."

Suzanne and Faith softened at her plausible explanation, their eyebrows lowering a notch.

Faith consoled, "Of course, my dear. We have probably worn you out with our questions and conversation."

Dinner arrived and they all tried to keep the conversation about light topics such as the weather and the upcoming Independence Day celebration. Everleigh wondered if she would be able to fit in without making a spectacle of herself. She really wanted to explore this time and the people as a little get away.

"Do you remember the Centennial, dear? Why you must have been just a child. What was it? Twelve years ago now?" Suzanne asked.

Everleigh did some quick adding in her head and it dawned on her that this must be 1888.

Good lord! How was it possible?

"Uh, yes, I don't remember much about it. Just a parade or something."

"We had a parade and a picnic. The whole town brought baskets of food. Oh my." Suzanne got a far-away look. "That's when my Edward proposed. We were married that fall."

Everleigh wished she had memories like that. Twelve years ago she was graduating college and looking for a job. No college sweetheart was there for her to marry like so many of her sorority sisters. She watched them all marry and begin families. She often wondered what that must be like. The pain of loneliness struck her again. Her eyes glassed over as she listened to Suzanne go on about the home Edward built for her.

Faith must have noticed because she interjected, "Oh, Everleigh. Your turn will come next. As pretty as you are, the men in this town will be falling all over themselves to have your hand. I bet you'll be married and with child by this time next year!"

Everleigh's mouth dropped open.

Could it be? Could I really get to have that life?

She had to stifle the urge to get up and hug Faith. That was the most wonderful thing she had ever heard. Suzanne and Faith began to list all the eligible men within a day's ride. Everleigh wondered if any of them was the man who was sitting behind her earlier.

Chapter Three

Everleigh felt the corn husk bed crinkle as she stretched out on the soft sheet. She was surprised how comfortable it was and cooler than a mattress from her time. The moonlight pooled on the wood floor next to her bed. It had been a fantastic experience dressing in period clothes and feeling like she was living in a history book. She wondered if she should just go in the bathroom right now and take a bath with her lavender soap. What was she doing here anyway?

The soap was tucked in the drawer of the bedside table. Maybe she should try it just to make sure it worked. But if she did, what if she couldn't come back to this time. What if it was just a round-trip ticket? Or worse, what if it was a one-way ticket and she was stuck here? Anxiety started to build in her chest and her mind raced. Like a calm island in a stormy sea, she could see the man's face in her mind.

Who was he? Where is he now?

She couldn't believe she was entertaining the thought of seeing him again. Would he have thought she was appealing if he knew what she really looked like? He was just looking at her because she had this Everleigh's body. A lump in her throat formed. She so wanted him to see the real her, but he would just turn away like so many men had before. Still though, he seemed to have looked through her eyes right into her soul.

Tormented, she slept fitfully, dreaming of drowning in a tub of water that had no bottom. She was lost in the deep water with only a narrow opening of the tub yards above her that she could not reach.

No one could find her.

***

The next morning Angela knocked as the sun was just beginning to send golden shafts of light into the room to beckon her from sleep.

"Come in."

"Good morning, ma'am. I've come to help you dress."

"Thank you, Angela." Everleigh sat up and stretched her arms and marveled at how good she felt. No back ache. No soreness. She actually felt like she had the energy to spring out of bed.

Youth is wasted on the young.

She got up and went behind the screen to use the chamber pot that sat under a wooden stool with a hole in the seat. An odd practice that felt a little like camping in the wild, except with a beautiful porcelain pot. She determined she would never make it as a chamber maid. Bleh!

She splashed some water on her face from the pitcher on the small dresser. Again she marveled at how ridiculously gorgeous her face was even first thing in the morning. She used a small brush she assumed was an antique toothbrush to clean her teeth.

Angela had her clothes fluffed and ready for her and began dressing her. Everleigh watched her in amazement as she tugged and pulled and smoothed. She sat on the small stool in front of the mirror and Angela brushed and swooped and pinned her hair. Before long, Angela was gone and Everleigh was perching in a chair by the window thinking about what to do today.

Should I try to find this aunt? How much

longer can I stay here? How is it being paid for?

She decided that if things got difficult, she could always excuse herself for a bath. With that, a rumble in her belly told her that her first order of business was breakfast. She left her room and lightly floated down to the dining room. Edward met her by the double atrium doors which were open and inviting the guests of the inn to come in.

"Miss Addison, good morning! Please come sit down. Would you care for tea or coffee?"

"Coffee please, with cream and sugar."

"Certainly!"

Everleigh settled in and admired her own gown while she waited. This one was pale pink linen with green embroidered leaves on the skirt below the waist. A square panel of lace covered her chest up to her collar bone. She didn't hear Suzanne approach and jerked her head up when Suzanne asked if she could join her.

"Oh, yes!"

"Your gown is lovely. Is it new?"

"Uh, yes! Yes. It's the first time I have worn it." She was winging it again and after all, it was true!

"I expect you'll be trying to contact your aunt today?"

"Yes, I suppose so." She thought for a moment and then decided to use her age to help her. A twenty-year-old probably wouldn't know what to do. "Suzanne, how do you think I should go about that? Without my mother," she cast her eyes down for extra pity, "I am just not sure what to do?"

Suzanne took it hook, line and sinker. "You poor dear. I will help you. We will go to the general store and see if Mr. Adams knows where she lives.

He can be difficult, but I think we can convince him to help." She looked over Everleigh's face and hair. "That will be a start. Maybe we can hire a carriage to take us there."

Everleigh was impressed. That seemed easy enough. Why hadn't she thought of that?

Because I would have only thought to Google her, that's why.

After they enjoyed a light breakfast of toast and eggs, the ladies made their way, arm in arm, to the general store down the dusty street. Everleigh noticed the piles of horse manure everywhere and wrinkled her nose as the smells of the 19th century found her.

"Mr. Adams, I wonder if you might be able to assist us."

"Certainly, Mrs. Clark, if I can." Mr. Adams gave Everleigh a top to bottom once over when he thought she wasn't paying attention, lingering a second longer on the curve of her backside with the extra lace adding bulk in all the right places. Everleigh wasn't sure if she should be offended or thank him for the attention.

Suzanne batted her eyelashes and Everleigh watched in amusement. Surely a woman in her late thirties couldn't still get away with that.

"Darlin'," she stretched out with a long southern drawl, "Miss Everleigh here is new in town since tragedy befell her family. She is all alone now except for her dear aunt Emory Heartwell. You know her, right?" She paused to let the pitifulness of the situation set in, pursing her lips and clutching her delicate lace handkerchief against her chest.

Mr. Adams appeared to be enthralled, nodded

and kept glancing at Everleigh as though he'd found a lost $100 bill and then tempering himself with an appropriate sad expression to match Suzanne's.

"So you see, Mr. Adams, we just have to help Miss Everleigh, here find her kin or who knows what will happen to her."

At this point, Mr. Adams was ready to offer her a carte blanche account to the store if it would help. Everleigh tried not to giggle and look like the pitiful thing she was supposed to.

It's amazing what a built body can do!

Suzanne glanced her way and winked discreetly.

"Oh! Oh my. That's just-, sure I will do anything I can to help." He smiled at Everleigh and puffed his chest out.

"Oh! I just knew you were the right man to come to, Mr. Adams!" said Suzanne. His face turned three shades of red at her gushing praise.

He composed himself and put his hand on his chin thinking.

"Yes, let me look through the list of accounts and see if I have an address. I believe she has an account. I think a farm hand usually comes and takes care of her business. Wait right here." He held up his hands to reinforce his hope they would not move.

After a few minutes in a back room, he came out with a slip of paper. Ignoring the other waiting customers, he headed right to them.

"I have it right here! She lives a ways out of town. You will need a carriage to take you." He scratched his head and it was apparent he was trying to figure out how he could drive her out there himself.

Suzanne reached for the paper in his hand

which he graciously relinquished.

"Oh my, Mr. Adams, you are amazing. We were hoping to talk to her right away and you seem so, so in demand." She stretched out that last word and he blushed again and glanced at Everleigh. "Perhaps, you could persuade your delivery driver to take us. I can't wait to tell Mr. Clark how kind you have been. I'm certain he will want to invite you to dine with us at the Inn." She nodded at Everleigh, who nodded back.

"Oh, please don't go to any trouble, but certainly, I would accept any invitation to dine with you, and Miss Everleigh," he added and looked at her with puppy dog eyes.

Everleigh felt like she was watching a movie about someone else. Never in her life had she been the object of such silly adoration. How fascinating it was the way people react to appearances. Mr. Adams told them to be ready to go in an hour and his driver would have the carriage ready. He was going out that way anyway for another customer so it was no trouble. He would just use the carriage instead of the buckboard wagon.

Everleigh and Suzanne left after expressing their appreciation. Suzanne said they would need to let Edward know and have the cook prepare a luncheon basket for them to take with them. Everleigh found herself sitting on the side porch waiting until time to go. She had a view of Main Street slightly obscured by a trellis covered in an ivy with white flowers. She watched the wagons and carriages go past and the people getting in and out of them.

The door of the law office opened and

Everleigh's breath caught when the mysterious man stepped out. He adjusted his black hat and looked up and down the road. His black wavy curls blew casually around the bottom of the brim. His mouth was downturned and his eyes squinted at the morning sun. He worked his shirt cuffs in a frustrated tug. Whatever had gone on in the law office had him frustrated. He stepped up into his carriage and closed the door. The driver lightly hitched the reins and the horses trotted away.

Suzanne opened the door to the porch and asked if she was ready. The ladies made their way to the carriage at the general store with their picnic basket on Suzanne's arm. The ride out of town was quiet. Everleigh hoped she didn't say anything wrong when they got to the aunt's house.

After the town was long out of sight, the carriage slowed and stopped. A worried look came over Suzanne's face.

"Everleigh," she whispered, "can you see anything out the window? But, be discreet."

Everleigh barely pulled the curtain aside. She couldn't see anything. They were out in the middle of nowhere on a dirt path where just two dirt ruts furrowed in the grass.

They heard the driver call out something and a man answered. Suzanne's eyebrows shot up even higher. Everleigh realized this wasn't good. If something happened to Mr. Adams' driver, they were helpless out there.

Again they heard the driver talking to a man but they were too far away to make out what was happening.

"We dare not stick our heads out the door to

see. Maybe the stranger will assume there's a man in the carriage."

Everleigh nodded. Another minute or two passed as they held their breaths. The door to the carriage swung opened and both of them jumped. The driver stuck his head inside.

Realizing their fear, "Ladies, everything's alright. Mr. Malcolm Steel will be joining us, if that is alright. His carriage lost a wheel and his farm is just past Miss Addison's aunt's estate. I'll take him and his driver home and then come back for you on my way back. Is that alright?"

Suzanne and Everleigh let go of a sigh of relief. "Certainly, sir. Mr. Steel is quite welcome to share our carriage." Suzanne nodded at Everleigh. The driver disappeared. Everleigh moved next to Suzanne to give her seat to the stranger.

"Mr. Steel is a local bachelor. A confirmed bachelor, I'm afraid." Suzanne whispered. "He dines at the Inn on occasion."

The carriage rocked and Everleigh turned to see the mystery man haul himself onto the forward facing seat. He tipped his hat at Suzanne and turned his gaze to Everleigh. Intending to tip his hat at her, he froze for a heartbeat before tilting his head down.

"Ladies, how kind of you to let me share your carriage. I trust it won't be an inconvenience." He said all this without ever taking his eyes off Everleigh's. Suzanne's right brow shot up and slowly looked between the two of them.

"No trouble at all, Mr. Steel. I assure you," Suzanne said with a questioning look. "It will be a pleasure to visit with you as we go."

Everleigh felt a hot zing of panic course

straight from her neck to her thighs. She heard Suzanne say something but the rush of her heart in her ears was a curtain of rain blocking out anything but her and this man. She was frozen to the seat but yet every fiber of her being wanted to lurch forward and into his arms. She was sure if he touched her, lightning would burst from the air.

They swayed with the carriage as the two drivers climbed to their seat in the front.

"Mr. Steel, I would like to introduce Miss Everleigh Addison. She is going to be staying with her Aunt Emory since the untimely death of her parents. I suppose you all will be neighbors of sorts. Everleigh, may I present Mr. Malcolm Steel. Mr. Steel is a Section Supervisor for the Louisville Southern Railroad at the Midway Station."

Finally breaking the hypnotic hold, he turned to Suzanne and said, "Thank you, Mrs. Clark, for the introduction." Then to Everleigh he reached for her hand which she placed in his. "Charmed," he lightly brushed his lips over the back of her hand, "I'm sure."

Everleigh decided that was probably the most sensuous moment of her entire life so far. If she could have melted into a puddle on the floor of the carriage she would have. If she had been standing, surely she would have collapsed. The electric energy of touching his skin was only topped by the searing burn of his warm lips on her skin. She could have jerked her hand away from the shock, but her heart would not allow any such sensible reaction. He released her fingers and she returned the pulsing hand back to her lap and managed a dopey smile. She was sure she looked like a goofy school girl.

As the effect of his touch waned and blood

returned to her brain, she wondered what kind of fool was she. A thirty-five-year-old woman from a time when hunks graced the covers of romance novels and even sold margarine and here she was swooning like a teenager over Mr. Wavy Locks. She tried not to stare and stole a glance without looking like a stalker. She wondered how old he was. By the fine lines around his eyes, she figured that he was probably in his mid-thirties. Possibly the same age as she was, in her own time.

He was more than just a pretty face, though. Something in her connected with this man on a cellular level. She was certain that even if she had any other body, she would have felt it. Something about him felt as connected to her as family. As though, she had been waiting to find him all her life. She had the deep feeling that she was looking at the man who would hold her heart forever.

"Mr. Steel," said Suzanne, "how is the railroad expansion coming along? I hear of such grand tales these days of travelling faster than a horse in a carriage that rides on rails. Is this true? Is it safe? I'm ashamed to admit I have yet to ride a train."

Everleigh stifled a chuckle at Suzanne's questions.

If only she'd seen 747s!

"Why yes! It's all true. It's the way of the future. Very safe. The train rides on rails to guide it. The passenger cars have every luxury. But the biggest benefit will be the ability to move goods and aid with the western expansion. All around this area rail lines are being laid to connect towns like Versailles to the whole country."

"I just don't know. It's hard to imagine. Such

speeds! And I see so many strangers at our new station." Suzanne dabbed her forehead with her handkerchief.

"It's true you must be careful. Many foreigners work for the railroad. But, have you not wanted to explore the world beyond Versailles and Lexington?"

"I'm afraid not. We are so busy with the Inn anyway."

The heat of the day was beginning take hold. She gazed out the window at the passing meadow of purple and white wild flowers.

Everleigh considered how much she should say. Of course she had ridden many trains. She had even done a consultation with a rail company that needed to make access to the station and rail cars handicap accessible. Yes, between her work and just living in the 21st century, it was quite possible she knew more about the railroad business than Mr. Steel did. One thing she didn't know, though, had never fully realized until now, was the sheer hope for the future that the railroad promised the people of this time.

She watched Mr. Steel as he looked out the same window that Suzanne did. She could see the daydreams of progress in his head. Change was coming and he was on the crest of it. Even with all the gadgets of the 21st century, hope was hard to come by. The Wild West was won. Women had equal rights. You could be anything you set your mind to. But, dreams like the ones reflected in Mr. Steel's eyes were usually not entertained anymore.

Sensing her gaze, he turned to her. She felt so old now, as though she had somewhere, sometime long ago, lost the ability to dream. Not dreams about a beach vacation or a bigger house, but dreams of the impossible. He did, though. She wanted so much to learn how to dream like that again.

"Mr. Steel," she started hesitantly, "what makes you so sure the trains will succeed?"

His face lit up, "Oh, Miss Addison, if you could feel the thrill of the wind in your hair," he looked at her hair as though surely a woman would never come that undone, "if you could see the billowing clouds of steam, feel the solid metal of the engine, or see the endless line of tracks that could carry you anywhere, then you would surely believe the train will succeed."

"I see. Perhaps I would."

Hesitating, Suzanne asked, "Mr. Steel, perhaps you could escort us sometime on one of your trains. I would feel most secure with you there for our first ride. Would that be possible?"

"Oh, yes. I wouldn't mind at all. In fact, you might enjoy a short excursion to a cave here in Kentucky. There are guides that do tours. You could ride the train there, stay at the lodge and then ride the train home. They call it the Mammoth Cave."

"Yes, I have heard talk of that. The cave is large enough that a whole house could fit in it. Imagine that, Everleigh."

Everleigh listened and remembered visiting Mammoth Cave as a child with her mother. Doing the math in her head, she realized that the National Park system hadn't even been created yet. She'd seen commercials that it celebrated its 100th anniversary. That would mean it would not be created for about another 25 years.

"What do you think, Everleigh?" Suzanne asked, "Would you join Edward and me if we went with Mr. Steel."

The thought of going anywhere with Mr. Steel was fine with her. "Oh yes, I would love to visit this Mammoth Cave and ride a train."

The carriage slowed and the driver hopped down and opened the door. He lifted Everleigh and Suzanne out and steadied them on the ground. They had apparently turned onto a dirt driveway and now stood in front of two story Italianate brick home. The porch was set with white gingerbread molding around thin white columns. There was no one to be seen. Large oak trees shaded the drive and lawn.

Mr. Steel climbed out of the carriage to stretch his legs and the horses whinnied for water. Suzanne and Everleigh climbed the three steps onto the porch to reach the front door. Suzanne looked around with knitted brows as though someone should have come out to greet them by now. She knocked soundly on the front door.

After what seemed like longer than it would take anyone to answer a door, it opened and a man in a butler's uniform greeted them.

"We are looking for Miss Heartwell. This is her home, is it not?" asked Suzanne.

"Yes, madam. You are correct. Miss Heartwell is not home at the moment. She has traveled to Lexington. You are welcome to come in and refresh yourself if you have need. But Miss Heartwell will not be home for several days. She had several business matters to attend to."

Everleigh and Suzanne looked at each other with a 'what now?' expression.

Suzanne continued, "This is Everleigh Addison, Miss Heartwell's niece. Was she not aware of her impending arrival?"

The butler now looked Everleigh up and down at this information.

"No, madam, I assure you Miss Heartwell was not expecting anyone. I do apologize if this causes you an inconvenience."

"Everleigh, a message was sent by the Trustee in Charleston, was it not?"

"Um, I think so. Uh," she looked from side to side not really knowing what to say, "I'm sure that would have been the case. At any rate, I'll just stay at the Inn until my aunt returns. Yes. That should be fine."

"Rate? I would expect there would be no changes in the rate, my dear." Suzanne looked puzzled.

"Oh, I'm sorry. I meant its no problem. I don't mind."

"I'm certain Miss Heartwell would not want me to turn away her niece. You are welcome to stay here," said the butler.

"Oh no," Suzanne interjected, "with her needing a chaperone, she is perfectly welcome to stay at the Inn. I will take care of her until Miss Heartwell returns. She can be my guest." She smiled pleased.

"As you wish, ma'am. I will certainly tell Miss Heartwell the very moment she returns so that she can make arrangements."

"Thank you. There is some family news she must be made aware of, but I'm certain it would be best to tell her in person when she gets in."

"Very good, then." The butler closed the door

and the ladies turned back to the carriage.

"That is unfortunate, but don't you worry Everleigh. You can stay at the Inn as my guest until your aunt returns. I have grown rather fond of having you around." She smiled sweetly at her.

"Thank you. I appreciate that and feel the same way about you."

Everleigh tried not to show it, but she was actually glad to have the chance to stay in town longer. She wasn't at all sure hanging around a house this far out of town with only an old aunt to talk to would be interesting.

The driver's eye brows poked up in question when they returned to the carriage.

"Apparently, Miss Heartwell isn't home so we will be returning to town. We will just ride along with you on your way." The driver nodded as though it made little difference to him.

Back in the carriage, they bobbed and swayed as it turned around and headed back down the long drive. Mr. Steel continued to steal glances at her and appeared somewhat uncomfortable shifting his weight and frowning occasionally.

"I need to check on some fields to see if that last storm did any damage. I think I'll signal the driver to let me out at the gate," he said.

Everleigh got the distinct feeling he was hiding something, but could say nothing. As they approached the estate, he rapped on the ceiling and the carriage stopped. He bid them good day and Suzanne asked him to stop by the Inn to let them know when would be a good time for them to plan a trip on the train. As the carriage pulled away, Everleigh could feel the tug of him getting farther away. He stood there until they rode away with his hands on his hips as though something was mulling around in his mind.

She leaned to look out the back window to get a view of his estate but the full green trees with summer leaves lazily lolling in the breeze blocked her view. She saw him eventually turn and head down the drive toward the house. She was certain he was not going to check on any fields. He was hiding something.

***

Malcolm needed some time to breathe. In all his days, no other woman had upended him like this woman. From the moment he saw her at dinner the night before, he had not been able to have a single thought that she didn't shine through like sunlight around a rain cloud.

He had determined years ago he would have to live the life of a bachelor. There was no other way. No woman would tolerate what he would ask of her if he were to marry. It was too much to ask. He understood his lot and took it willingly. It was his choice. But to force it on a wife would be unfair. Any woman he got close to, would come to love, he would have to let go and therefore, it was easier to close himself off. He knew people talked about him. He didn't care. They did not have his life to live.

But here was this woman. Everleigh Addison. What was it about her? Certainly she could make him melt into molten fire just looking at her, but it was something else. When he looked in her eyes last night, he could see eternity. Her very soul reached out to him. What if she could understand?

"No!" he said out loud. "I can't do that to her!"

He couldn't let himself think about it. He couldn't let himself think about wrapping his arms around that tiny waist, pulling her to him, and kissing her rosebud mouth until he lost control.

Stop it, Malcolm!

He felt the conflicting emotions of his rock solid resolve and the animal inside him that seemed to be growing by the minute. He raised his fist and was about to abuse a tree trunk to vent his frustration when he heard Bethann call from the front door.

"Oh, there you are! I'm so glad you are home."

***

Everleigh, Suzanne and Edward stood on the platform at the Elizabethtown Station. The enormous black steam engine hissed and groaned as it inched toward them. Everleigh watched Suzanne. Her eyes got as large as saucers. She held on to Edward's arm but looked ready to bolt at any minute. She was like a little child.

"Everleigh, my dear, don't be afraid," Suzanne said with as much courage as a mouse in front of a lion. Everleigh had to hold back a chuckle. Suzanne turned to look at Everleigh.

"You are so brave, my dear. You don't look afraid at all."

"No, I suppose am not. It's kind of exciting really." Her eyes turned up to the big steam engine with a twinkle of excitement.

"I'm glad to hear you say that, Miss Addison." Mr. Steel appeared out of the billows of steam rolling onto the platform. Everleigh's heart leapt right up into her throat. The enormous hissing train engine didn't hold a candle to what this man could do to her.

"Mr. Steel," she breathed.

"Come, let's find your seats so you can settle in." He bowed slightly and motioned with his hand for them to step up onto the passenger car.

Suzanne looked at the step and how high the car stood off the ground.

"I'll never be able to get up there."

The conductor raced up just then and placed a small stool in front of the train step to make it easier to climb aboard. Edward took her left hand and she reached up with her right hand to grasp the red handle bar. Pulling herself up, she managed to step onto the train car and look around. Mr. Steel stepped ahead of Everleigh onto the train and reached his hand down to her. She took his hand and lifted her skirt enough to not trip on it and stepped up. As she did, he pulled gently so that she nearly floated up onto the passenger car. Mr. Clark followed and they all made their way in. Rows of seats stretched on both sides. Everleigh watched as the porter moved seat backs forward or backward to create seating groups of four with two people facing backward.

"My word! How many people can all fit in this, what do you call it? A carriage?" said Suzanne.

"About forty, but there are three more passenger cars," said Mr. Steel.

"I think our whole town could fit in one train!"

Mr. Steel chuckled. "As I said, you will be amazed! Trains will revolutionize travel and the movement of goods. This is such an exciting time in which to live!"

He motioned for them to sit and sat next to Everleigh on the bench seat. The heat from his thigh permeated her dark linen skirt causing her a pleasant discomfort. He turned to her and his lips turned a sweet dimple on each side. She suddenly felt flush all over and stopped breathing.

"Miss Addison, you must breathe on this trip. I'll not have you falling ill and discrediting the train's reputation. Don't be afraid."

She then blushed deeply and opened the fan hanging by a ribbon on her wrist. If he only knew it was not fear that kept her from breathing. She tried to extinguish the fire raging in her belly as her insides seemed to twist and pull. The soft wind of the fan on her chest felt wonderful and she breathed deeply and closed her eyes to block the barrage of emotions the sight of him caused. It didn't help because she could still feel the heat of his leg and the intoxicating mixture of the smell of his skin and the lingering sandalwood apparently from his soap. She had never felt this overwhelming desire in her life. It was frightening.

"Are you warm? I can open the window and let some air in."

He leaned across her with arms outstretched, enclosing her in front and behind in a bubble of his presence and slid the window down above her head.

Oh god. I'll never make it. Maybe I should just run while I can.

She jumped up, stepped around him and made it half way down the aisle before the train lurched and she lost her balance. Panic struck her as she realized she was going to fall and she let out a fearful cry. Her fear of falling was unwarranted, though, because the next second she found herself rooted to the rock-solid frame of Mr. Steel as he reached around her waist with one arm and pulled her against him.

Heat flashed down her back, across her backside and down her thigh as the boundary of where she stopped and he started seemed to get lost in the haze of her brain.

"Whoa, there, Miss Addison. There is nothing to be afraid of. Truly! I won't let anything happen to you." His voice was as gentle and strong as a peaceful river. She was falling and fast. At this point she would have followed him to the ends of the earth and not been afraid of anything, except for how her body was acting completely on its own accord.

"Uh, buh, hm." She was mumbling non-sense.

He smiled and his green eyes crinkled at the corners. It was getting worse. The passenger car seemed to be spinning around her. She was afraid she might actually faint. With his arm holding her up, he pulled her back into her seat and went to get a glass of water.

With him away from her, her mind seemed to clear somewhat. Still dizzy, she looked up at Suzanne and Edward whose mouths were downturned in obvious concern for her well-being.

"Dearest Everleigh, are you quite alright?" asked Suzanne laying a delicate hand on Everleigh's knee.

"Uhhmm. Yes-m-s-sorry," slurring her words.

"Poor dear. Edward, she looks utterly traumatized. Perhaps this was a bad idea."

Edward nodded unsure of how to help. Mr. Steel returned and handed her the glass of water. She nodded gratefully and took a little sip. Now thoroughly ashamed of herself, she couldn't look up at him.

"I'll be fine, really." She took some deep breaths to clear away any more dizziness.

"I need to speak to the conductor, so I will return shortly, if you think you are alright now." He waited to see if she was recovering.

"Oh yes, yes." The reddening anxiety blotches on her chest betrayed the truthfulness of the answer. "Please, don't mind me. Just so exciting, you know, the train." She fanned herself again and hoped she was believable.

Please, Lord, help me control myself.

"Don't think twice about it. You're not the first lady to swoon on her first train ride. Nothing to be ashamed of." He smiled a reassuring smile that didn't help her recovery at all. He disappeared out the back door of the passenger car and Everleigh concentrated on her breathing.

***

Malcolm walked through all three passenger cars to the very back of the train. He gripped the handrail and stared out at the stretch of tracks behind them. What was he thinking, escorting them like this? He could barely handle sitting next to her. Lifting her onto the train, she was as light as a bird. Then when she darted away, panic seized him. What if she made it outside and fell off the train? Then she stumbled, his instincts kicked in and he had his arm around her before his mind was engaged. Her body pressed against him was maddening. He had to get away under the guise of getting water to let all parts of him cool down. The lady was intoxicating. He was certain he had no control over himself around her.

God, I must flee from this temptation!

He took a deep breath and determined he would get through this trip and refuse any more contact. The last thing he needed was this woman under his skin. His life was complicated enough. Besides, he could not bear to see the look in her eyes if she knew the truth about his home life.

***

When they got to Glasgow Junction, they had to change trains to the new Mammoth Cave Railroad. This much smaller excursion train went straight to the Mammoth Cave Hotel. There were only two cars: the engine and a red passenger car. She looked at the small train and hoped it met at least some of the requirements of the Transportation Safety Board which she was certain did not exist yet. The small engine didn't look strong enough to pull a bus, despite its name "Hercules" proudly emblazoned on its side. Everleigh overheard other guests talk about how this was so much nicer than having to take a carriage for the last leg of the trip. She lifted her long dark skirt and stepped up onto the wooden step holding on to the metal bar on the train car. She noted that only a thin metal bar served as a railing to keep people from falling off the landing. Grimacing at the antiquated rail car, she stepped onto the dusty wood floor of the passenger car. The seats were plain wooden benches. She sat down across from Suzanne and Edward. Suzanne was chattering away about the difference in the two trains and how fast the first train was. She couldn't imagine it was safe to move along at that speed.

The train lurched forward and soon Everleigh watched the forest fly past in a blur of green and black occasionally opening to a meadow where a small farmhouse would come into view. At one house children squealed and jumped and waved as they went past. Mr. Steel had made himself scarce by staying in the engine for most of the ride. Everleigh wondered if he had become annoyed with her. After her behavior getting on the train, she had no doubt that he wanted nothing to do with her. She could not see him from her seat as the tinder was too high.

She chided herself for acting so silly. She was not a ditzy little girl. What was wrong with her, she wondered? One thing she knew, no man had ever looked at her with that yearning in his eyes. Obviously this body helped in that regard. She didn't have a great deal of experience when it came to men. Maybe the first pretty face that paid attention to her had sent her reeling.

She thought back to Luke. They had been a couple for a year in college. Of course she was younger and thinner then. Still a bit dowdy but she enjoyed sorority life even if mostly it was to live vicariously through her sorority sister's stories. Luke was cute with an average build. He seemed infatuated with her at first but as time went on and she got clingy, he pulled away. Finally he just cut ties with her and moved on. She had been crushed for months. He was her first love. How could he just walk away? Wasn't love supposed to last forever?

A dirt road followed the train for a while before disappearing around a bend. She wondered about the people who lived in the houses out here. How hard must their life be in 1888 with no electricity and no phones?

Her mind drifted back to Luke. After he left her, she didn't look at guys for a long time. It hurt too much. She felt like she had put all of herself in that relationship and he just threw her away. If that was dating, she wanted no part of it. Still, she always wished for that perfect love. Perfect love - even thinking it sounded crazy. She knew there was nothing perfect about relationships. That's where she couldn't make sense of it. She wanted perfect love but knew logically there was no such thing except love from God.

Chasing that never ending argument had not gotten her anywhere and she focused on pleasing herself. She ate what pleased her, did as she pleased, and vacationed where she wanted to without ever having to think about anyone else. For a long time that fulfilled her, or so she thought. Then she turned thirty and reality sank in. She was still alone and youth was fading away. The woman she saw in the mirror didn't match the free spirit inside her. How would she ever find the impossible perfect love now? How did her friends seem to find it so easily?

The train slowed and as it curved around a bend of trees, a white inn came into view. It had a large front porch and seemed to invite you in with a whisper of secrets hidden below the grassy meadow in front of it. With a lurch forward as the brake was applied, she looked around for Mr. Steel. He bolted up the up the steps and into the passenger car ready to escort them to their destination.

Mr. Clark picked up his bag and Mr. Steel picked his and Everleigh's. The men descended first and set the bags down to help Everleigh and Suzanne depart the passenger car. Mr. Steel took her hand rather than lift her down. Everleigh brushed her long skirt with her hands to smooth out the wrinkles before the crowd of passengers made their way to the inn. She marveled at how different it would look here in 2016. The inn would be completely gone and replaced by a plain one-story brick lodge and motel-like structure. A visitor center with post-modern lines and beautiful rock walls would house a museum, gift shop and rangers information booth. Millions of people would file in year after year to be led on tours into the earth.

There were no rangers here now since the Park Service had not been created. Mammoth Cave was not a National Park. It was a fascinating site owned by a private individual. Now that she thought about it, the 414 miles of cave had not even been fully discovered. At this time, they probably had very little of the cave mapped out.

On the porch stood an old black man wearing dusty pants, a shirt, and brown coat. He had a short beard and a kind face under a round black hat. He was short and stout. His solemn eyes searched the group, taking them all in. He seemed neither eager nor annoyed they were there. In fact he looked us over as if we were the spectacle on display rather than the cave. He leaned on a cane and Everleigh wondered how such an old fella was going to make it on the tour.

"Ladies and gentlemen," he started, changing his gaze to a place past them up in the meadow, "my name is Nick Bransford. Welcome to Mammoth Cave. I will be your guide. I have lived here since 1838 and I know this cave, what we know of it, like the back of my hand. You have no need to fear. We will be perfectly safe as long as you follow my instructions. You ladies can speak to the matron of the inn about what to wear so that you have an easier time."

Suzanne looked at me with a concerned glance.

"Dinner will be served soon in the lodge after you have settled in. We will leave on our tour first thing after breakfast in the morning. There will be a late picnic lunch afterward and then the train will take you back to Glasgow Junction. I hope you enjoy your stay and find the cave as majestic as I do. After dinner, I will be available on the porch for your questions."

With that he smiled a slightly staged expression, then turned and strode down the stairs and started around the side of the inn.

"Odd man, wouldn't you say, Everleigh?" Suzanne puckered her lips as she stared toward the back corner of the inn.

Everleigh sighed. "I suppose. He just seems like he cares for the cave a great deal and we are strangers."

"I suppose. It is good to have an experienced guide. I certainly don't wish to be lost underground."

Suzanne picked up her long skirt a few inches to step up onto the porch.

***

Mr. Steel was nowhere to be found at dinner. Everleigh knew it had to be her fault. Obviously she had made him uncomfortable and now he was just trying to stay clear and get this trip over with.

Looking for a breeze to cool the stuffy July air, she excused herself to go out on the porch. The quiet night gave way to a rush of natural sounds. Wind rustled the tree leaves with a sound not unlike the rush of a waterfall. An owl hooted in the darkness. Above, the Milky Way pulled together a million glittering points of light in a hazy frozen river.

The air lifted the fallen tendrils on the back of her neck and she couldn't stop a quiet moan of relief. Leaning against the handrail, she caressed the back of her neck and wiped away the sheen of moisture that left her sticky. She closed her eyes to soak in all the sounds of the 1888 night. She wanted to remember. When she finally went back to 2016, she wanted to be able to pull up this memory as her own meditative escape from modern life.

She wrapped her arms around herself hugging her abdomen. The tiny waist was such a new delight. She didn't feel frumpy or embarrassed finally. How wonderful to not have the ever nagging self-consciousness weighing her down. In all the times when she thought she was so free because she was doing what only she wanted, she was never really free. The oppression of self-doubt always clouded her. She never quite matched people's expectations. Where was her husband? Her children? Who did she talk to at dinner? She could see the questions in their eyes even if they never fully formed out of their mouth.

Hearing a twig snap, she opened her eyes. A fat raccoon froze in the shadows. She stood very still so as to not scare it away. Slowly it began to waddle around the yard, stopping occasionally to pick up something with its tiny hands and turn it over. A thought dawned on her that that was who she was before. She was alone and fat and just exploring around. How could she go back to that? A pang of ache gripped her heart as she thought of her mother. If she never went back, if she just enjoyed life in this body and started new, she would never see her mother again. What would her mother think? Would they think she was a missing person? What happened to her body? What if it is still in that tub in 2016? Is it alive without her soul in it? Had time moved on like it did here or was it frozen, waiting?

She envisioned the police investigating her questionable death. Would they think it was suicide? Her mother would be so sad. Maybe she should go back now. She could go back and see what was happening and maybe leave a note for her mother. She had plenty of the soap. But, what if it only worked this one time? No, whatever was happening, this was too great an opportunity to risk losing it. She would stay a little while longer and then try to go back. Hopefully time was standing still on the other side. She shook off the worry that her mother was grieving for her.

She saw a large rock in the distance reflecting the light of the moon. It sat in the middle of dark meadow. Compelled to experience the night fully, she picked up her skirt lightly and stepped down the steps onto the dirt and made her way in the moonlight. The owl hooted again. She felt like all of the forest was watching her. She could imagine deer and birds turning to see the stranger moving silently through the tall grass. The wind pulled at her skirts now and tingled a dry softness on her moist skin even under her shirtwaist. The cool tickle on her spine was delightful.

She reached the rock. It was just about two feet high with a flat top, perfect for sitting. She climbed up and sat crossed legged under her dark skirt. She looked down and realized that the bottom half of her body in the skirt completely disappeared in the darkness. Her white blouse on the other hand, glowed a purplish brightness. She thought about how from the lodge, she must look like a floating shirt.

Leaning back on her hands, she looked up to see that half of the sky was now obscured. A bank of clouds had crept in with the wind. A tiny glow of lightening flashed deep inside the dark cloud. The air seemed full of life, crisp, and sweet smelling. A sudden rush of wind tugged harder at her hair and, despite her quick reaction to reach up and protect the heavy bun, the pins slid out and waves of blond wrapped around her and rose with the wind. Like being caught in sheets on a line to dry, her hair glowed in the moonlight and wafted wildly. The cool massaging of the pulling on her scalp was heavenly. A giggle erupted from her lips.

Lost in the reverie of the natural world, she was jolted back to reality when huge glops of water instantly poured all over her and the rock. She jumped to her feet and quickly calculated that the tree line was closer than the lodge and maybe she could wait out the storm under the protection of a large maple tree. Gathering her now heavy rain soaked skirt over her arm, she ducked her head and ran. She marveled that it felt like floating as she ran with these delicate legs.

She was halfway across the open expanse when a blinding surge of light stabbed the ground not ten feet in front of her. The hum of electricity filled her ears. Coursing fingers of tangible energy grabbed at the grass. Steam sizzled and she halted terrified. A scream left her mouth but buzzing like a million bees blanketed all noise.

She fell backward as the air whooshed past her and then a clap of thunder was the last thing she heard. Darkness closed in as cool rain pelted her face and heavy skirts pinned her against the grass.
***

He had seen her on the rock as he came around to the porch. He'd had an enlightening conversation with Mr. Bransford as he ate dinner on the porch of Mr. Bransford's cabin. His wife Charlotte served them food and drinks. The smile was still on his face as he chuckled remembering Mr. Bransford's stories of visitors who had taken out on their own to visit the cave and how he had found them in various states of ignoble distress.

He froze mid-step when the illuminated blouse caught his attention. Thinking it was a ghost or some hellish demon, he couldn't move. Then he made out the delicate swoop of flaxen silk atop her head. In an imprudent display of reverie, she had leaned back on her arms and thrown her head back. She looked like a sacred goddess or a forest fairy. His sigh of relief hitched in his chest.

Like a magnetic pull, his body yearned to move toward her, to wrap his arms around the ethereal torso, to let his lips roam up her graceful neck until they found the fount of life of her mouth. He fought the urge with all his strength, digging in his heels. Testing his resolve further, he watched her reach with graceful arms to hold her hair from the risk of being undone by the wind. Not fast enough, he watched it pull apart in a cyclone of silk and wildly wrack her face.

The sight of her being pummeled by the passion of the wind sent a gripping jab of white hot shock from his chest to his loins. His body reacted to the sight of her on its own accord and he felt as powerless to resist as her golden tresses in the wind.

Fighting with all his resolve, he was about to turn away and go the other direction when the wind swept through his hair, lifting the dark silky curls around his ears. The curtain of rain moved across the meadow and reached her before him. In the same instant, he saw her jump up and look at him and then the forest and back.

Apparently deciding the forest was closer, she leapt like a gazelle from the rock and sprinted toward the trees. With a blinding flash, his breath caught as lightening struck not ten feet from her. In the blink of an eye, he watched her delicate body flung backward and disappear in the tall grass. The crack of thunder rang in his ears. Without thinking, his legs propelled him across the meadow with the speed of a lion.

He reached her in the grass and his heart tore in two, the physical pain he felt gripped him. She lay like a rag doll left outside. He feared she was surely dead, but even in death she looked like an angel. He knelt down and gently pulled her body to him, the soaking rain pelting them both. Her head lolled and his fears seized him. The warm softness of her thighs on his arms made his mind swim. Sucking in a breath of strength, he turned to finish her sprint to the trees.

Under the umbrella of the maple, it was dry

and cool, even though the boughs above creaked and groaned. With the gentleness of a father with a newborn, he set her down and cradled her head on his lap. A tear threatened to fall and he dashed it away. All of the emotion that he had stamped down in his heart, all the resolve that he had made as a scab to protect him, let loose and he crumpled.

"Miss Everleigh! Please wake up!" He tapped her cheek and rubbed her arms. Drops of rain escaped from her forehead and ran rivulets down her face. Reminding him of tragic teardrops, he let go and sobbed. He hadn't realized how real his feelings for her had become. How was it possible to fall in love so quickly? He knew she had touched him in a way no other woman had. Even sitting there on that rock soaking in all the natural wonder as though worshipping God's creation in a church, she moved him. It had been so easy to turn a blind eye to women before. The constraints of proper society gave him a safe distance to guard his heart. Every other lady he had ever met was so bound to convention that he was never caught in the dangerous throws he was now. And now, this singularly vibrant creature was slipping out of life. As though his life could not have been any more tortuous, even by his own choice, now he had to hold this treasure of life while she slipped away.

Tears now streamed freely down his cheeks as he railed at the impossible-ness of his life. Even if she had not been struck by lightning, how would he have gone on? He surely could not take her home to be his wife, not with his shameful secret.

***

Lost in his misery, he didn't see her breath

suck in and her chest rise. Her eyes opened and she looked at the incongruous vision of raw masculinity as he cradled her and cried defeated. His rain soaked shirt revealed a wall of chest and muscular arms. His stubbly jaw framed a grimace and he quietly sobbed. Did he cry for her? Confusion swept her. His reaction at her obvious near death experience did not match her understanding of his annoyed revulsion of her.

As she pondered this, he opened his eyes from the contorted twist of grief and saw she was alive. He transformed in one fluid image from sheer agony to elation to hunger for her mouth. Pulling her up into his arms and encircling her back and head, he paused once with his mouth so close she could breathe in his breath, and then pressed his mouth to hers with all the fierce emotion that had been bottled up inside his.

She wound her arms around his strong neck and succumbed to the torrent of passion. Every fiber of her being screamed to merge with him. She pressed herself against his abdomen and the heat from his skin seared a path from her breasts to her hips. Her senses at once become hyper-aware of every touch and also deaf to anything around them. The storm around them raged with rain coming down in sheets around the tree, dripping in streams from the leaves above them, flashes of lightening and cracking of thunder.

Nothing mattered but their souls, blindly bound by flesh and earth, finding each other.

He pulled back and looked into her eyes. A smile curved the delicious lips that she had just tasted. She reached up and caressed his cheek. This wonderful man loved her and she could love him back. He pulled her close into an embrace. His scratchy stubble grazed her neck, tickling and causing her to convulse into him further. Heat from his mouth branded her collar bone right through the fabric of her shirt. Dizziness left her weak and she melted in the safety of his arms.

Breathe, Everleigh, breathe!

He stiffened slightly and, as though another person invaded his body, he quickly rose and pulled her to her feet. Brushing dirt and leaves from his trousers, he looked away.

"Miss Addison, I beg your pardon. I- I lost myself. Please forgive me." He still would not look at her and after looking slightly alarmed and ashamed, he stiffly held out his arm for her.

Embarrassed, she tried to smooth out her skirt and twist her long, tangled mass of hair into order over her shoulder and down her chest. She couldn't help herself from staring now. His behavior had so abruptly changed. What had she done? Was she wrong when she thought she saw love in his eyes?

"Mr. Steel, um, thank you for rescuing me from the storm."

"Oh, yes, of course. You really scared me there." He coughed under his fist.

"I'm terribly sorry to scare you." Then she hesitated and added, "Mr. Steel, it seems you had another reaction besides fear. I..." she stumbled on her words, wanting desperately to affirm what she thought he felt.

"Please! Please accept my sincere apology, Miss Addison. My behavior is unforgivable. I will endeavor to keep a distance between us so as not to, not to..." He glanced at her once and then turned away in obvious pained grief.

Unsure what to think and wanting to free him from his guilt, "Certainly, I don't hold it against you. I, uh, don't want you to avoid me."

"Thank you, but I think its best. Now," he straightened and held his arm out again, "Let's get inside before you get chilled."

She took his arm and let him lead her through a path under the trees to the lodge. A chill was the last thing she worried about. It had been in the 90s before the storm and even now couldn't be any less than 80. Even so, it could have been ten degrees and she would have melted snow with the heat radiating from her skin. Every hair on her body stood on end with attention. She was certain her face had to be a scarlet blush. She had never been kissed like that in her life. She wanted so much to stop him now and pull his mouth to hers again. As her heart thudded to a normal rhythm, her head cleared its fog. The rain slowed as the storm was passing by. She was left with a confusing jumble of memories of the last half hour and a pain in her heart that ached a little too familiar.

He ensured she made it safely to her lodge room and ducked away before she could say a word. She closed the door and leaned against it. Her mind reeled. She tried to push away the pain that threatened to creep into her heart. The old familiar pain of rejection. She had kept it away for so long by hiding herself away. Now here it was again. With stretching and contorting, she managed to undo the buttons down her back and slip out of her wet shirtwaist and long skirt. The fabric clung to wet skin and resisted being pulled away. Only the sheer weight from being water-logged managed to pull it to the floor and off of her. She stepped out of the pile of skirt and slid the bloomer underwear off her and lifted the slip over her head. Hooking her thumbs into her stockings, she slid one and then the other off onto the floor. The bar of soap wrapped in its delicate paper bounced on the wood floor. She picked it up and set it on the vanity.

The air on her skin felt wonderful. She sat on a woven grass stool at the vanity table naked and began the process of brushing out her damp matt of hair. At last, she sat staring at her face in the vanity mirror. She wondered how she looked through his eyes. She puckered her lips and recomposed herself as if in a slight faint, head thrown back and peeking at herself in the mirror through half closed eyes. After deciding she must have looked like an idiot, she let out a "pfft!" and picked up the soap.

The label read,

Lady Clara's Fine Soap
For Cleansing Away All that Ails You

"Guess what, Lady Clara? What ails me seems to have followed me even to the 19th century."

She crawled into bed naked and had fitful dreams of storms chasing her.

***

Malcolm needed air. There was no way he could sleep anytime soon. His mind was reeling with elation and grief at war with each other. How could he have lost himself like that? But on the other hand, what man could have resisted her? *Damnation!* He cursed in his head! What was a proper lady doing out there in the dark alone anyway? Senseless woman!

And then nearly getting struck by lightning. That's what happens to women given to hysterical notions to wander around in thunderstorms.

He sat in a rocking chair and rocked furiously. Then he stopped and leaned forward gulping air. He sat back again and ran his hand through his dark waves of hair. She had gotten under his skin and now he was having to fight it. How could he have let her in? Suddenly still in his chair, he gazed off into the dark night. In his mind, he could see her face. She reached up and caressed his cheek and he nuzzled his face in her soft palm, kissing her silky fingertips.

He shook his head to clear away the vision. She was more than a pretty face. He had seen hundreds of pretty faces. Society matrons had paraded their daughters before him like cattle at auction. They were all lovely. Most anyway. Loveliness had been nice to look at but never pulled his heart. It was as easy to turn away from the parade of eligible young ladies as it would be to turn away from a field of flowers.

He had to anyway. He had envisioned their expression when they found out what came along as part of the marital bargain. He couldn't bear that. He couldn't bear seeing their disgust, not for something so much a part of him. He grimaced at the idea of what sharing his secret would mean.

Part of him asked *what if*, though. What if Everleigh was different? She was, he could see that. She seemed so free. Not stifled like so many women he knew. What if she truly did not recoil in revulsion? He slammed the door on this thought and closed his eyes. He would have to shut her out. He hammered down the lid to the box in his head that held all his desire for her. He was stronger than any emotion. He was no weakling.

He pulled out thoughts of forging ahead with the railroad. He could feel the wind in his hair as he leaned out of an engine car. He thought of the billows of white steam escaping to the heavens. He could feel the power under his feet as the train ate up the track propelling them into the future. Progress was his work for this country. That was much more important than fantasies of a woman. He had chosen his lot and now he had to make it work.

***

The next morning, a maid for the hotel brought her an unusual outfit.

"It's a Turkish dress, ma'am. You wear it in the cave so you don't trip on your skirt. You wear your stockings underneath to cover your legs."

"Oh, ok! Thanks!"

The maid left with her armload of Turkish dresses to deliver to the other ladies in the party. Everleigh closed the door and held up the odd garment. It look like a giant version of what you might put on a baby. Poufy billows of fabric for the torso and gathered on each leg with a band at the knee. She was certain she would look like a marshmallow with black legs. The image in her head made her chuckle.

She pulled her thick black stockings up.

"Man, how I would love to just wear a pair of shorts."

But then she remembered how cold it was down in the cave and decided the stockings would probably be useful.

Then she stepped into the unbuttoned opening at the neck and pulled the giant romper up over her shoulders. She buttoned the front and turned to look at herself in the vanity mirror.

Bleh! Hideous!

She sat on the stool and slipped her feet in her short, black leather boots. With a final check of her hair to make sure it was pinned securely, she turned to go downstairs.

A buffet board was set out with toast and coffee. Mr. Bishop told them to be prepared to leave for the cave in just a few minutes. She looked around and saw Suzanne and her husband on a couch by the large rock hearth drinking coffee. She sat opposite them in a chair.

"Everleigh, love! I worried about you last night. You'd gone out for air and then we had that dreadful storm. You didn't answer when I knocked on your door." She gave her a little knowing eye.

"Uh, yeah, I had gone for a little walk and got rained on, but no big deal."

"Big deal? You say the strangest things, child. Is that normal lingo now in Charleston?"

"Oh, oops! Sorry. I guess so. I meant that it wasn't too bad."

She looked at her questioningly, and then added, "Have you seen Mr. Steel this morning, Edward?"

Everleigh felt the reddening of her cheeks betraying her. There was no way to stop it.

"What darling?" Mr. Clark had not been paying any attention to them. "Mr. Steel, did you say? Yes, he was up getting coffee when I came down here. The first guest for breakfast, I daresay."

"Hm," was all Suzanne said as she continued to eye her.

"Suzanne, whatever are you looking at? Am I not dressed correctly?" Everleigh had had enough of her insinuating stare.

Suzanne pursed her lips and turned her chin away and said, "No dear. In fact you look perfectly rosy this morning. You're probably the only one that looks like a beauty in these get ups."

Everleigh smiled enjoying being complimented for once in her life. Mr. Bransford called them all to the porch. He gave them each a lantern and before picking up a woven basket with refreshments. Before long, the small assembly paraded across the meadow.

As they passed the rock, Everleigh cast her eyes down, flashes of the night before coming to mind. She looked around but didn't see Mr. Steel. Apparently he was skipping the cave tour.

At the edge of the trees, they came to a trail with a gradual downward slope. Everleigh superimposed in her mind the bridge that would connect the two hills. The lodge and restaurant would be to the left and visitor center on the right. She imagined a forest ranger in his or her green uniform and official-looking hat leading the way. The ground would be a smooth wide asphalt path instead of a narrow dirt path with poison ivy threatening to get your ankles. The ghosts of the future colored her descent into the forest.

Eventually they came to a gaping hole of rock. No concrete staircase that would be built to code sometime in the future. Foliage grew right up to where the sun no longer cast its life-giving rays. A steady stream of water cascaded from a place at the top. There was no light inside. It could very well have been a hole to the center of the earth.

Mr. Bransford went to each person one by one and lit their lantern with a small torch of rolled leaves. He told them to stay together and not wander off alone. If they got lost, just sit and wait. Don't try to find a way out. You would likely just go deeper in the cave and be harder to find. He reassured everyone that they would check their numbers frequently so if someone did go missing, they would know right away.

One by one they passed through the mouth of the cave down the slippery rocks. Everleigh was privately praising whoever put in the paved steps in the future and wished for them now. From her recollection she was only half way down to the cave floor and she already had mud on her stockings and hands.

Mr. Bransford was exceedingly patient, stopping several times to talk about the cave and what he had found in it. It was a slow process getting the group, small as it was, all into the cave.

Soon they were all inside the dry dusty mouth. She could no longer see the light of day and beyond Mr. Bishop it was black as pitch. Fear gripped her at the wildness of it. How could it have seemed so safe and benign in the modern age? She really had felt no fear at all following the ranger inside. The cave had been well lit and fascinating. Now, it was still shrouding its secrets.

They made it to the great dome room. Their lanterns did illuminate most of the room but she could not see back into the corners. She marveled at how brave Mr. Bishop must have been as a boy to explore in here.

Without the nice pavers and handrails, it was strenuous to get through the tour. They had to climb over boulders and squeeze around rock walls. They traversed a scary bridge over the bottomless pit and wound around the path in Fat Man's Misery. They went down to the underground river and Mr. Bransford used a net to scoop up the blind fish swimming in it to show them. They sat down and had a refreshment and then continued until they finally made their way back to the great dome room.

They climbed up out of the mouth of the cave, slipping on mud and loose rocks. Everleigh felt exhausted. She imagined Suzanne must have felt far worse in her older body. She thought about how a normal 20-year-old would have no idea what it felt like to move in an older body.

Back at the meadow, the group was happy to see tables and chairs set up under the trees and a buffet table with pitchers of lemonade, congealed salad, and cold sandwiches. Everleigh felt completely refreshed with the soft, albeit humid, breeze tickling her neck. She did wonder what happened to Mr. Steel. Had he really taken it so hard that he was staying away from her? She hated to think that.

Eventually, feeling renewed from the cool luncheon, they all ambled into the hotel to change and get ready for the trip home. As she was packing her bag, she heard the whistle of the train as it chugged into the meadow up to a small platform for boarding. She peered out her window. The wavy imperfect glass distorted the landscape but she could make out the broad shoulders and dark hair of Mr. Steel as he jumped into the engine car.

So he hadn't disappeared from thin air.

Her heart leapt a beat and felt as though it stuck in her throat. With a mind of its own, her hand slide up her neck and touched the spot where his fiery hot kiss had melted into her. She could almost still feel the warmth of his breath on her. She felt that visceral pull again like a magnet drawing her to him. As though the same tug, the invisible cord between them had been drawn, he turned on the step of the engine and looked at her window. It was too far and the glass too imperfect for her to see his expression.

For a brief moment, she selfishly enjoyed the connection. She could almost feel his lips on her ear whispering for her.

A knock on the door jolted her back to reality.

"Come in."

"It's me, dear. Are you ready? Can I help with anything? This has been such a fascinating excursion. The study of the earth, so much science! I say, we will have things to think about and discuss for weeks now."

Suzanne prattled on and Everleigh turned back to the window. He was gone now. He must have gone inside the engine.

"Whatever are you looking at, my dear? We must get going." Then as though reading her mind, "You poor dear. I suspected as much. You are falling for our friend, the heartbreaker."

Everleigh jerked around at this. What could she mean, heartbreaker?

"I told you, sweet child, he is a confirmed bachelor. No maiden has made head way with him. Ever. It's like he is immune to any ways of femininity. Down right off, if you ask me. I was actually hoping maybe you had made a dent in his armor last night. I was sure something had gone on."

Everleigh's eyebrows shot up and a blotchy rose hue crept across her chest.

"Oh come, come. No need to pretend with me. I can see how you look at him. I was hoping with your looks that maybe he would finally let go of his iron resolve to never marry."

"His resolve? He doesn't want to marry?" said Everleigh choking on the words.

Suzanne got up and took her hand. Her expression of motherly sympathy seemed sincere.

"No, honey, he's never actually said as much, but it has puzzled many a mother and daughter. Some have speculated that maybe he had been a widower. He has only lived in Versailles for two years. He moved here when his aunt and uncle passed from consumption. He took over their estate. If I had to guess, I would say he is about 34. He would have been old enough to lose a wife. Heartbreaking as that could be, I can't see how a vigorous young man like that could give up on women forever."

"Do you really think that's it?"

"I'm not sure." She pulled the curtain back to see the view for herself. "I know he keeps to himself. No one has been out to his estate since his aunt and uncle's funeral. Some people say he is hiding something, but I think that is just tongue wagging."

"Suzanne, you remember the other day, when his carriage broke down?"

"Yes, sure I do."

"He said he was going to check his fields, but I watched him through the back window as we pulled away. He didn't. He went straight back to his house."

Suzanne puckered her lips thinking. "Ah, that doesn't mean anything. Maybe he changed his mind or something."

"I suppose." Everleigh puzzled over the mystery of Mr. Steel.

"But right now we will miss the train if we don't get downstairs. Let's go."

Everleigh smiled at her friend. She hadn't had a good friend since college. Most of her friends were busy with families now and didn't understand her carefree lifestyle.

***

After he took her to her room, Malcolm had paced the porch until nearly dawn. Never before had a woman captivated him like she did. Even the very scent of her wet skin mingled with the scent of rain and earth cut him to the core. Every time he would push her from his mind and resolve to just stay away from her, the memory of her scent would invade his mind. A soft rain shower fell just as the sky turned to midnight blue before dawn. The soft smell of rain and flowers wafted through his lungs and reminded him of her again. That's when he knew, his heart was imprinting with her face. He may have to stay out of town on work or not leave his estate, but he would wait until she was gone from the Versailles Inn and couched safely at her aunts. Surely in no time, another man would sweep her off her feet and make her a missus and that would be that.

That seemed so logical but even the thought of another man with his lips on hers made him clench his fists until his knuckles went white. Feeling utterly defeated by his own heart and knowing that for the sake of another, he must be strong. This was about more than just him.

He went inside and saw that the hotel staff was already setting out coffee. He poured a cup and nodded to Mr. Clark on his way upstairs. In his room, even the coffee left a bitter taste. He shucked his shirt and trousers and climbed into bed.

Bright sunlight hot across his face woke him from the dead sleep. The hotel was quiet except for the tinkling of dishes downstairs. He determined the staff must be setting up for lunch. It was much too bright for breakfast. He crawled out of bed and held his head. The pain of being away from her was leaving an aching hole in him.

How am I going to do this, Lord?

He washed and shaved and got dressed. He packed his bag and heard distant voices outside. At the window he watched the group of visitors slowly drag across the meadow. There she was, muddy and gorgeous. His eyes fell on her and would not let go. He could make out the scandalous shape of her calves and ankles as the black stockings contrasted with the bright green grass.

Lord. I never would have made it on that tour.

He pulled himself away from the window with all his might, he grabbed his bag and headed downstairs. He found Mr. Bransford coming into the lodge as he stepped off the staircase.

"Heading out to the picnic, Mr. Steel?"

"Uh, no. I was hoping to beg the cook for a sandwich on the back porch."

"Nice coincidence. So was I!" Mr. Bransford smiled a wide friendly grin and the two men made their way to the kitchen.

As soon as the train whistle blew, he thanked Mr. Bransford for his company, picked up his bag and strode around the house to the platform. He had almost made it, stepping onto the step of the engine when a pulse hit him like a spear. Without even looking he would have known it was her. He couldn't stop himself from looking, though. He turned and his eyes roamed across the grass, up the front of the hotel and centered on the window. At first he couldn't make her out. The glare of the sun on the window obscured her. But then he saw her. What kind of power was this love? He could feel the pull of her as though the cord were wrapped around his very heart and she held the other end in her hand.

Just as quickly as it came on him, the feeling released as she stepped away from the window. He took his leave before the ache consumed him.

Chapter Four

Everleigh was glad to be back at the Versailles Inn. It was beginning to feel like home away from home. She soaked in the warm water of the uncomfortable little tub.

When were real bathtubs invented?

Using a bar of the sandalwood soap the Inn provided, she lathered a washcloth and rubbed the bubbly silk over her arms. The spicy sandalwood scent tickled her nose. Cleanliness was hard to come by apparently. With no Suave deodorant or regular hot water-running showers, bathing was a must. However, with no indoor plumbing, bath water had to be brought upstairs for her and she hated to bother Angela. Sponge baths were the only saving grace from keeping her from not being able to stand herself.

She did find a fairly nice assortment of powders and lotions in the trunk. She had found some scented oils to rub under her arms that helped mask the body odor. Her favorite powder had a gardenia scent. The paper over the cardboard container said it was from France. She wondered if it cost a fortune. Goods would have to come by sailing ships these days, not the cargo ships filled with rail containers that spread goods worldwide in her time. Once it did reach the coast, she thought, it would have to be transported by wagons. Of course trains were making great in-roads to connect the middle of the county to the east coast, but even that was a new development.

She wondered if maybe the powder had been a

gift from Everleigh's parents. Or perhaps a suitor. She wondered why a girl this pretty didn't already have a husband. From what she knew, girls were old maids if they were not married before their mid-twenties in this time. She had found papers for her carriage passage in the trunk that clearly showed she was a "Miss". She was not a widow.

What happened to this girl's soul?

She wondered if maybe something tragic had occurred and left an empty place for her soul to land. Maybe the Everleigh of 1888 had gone on to the Promised Land. She'd left behind all the mortal and worldly parts one doesn't need any more in the afterlife.

The answer was unfathomable to her. Sometimes there just are no answers and you just have to live life and make the most of it.

Make the most of it.

Such an interesting proposition. Here she was with the second chance. What would she do if anyone had ever told her she could go back to twenty and have another go at it?

She lifted her knee and rubbed the delicate bubbles across her thigh.

Would you just look at that leg? How beautiful!

She wondered if this Everleigh ever felt self-conscience. Surely not, but then she remembered her bombshell sorority sisters saying they were fat or they hated their nose or their feet. It seemed that even the beautiful were not immune to the whispers in their head that can crush a girl.

She lifted her foot out of the warm water sending a swirl of soap into a mini-typhoon. She held her leg up to look at the length of it.

Wow! How many times had I dreamed of having legs like this?

A thought occurred to her. A positively against-the-laws-of-nature thought: here she was and she loved the body she was in. By whatever magic that had put her here, even though it was not her body before, now it was and she could freely love it. All the guilt of her own deficiencies were evaporating like the steam rising out of her bath.

How many times had she sabotaged her own efforts at weight-loss or exercise or just given up because she didn't think she could do it. She hugged herself with the very arms she now delighted in. This precious body that she needed to protect and cherish changed how she saw herself and allowed her to love herself. She closed her eyes and breathed deep in the peaceful confidence. Gratitude welled up in her chest to the Everleigh before for sharing this gift even if she'd never known she did, perhaps would never have known it would have this effect. Wherever that Everleigh was, she wished she could thank her.

The water cooled and she stepped out onto the soft rug covering the cold tile floor. She hugged a pressed piece of linen around her to dry off. Padding around the screen, she picked up a sleeping gown and pulled it over her head. The soft cotton stuck to her hips and legs where the moisture still clung to her. Her long flaxen hair resisted being brushed, instead preferring a wet tangle. Starting at the ends, she smoothed it all the way up to the crown of her head.

She studied her face in the mirror. She looked kind, even sweet. Without having ever met the other Everleigh, she had no idea what personality she had.

She softly caressed the face that now functioned as the focal point to all her human encounters. She loved every part of it. The small nose. The high delicate cheekbones. The long eyelashes.

A strong urge filled her. She looked into the mirror and spoke to the body itself:

"I will protect you. I love you."

With all the fierceness of a mother protecting a fragile babe, she resolved that she would protect this body and love it. She realized for the first time that she had taken her body for granted before. She'd acted like her body was hers to do with as she pleased. Now she'd discovered that we are passengers in our bodies which deserve to be cared for as our home.

She crawled under the light summer bedspread and sank into the soft pillow. Feeling her arms, legs and back muscles give in to the lull of impending sleep, she smiled because she knew that this was what her body needed. She made a promise to listen more, be more aware, of the clues her body gave her about what it needed.

The next morning, ambient light from the summer day already blaring outside gave the dining room a feeling of promise. She really hadn't thought of what she would do today. She ate a good breakfast and leaned forward on her arms to watch guests come and go. The room got more crowded as the morning got into full swing. She hadn't seen Suzanne yet.

She remembered all the interesting "antique" things at the general store and decided to see what all they had. She got up and made her way outside and across the street, dodging horses and carriages that didn't seem to abide by any rules of the road or pedestrian rights.

Dusting her skirt and taking a deep breath she paused before opening the door. A carriage pulled up near her and a young woman was lifted down. She had a paper in her hand that looked like a shopping list.

"Mr. Sloan, I won't be long. Please wait here. I'll need help loading the items in the wagon."

"Yes, ma'am." He went around her to tend to the horses.

"Oh, and if Mr. Steel comes out of the law office, ask him if he would like a ride back with us to the house. I need to talk to him."

"Yes, ma'am," he acknowledged again.

Everleigh fought the urge to stare the woman down as her skirt swished against her as she went on into the store. The words "back with us to the house" kept circling her brain.

What is that supposed to mean?

It sure sounded like this lady lived at the same house as Mr. Steel. Everleigh glanced at the man tending the horses. He seemed like a hired hand. The lady had on a light green day dress. She didn't look like any maid or kitchen help.

Heat rose up Everleigh's chest and spread to her cheeks. The lady had said Mr. Steel was at the lawyer's office. She glanced down the dusty road looking to see if she could see him anywhere. No Mr. Steel presented himself. Her forehead crunched in a scowl that went down to her lips and formed a frown. Who was this lady? Did he have a girlfriend? No. They didn't 'live' together in this time. Surely he wasn't married after all Suzanne had said. There was no explanation for this woman to be *living* at his home.

Jealousy and curiosity twisted in her stomach. She turned and quietly stole into the store. The lady was at the counter talking to Mr. Adams going over her list. Everleigh dared not look their way and appeared keenly interested in some thimbles, hoping she could make out their conversation.

Without turning her head, she glanced with the corner of her eye and saw that she had light brown hair and pale creamy skin. In a stab of jealousy, she imagined Mr. Steel nuzzling his mouth into her neck. The rise of heat on her face got hotter. She had to get a grip on herself.

The woman asked for several herbs, lotions, and medical supplements for sleep. Then she asked if they had any tubing for enemas. Everleigh wondered what on earth she needed all this for. She got coffee and soap. She asked if they had gotten in any new spectacles. Mr. Steel seemed to have good vision and this woman didn't wear glasses. Finally the woman asked for several bolts of linen and calico fabric.

The stock boy loaded everything into their wagon outside and the woman asked Mr. Adams to add the purchases on Mr. Steel's account. Mr. Adams didn't give her any look when she asked so Everleigh surmised this must be a regular occurrence.

The purposeful lady turned and left the store without ever glancing Everleigh's way.

"Can I help you find anything, Miss Addison? We have some new ribbons there."

Everleigh swung her head around at his voice, "Oh, no. No thank you. I was just looking." Wanting to see what was happening now outside and if Mr. Steel had joined them, Everleigh moved closer to a window. The distorted glass made it hard to make out but it did appear Mr. Steel had joined them.

Not daring to find herself in an awkward scene, she couldn't go outside. She watched the smudged images move around to get up onto the seat of the wagon. Mr. Steel lifted the girl up by her waist and she sat between the two men as Mr. Steel agilely propelled himself up to the seat. In the blink of an eye, the horses were already trotting down the dusty road. The girl had pulled a bonnet up over her head obscuring her face.

Everleigh stood there like she'd been hit with a wet blanket. What on earth could this mean? It was apparent a lady was living at his estate and charging to his account. She didn't have on maid or cooks attire. Maybe she was a relative? But, he never mentioned this. Neither had Suzanne. Suzanne definitely would have known. A relative would have probably come around to eat at the Inn. She had suspected Mr. Steel was hiding something. Was this what he was hiding? A woman?

That would certainly explain his odd behavior before at Mammoth Cave. He must have felt guilt after kissing her. He had betrayed this other woman. Fire scorched her cheeks. She decided she would make it easier for him so he didn't feel guilty anymore. She would have nothing to do with the two-timer.

With her mind reeling she pushed her way through the store doors and dashed across the road. A horse reared and she looked up just in time to see the whites of its eyes and its front hooves bicycling. She dashed out of the way and heard the man on the horse curse her.

"Are you an idiot? Mind your way, girl!"

Terrified at nearly being trampled, Everleigh never looked back and burst into the Inn foyer.

"Everleigh, dear girl, you look perfectly ill. Come sit down. Edward, get her a glass of water!"

Suzanne pulled her over to a velvet couch with dark wood scrolling around the edges of the back.

"Now, tell me, dear, what is the matter?"

"A horse! It was so big. And the hooves. The carriages! And Mr. Steel and that *woman*!"

Suzanne gazed at her with her mouth open trying to make sense of what all that meant.

"Hooves? Did you get trampled?" At this realization, Suzanne started to examine Everleigh's arms and her gown looking for evidence of injury.

Calming a bit, "No. I ran. I ran away. Oh my word, Suzanne. How *do* you survive around here?"

"Granted it isn't Charleston, but surely the streets are just as dangerous. More so I would think"

The stab of adrenaline subsiding, she could breathe a little better.

"Oh! Yes. That's true. I don't know what I was thinking."

Mr. Clark came around the corner and handed her a glass of water. Apparently not wanting to wait to see what female drama she was having, he excused himself and darted away.

Suzanne waited until he turned the corner back to the parlor before continuing.

"What did you mean about Mr. Steel and the woman?"

Everleigh regretted her senseless blabbering now.

"I, uh, I am sure I just over reacted"

"To what? Tell me, dear? Was he with a woman? This in interesting news."

All the color drained from Everleigh's face now. The jealousy, then terror, and now humiliation at being caught being jealous made her stomach churn. Her breakfast threatened to return.

She straightened and smoothed her skirt, "There was just a woman at the general store picking up some items, that's all. I am sure she is part of the kitchen staff or maybe she supervises the maids."

Suzanne lowered her eye lids and furrowed her brows. She was quiet a minute as she pondered this new tidbit.

"What was she wearing?"

Suzanne was quick. "A day dress."

"Not a black or gray work dress?"

"No. Oh, Suzanne, who was she? Could she be a relative?"

"Not likely." Suzanne tilted her head considering possible options. Then her face changed to a sympathetic motherly smile.

"Don't you worry, sweet girl. I'm certain I will find out who he has hiding out there. This would explain a great deal. You go upstairs and freshen up. I daresay you look like you have been in a tornado!" She chuckled a light laugh obviously intended to redirect Everleigh.

Back in her room, Everleigh splashed water on her face and smoothed her hair back into the swirling bun. She chided herself for acting like a school girl. She was too old for such silly nonsense. But yet, she wasn't now, was she? It was perfectly normal for her to have her insecure drama about a guy. That's what inexperienced young women did, and she was inexperienced and now young, again.

She grinned at herself in the mirror and enjoyed the feeling of being okay with her feelings. She felt true to herself. She was jealous. She had a right to. He had kissed her and she did have feelings for him. She closed her eyes and remembered the delirious dizziness of being in his arms.

A knock made her jump as her eyes flew open.

"Who is it?"

"It's me, Suzanne. May I come in?"

Everleigh jumped from the stool and headed to the door.

"Of course!" she said as she swung the door wide.

"You look much better! Now, I have something to share." She looked like the cat who had swallowed the canary as her mouth twitch up in a curl on one side.

They sat at the settee of chairs.

"What is it? Do you know something?"

"No." she paused for dramatic effect. "But we will. I just had a messenger take out an invitation inviting Mr. Steel and his 'house guest' to dinner."

"You didn't!" Everleigh's eyes bulged and she covered her mouth. "Suzanne, you didn't!" she breathed the words like it was all a secret.

"Oh, I did!" she crossed her legs under her skirt and draped her arm across the back of the chair proud of herself. "That ought to blow his little secret wide open."

***

The butler brought in a letter on a silver

platter while Malcolm was reviewing a ledger in his library.

"A letter arrived, sir."

"Thank you, Jones. That will be all." The butler silently disappeared through the door.

Malcolm looked at the delicate cursive handwritten name. No doubt another matron trying to arrange a marriage. He sighed, tearing open the envelope. He read the short note on the white parchment and sat frozen. Mrs. Clark. She had seen Bethann, apparently. He knew it was a bad idea to ride home with them. He usually tried to not ride with her for fear of wagging tongues. No one ever thought anything of a woman and a man servant coming to town to buy goods. She could have been from anywhere.

Why had he not told her he would talk to her when they got home? Blast it all anyway. How was he going to explain this? There was no way in the world to explain it without everyone finding out. His world would be torn apart if it got out.

He raked his hand through his hair and rubbed his face.

Damn!

He read the note again:

Dear Mr. Steel,

Please accept our invitation to dinner this evening at the Inn. Please bring your lady guest at your home. We would love to show her how friendly Versailles can be. Dinner is at 7:00.

Until then,
Mrs. Clark

He threw the parchment on his desk with a violent flick and sprawled his legs out and threw his head back. There was no way around this. He simply could not deny there was a lady in his home, and that was the tip of the iceburg. He turned his head toward the ceiling and looked as if he had x-ray vision and could see the hidden reason why this was so difficult.

He picked up a stack of legal papers bound in a folder and sighed again. As if it couldn't get worse, he had to figure out a way to keep the house. The government was trying to seize his estate saying there was no blood relative to inherit his aunt and uncle's estate. The estate had been a part of a land grant to his uncle's great grandfather after the Revolutionary War. It had been passed down from one generation to the next. Unfortunately, he was his Aunt Cecelia's kin, not his Uncle Jasper's. Legally, Malcolm was not a blood heir. Normally this wouldn't be an issue, explained the lawyer, except that Jasper's great grandfather was a patriot that was off the deep end with conspiracy beliefs. He swore the Red Coats would never get his land by hook or crook and added into the title that only blood heirs could inherit the estate. He was certain the Red Coats would secretly marry Americans and kill them to inherit their land and take over again. At least he could insure that only his Rebel blood would control the estate.

That last thing he needed right now was to play social curiosity to Mrs. Clark. He needed to figure out what to do to keep his home. Without the estate, there would be nowhere to hide. The authorities would step in and he could not bear that.

He decided a good ride on the fastest horse he owned would clear his mind and help him think. He strode to the stable and saddled his horse. He would have had a stable boy, but he had to be careful about who and how many people were on his land. The few that were there he had either brought with him from Louisville when he moved or he paid them dearly for their tight lips. He pulled the strap to tighten the saddle and swung himself up. The majestic thoroughbred whinnied and pranced. He was built for racing with long muscular legs but had the temper of a wasp. He really didn't feel good unless he was running at full sprint.

Malcolm bought General at an auction when he was a yearling. He named him General after the great steam engine in the Civil War that the Union captured to thwart the movement of goods for the Confederates. The steam engine Texas gave pursuit in a race and eventually the General ran out of wood for the engine and would not let the Union get away with it. Granted, running out of wood is a practicality, but Malcolm liked to think the General refused to move being the Rebel train it was.

Malcolm pulled the reins and kicked his heels mildly. That was all it took. General shot from the yard and down the dirt path beside the rows of blowing corn now six feet tall. Malcolm raised his back end up off the saddle to give the horse freedom to let loose. Wind whipped his face and he had to squint his eyes. He felt like he was flying over the corn and from a distance he probably looked like he was since the horse would be obscured.

The estate was 200 acres with the house sitting on one side. Fields and fields of corn, tobacco, potatoes, and wheat grew. Malcolm had field hands that lived on the back of the property to help him harvest and never came to the house. The rich dark soil with limestone minerals turns seeds into gold. The estate more than paid for itself and he was able to set aside an amount for saving.

As the horse dashed and pulled, Malcolm wondered if there was any way he could just buy the property out right. The title specifically stipulated the land was to go back to the federal government if there were no more blood heirs. He knew the government had no use for it and would turn around and sell it to the highest bidder.

But there is a blood heir, damn it!

***

Everleigh wrung her hands as she sat on the side porch. The last thing she wanted to do was sit at a dinner table with Malcolm and his secret wife. The thought made her sick at her stomach. What was Suzanne thinking? Why did she have to involve her? There was no way of getting out of it.

A tall man in a cream suit stepped out of a carriage that pulled up. He brushed his coat down and carried a small bag. His white blond hair was combed perfectly with a part at the side and jaunty angled sideburns. He took a big breath and puffed out his chest. He looked like he was about to be heard or know why. Everleigh wondered what was going on in his mind. What did people in this time worry about? There was no terrorism or Zika viruses, even the White House and the President seemed far away. It almost seemed like a person could actually just worry about normal things, whatever normal things were. She looked down trying to figure out what one would worry about if they didn't have all the problems of life in 2016.

"Everleigh? There you are. Just who I was looking for."

He said this, not with the tone of a friend calling, but like someone slightly miffed they had to track you down.

Everleigh looked up surprised, obviously he knew her, or at least knew the old Everleigh. She, however, had no idea who he was or why he would be annoyed.

She stood and, as she had learned, offered her hand knuckles up in greeting. Not knowing what to say, she stammered.

"Uh, uh, yes, here I am! And how are you doing?"

She smiled pleasantly, hoping that would pass as a greeting, and looked up into his eyes. It dawned on her he called her Everleigh. He must be very familiar. He couldn't be family because she had found out her aunt was her only family. Who else would call her by her first name? That was frowned on, men calling ladies by their first name, unless they were married or... oh god, unless they were betrothed.

Her breath caught in her throat. She looked over his translucent skin which nearly had a bluish tinge and his watery blue eyes. The fact that he looked like he lived underground could have been overlooked but his expression had a downright domineering tone. He was smirking. It was like it was a game and he'd won.

"How am I doing? Is that what you ask? Hm. Did you think you could take off and I wouldn't find you?" He laughed sarcastically and put his hand on her bicep, looking to see if anyone could see them and then jerked her toward the back of the porch to a wicker love seat.

"Ow!" She let out as the pain of his fingers digging into her arm shot through her shoulder. "What are you doing?"

"Shhh! You'll not make a scene. I have come for what is rightfully mine."

The words hit Everleigh like a smack in the face.

Rightfully his?

"Apparently by the look on your face, you are not charmed to see me. No matter. It would have been easier if you were," he trailed off. And then, "But anyway. In time you will learn to be at least respectful of my … demands."

Everleigh was nearly sick now. Her stomach roiled into a thick knot. She tried to scoot away from him but he put his arm on her wrist and smiled a sickly grin.

"I don't know what you are talking about, but I am not doing anything with you!"

He chuckled and reached into his breast pocket. He pulled out a folded set of papers and held them out to her, but just before she took them he snatched them away.

"No, no! I'm not letting anything happen to these papers. They are worth gold!" He laughed out loud. "That's funny. Gold."

"Are you out of your mind?"

"Everleigh, stop this idiotic game where you act like you have had a blow to the head. I will marry you, this very day," he looked around at the shadows of twilight creeping up, "or perhaps tomorrow, either is good. But I will marry you and take you back to

Charleston on the next stage."

"What makes you think I will marry you?" Her mouth contorted in disgust.

"For one thing, these papers that bound you to me fifteen years ago. You can't think I am going to walk away from that do you? Besides," he got a cartoonish sympathetic expression pulling his face into a frown, "you are all alone." His face resumed the sardonic smile. "Anything could happen to you. You need me to take care of you."

That was it! She wasn't listening to one more minute of this craziness. She stood and crossed her arms.

"I'll have you know, I am perfectly capable of taking care of myself, you boor!"

He laughed at her. As though she was a little girl stamping her foot demanding to not take a bath. He laughed at her and shook his head.

"Anyway, my darling soon-to-be bride, perhaps you could," he entertained the thought, "but according to the betrothal papers, if you do not marry me, your parents fortune will be taken from you and the courts will decide where it goes. So you see, we are in the same boat."

He continued, "I don't like you, but I want your money and you don't like me, but you want your money. So you *will* marry me and both of us will go on just like most married couples."

She stood there aghast. What an outright cad! He admitted he didn't like her. How could he not like her? She was beautiful. Was the other Everleigh hateful? She could understand if he just wasn't in love with her but, seriously, how could he dislike her?

"You don't like me?" she stammered.

He pinched the bridge of his nose and took a breath like having to explain the obvious to a child and his patience was gone.

"Everleigh, dear, I am sure the death of your parents has been hard on you. I'm not totally insensitive. But, you have known for quite some time that, I will probably never forgive you for getting in the way of me and Cherise being together."

Deep horizontal furrows appeared on her forehead. Her legs trembled at all this and she eased herself down onto the seat.

She looked at him quizzically trying to get this straight, "So, you don't like me because you really want to be with this Cherise, but you can't because it's my fault that if you don't marry me, you won't get my parents' money?"

He put his index finger on his lips and looked up a second and then nodded.

"Yes! I think that sums it up. See what you have done to my life?"

"Oh, good grief. Now I have heard it all. Look. Isn't there anyway we can work this out? I mean, if you need money, maybe I could pay you to break off the betrothal? Sounds reasonable."

His mouth fell open horrified.

"No! You'll not pay me off like a villain! I do have honor to uphold."

"So you would rather spend your life married to me instead of being with Cherise?"

"Oh!" he laughed again. "I won't be without her. She is willing to be kept in an apartment in Charleston. Frankly, you and I can live in different homes for all I care."

Everleigh saw the inequity of gender

discrimination right before her eyes. She would have to remain chaste or probably be thrown in jail while he could have her money and his lover, and Cherise would lose her reputation in society as a tramp. And really, there was not much she could do about it. She needed to speak to Suzanne. Maybe she knew something.

In a tone of defeat that would hopefully get him to give her some space, she said the first thing that came to mind, "I need to pack, then. So, I'll see you at dinner I suppose."

He smiled an oily smile of triumph and she turned and went into the Inn and straight to Suzanne and Edward's apartment.

Knock knock knock!

"Suzanne! I really need to see you. Are you in there?"

***

She was so mad at this guy she hadn't even gotten his name. On top of that she told him she would see him at dinner. Mr. Steel and his, what? Wife? Would be there. This was setting up to be a real nightmare. She thought about just stripping off her clothes and taking one of Miss Clara's lavender baths right now and high tail it out of there. Surely a sponge bath would be enough to make the magic happen.

Suzanne thought the whole turn of events was perfect for stirring up some jealousy in Mr. Steel. Besides, she'd said, what did she have to lose? She finished the last touches on her hair for dinner and looked at her reflection. The gold and cinnamon colored silk gown with drop shoulder sleeves made her look like a fairy princess. Delicate handmade lace fell from the hem of the sleeves. She ran her hands down her torso and lingered in the appreciation of her figure. The sensation of loving herself was blissful. The bosom-exposing neckline was different than her usual day wear but appropriate for dinner.

A sound outside of the Inn caught her attention. A man was yelling. She moved to the window and peered between the narrow partings of the sheers. She could see the head of the man who called himself her betrothed below on the path to the front door. He was waving his arms wildly and speaking harshly to Mr. Clark. She could make out the top of Mr. Clark's rounded hat and his brown suit jacket as he stood unimpressed in front of him.

"Mr. Peeble," he sighed patiently, "I can assure you that if the Justice of the Peace says he is not available, he surely isn't. There is no conspiracy against you."

"I will not tolerate your hick town discriminating against me. I know how you Kentucky mountain people can be!"

Everleigh sighed embarrassed for the man.
What an idiot!

She crossed the room to head downstairs thinking this was going to be an interesting evening. She descended the stairs in a glide and found Suzanne in the foyer wringing her hands.

"Oh, Everleigh, that man! Have you seen the likes of such a man?"

"I suppose there are creeps wherever you go."

"Creeps?" Suzanne looked confused.

"Scoundrels?" Everleigh tried to think of an old word for a loser.

"Oh, yes! This should be an entertaining

dinner, I would assume."

Mr. Clark and Mr. Peeble came inside both looking perturbed. At the site of Everleigh, Mr. Peeble's expression changed from perturbed to gloating. His chest swelled up and he looked down his nose at her.

"There's my bride to be. If it weren't for these backwater fools, we would already be married."

"There you are... again, I suppose." Everleigh's mind scrambled trying to think of something pleasant to say but nothing at all came to mind. Suzanne looked at her with raised eyebrows.

"Gentlemen, why don't we wait in the parlor for our other dinner guests?" Suzanne strained to sound hospitable.

"Mr. Peeble, let me pour you a drink." Mr. Clark led Mr. Peeble into the parlor and offered him a glass of whiskey. Everleigh wondered if that was sensible but perhaps it was the polite thing to do anyway.

Mr. Peeble, seriously? What a mamby-pamby name.

"Everleigh, when Mr. Steel gets here, try to seem like you don't care for Mr. Peeble's advances. That will clear the way for him to let his manly pride have its way."

Everleigh giggled, "I should be able to handle that!"

The door swung open and there he stood. The breath sucked out of her lungs. An invisible magnet tugged at her visceral core. A shot of heat bolted through her. She was about to step forward when she remembered that he hadn't come alone.

Suzanne shot a look around him and her

mouth fell open. "But," she paused searching his face, "where is she?"

"Oh, you must mean Mrs. Monroe. I really wasn't sure who you talking about but I assume you had seen Mrs. Monroe in town this morning."

"Mrs. Monroe?" she shook her head.

"Yes. Mrs. Monroe is, well, the wife of my farm manager. She often does shopping for my estate even though she is not my employee. It would be inappropriate for me to take her out to dinner."

"I suppose so." Suzanne was crestfallen. Her mouth turned into a sour downcast. She shot a look at Everleigh.

"Then. I suppose we can go into the parlor." Everleigh winked at Suzanne. Everleigh detected a slight sense that he was not telling the truth but couldn't pursue it.

"Oh, yes" Suzanne appeared to remember the other guest and resumed her satisfied look. All was not lost. She looped her arm into Mr. Steel's and led him into the parlor.

Mr. Clark was already looking weary as he rubbed his temples. Mr. Peeble was droning on about changes that should be made to the Inn to bring it up to the current standards of civilized townspeople. Hearing the group treading across the carpet, he looked up and gave Suzanne a watery smile.

Standing and reaching out his hand, "Ah, Mr. Steel! How good of you to join us. Suzanne said you would have a lady friend with you," his eyes darted around expecting to find someone else.

"Oh, I think there was a misunderstanding." He smiled politely and clasped his hands in front of him indicating he didn't really want to discuss it further.

"I would like to introduce Horace Peeble. He arrived today to discuss some business with Ms. Addison.

Horace? This is getting worse by the minute. Mrs. Horace Peeble. God save me.

Mr. Peeble stood and barely came to Mr. Steel's shoulder. He had to look up to speak to him.

"Business? Not exactly, Mr. Clark. I came to collect my betrothed. We will be married by tomorrow at dinner, if I can get your justice of the peace to do his job."

Mr. Steel's jar clenched, the muscle under his ear tensed. Slowly his face turned toward Everleigh before his eyes did. She could see a fierceness below the surface of his expression as he watched Mr. Peeble speak. Then his eyes shifted to her and changed to pain. His whole face exuded a controlled grief.

"I suppose congratulations are in order," he quietly enunciated.

She looked away. She couldn't bear to look in his eyes.

"That's right. We will celebrate, won't we, my *darling*." He nudged her and she brought up a hand to her stomach as the nausea threatened.

"Shall we move to the dining room, then?" Mr. Clark held out his hand to direct them through the doorway to the dining room.

The last thing she felt like doing was celebrating. In fact, it really didn't look like any of them did. Even Mr. Peeble looked more annoyed than anything.

As they gathered around the table, it became

clear to her that this was going to be a trying meal. She had lost any appetite she might have had. Suzanne and Edward stood next to each other. Mr. Peeble stood to her left and Mr. Steel stood to her right. She would have to sit between these two. One side of her vision filled her with nausea and the other side of her vision made her heart lose track of its rhythm. When Mr. Peeble stood there and did nothing but hold his face in contempt, Mr. Steel reached over and pulled her chair out for her. She smiled sweetly and tried not to look in his eyes.

She sat and his fingers grazed her bare skin on her shoulder as he pushed her chair in. Like the shock of a frayed wire, the spot burned long after he sat in his own seat. Whatever it was that they shared seemed to be more than either of them could deny. Discreetly, she cast her eyes to her left to catch a glimpse of him. She could feel the heat radiating from his body like a furnace. She could see him gently rubbing the fingers that touched her. With his mouth turned down in a frown, he seemed lost in his sadness.

He glanced up at her and held her gaze for just a second. The torment warring in him pleaded with her. She wished there was some way she could speak to him. If they could just talk, maybe they could find a way to make it work. She couldn't understand his hot and cold attention and now this. He was obviously affected by this news. If he didn't care about her, why would he look so disturbed?

"So Mr. Peeble, what do you enjoy most about Charleston?" said Suzanne making conversation.

He leaned back and thought a minute. Before he could speak the server came and brought them tea.

He waited until he was finished.

"Charleston has beautiful ladies. I enjoy the scenery."

Everyone at the table just stared at him. Had he really said that? Everleigh was even more convinced this was the vilest man she had ever met. If she married him, she was certain he would be a complete embarrassment of a husband.

"But, of course, Mr. Peeble, you will only have eyes for Miss Addison now," said Mr. Steel.

Mr. Peeble was taking a sip of tea and nearly spat it onto the table. Regaining his composure, he smirked a knowing glance at Mr. Steel as though this were a secret among men.

"Oh, to be sure. Of course." Then he chuckled.

"Will you take a honeymoon?" Mr. Clark asked while stirring sugar into his tea. He apparently was not aware of Everleigh's disgust for the man or surely he would not have asked. Suzanne ribbed him with her elbow and Everleigh gave him a look that could maim. Mr. Steel sucked in a breath. Suzanne brought her napkin to her mouth to cover the shock on her face.

"Oh, you know. I have much to attend to at home. I have already been away for too long. I see no need for such a silly notion."

Everleigh realized that Cherise probably would not care for him to run off with a new bride. In fact, he probably had plans to go on a trip with her. This guy was a piece of work. She had to figure out how to unload this guy and fast.

She could just refuse to marry him. Of course she would be penniless, but she didn't know before she had any money anyway. Besides, she would probably be returning to her job in 2016 before long.

The server brought them menus to select an entrée and then served soup. She picked up the long narrow parchment in front of her with a selection of three entrée's to choose from. The paper triggered her memory of the legal papers Mr. Peeble had waved in her face. He wouldn't let her see them.

What if there was something on them he was hiding from her, she thought? She glanced at Suzanne. Suzanne was watching Mr. Steel. Everleigh could tell her wheels were turning to somehow press Mr. Steel into a jealous fit. Mr. Steel looked more tortured than ever as he had his elbow on the table and was chewing on his left index finger as he read the menu. Seeing her look at him from the corner of his eye, he turned to her and gave her a weak, distanced smile.

So this side of him was back. Rather than become jealous, he was pulling away. It would be easier, she conceded, for him to just let go, especially if he was so torn. If there wasn't another woman, then what? What was he hiding? She turned back to her menu and decided she needed to focus on one thing at a time. The papers. How could she get to the papers? Surely he didn't have them with him now. If he didn't, that meant they would be up in his room. If she could slip out now, she would know he was occupied and she could find them without his knowing. Her mouth went dry thinking about it. What if he caught her? His behavior earlier showed her that he had no compunction about strong arming her. She shivered at the vision of him finding her in his room with no one there to help her. This was the only plan though.

She picked up her tea for a sip and the thought came to her. She let the handle slip on her finger and the tea spilled down her dress. With mock surprise she let out a gasp and jumped from the table.

"Oh, clumsy me! I'll need to go change. Please excuse me." She gave little curtsies as she backed away. The men jumped up with nothing to say but Suzanne gave her a side glance and a pucker of her lips. Everleigh could tell she knew something was up.

"Do you need a hand, dear? Do let me help." She excused herself and followed Everleigh out the dining room door. "What are you doing?" she whispered as they went up the staircase.

Everleigh breathed a sigh of relief. This was better than she expected.

"I got to thinking. Those papers he had. He never let me see them. Maybe he is hiding something? Maybe there is a loophole."

"Loophole? I don't understand."

"I mean a way out of this crazy betrothal. Surely Everleigh's, I mean, my parents," she corrected herself, "wouldn't have forced me into anything I didn't want, right?"

"I don't know, honey. Don't get your hopes up. Parents often think they are doing the right thing when they make decisions for their child."

Everleigh grimaced. Times sure have changed, she thought.

"I am going to see for myself anyway. Will you help me?"

"Of course I will. That man is awful! Frankly, I am not sure what he has to offer you. What sort of exchange could he have made? Maybe it was a business deal among the fathers."

"Alright. You wait at the top of the steps and if he comes, try to head him off until I can get out of his room. By the way, which one is his room?" She was suddenly glad Suzanne followed her. Going from room to room might have been a nightmare.

"Sounds good. It's room number four." Suzanne posted herself guard at the top of the steps and shewed Everleigh on.

At the door of room number four, she paused a minute and then turned the knob. The room was dark with the light of day fading away. A faint moonlight was cast on the floor beside the window. The curtains billowed in and out with the gentle summer breeze. As her eyes adjusted, she could make out the bed and dresser. His case was open on the bed. She could see clothes inside. She pawed around the sides when something cold touched her hand. She pulled it out. Metal buckles over leather cuffs. The hairs on her neck stood on end.

What did he plan to do with these?

She turned to the dresser. Some coins were scattered next to a pair of glasses. She slowly opened the top drawer. Empty. He hadn't had time to unpack. He probably assumed he wouldn't be here long enough to get comfortable.

Turning back to the bed, her eyes landed on the night table. A small drawer was slightly open. She pulled it open and saw the legal papers inside. Snatching them up, she closed the drawer and turned to go. Voices carried up the steps. Her heart lurched. She listened through the door.

Suzanne loudly made conversation with a

guest and his wife in the hallway. Before long, the couple's footsteps went farther down the hall and she heard the click of the door closing.

She darted out the door and closed it silently behind her. Suzanne tiptoed to her quickly with a look of glee and ushered her to Everleigh's room.

Inside, Suzanne lit the oil lamp on the dresser and Everleigh laid the papers down for them to look at. The yellow glow of the flame made a circle of light around them. They both read as fast as they could. It looked pretty straight forward. Everleigh would gain the inheritance if she married Mr. Peeble. If she did not, the entire estate would go to the only other living relative, Everleigh's aunt, Emory Heartwell.

Everleigh turned to Suzanne with a serious gaze.

"He didn't mention this. He just said I would not get it. I think he said the court would decide. That liar!"

"Don't get too excited. Just because it goes to your aunt doesn't mean it will help you."

"Surely my aunt would not leave me penniless! In fact, I am going to live with her, so that will work out."

Suzanne gave me another matronly smile.

"You innocent babe." She sighed. "I am sure your aunt will keep you until you are wed to a man who will take care of you, but she will likely keep the majority of the inheritance. Do you have any idea how big it is?"

Everleigh shook her head. There was no way she would know. Suzanne rifled through the rest of the pages. At the back was a statement from the bank dated the day the papers were drawn up. She gasped.

"No wonder he wants to marry you! You may as well be royalty."

"What do you mean?" She took the papers and read them. Her eyes got as big as saucers as she read the statement. Apparently, her father had invested in Alexander Graham Bell's telephone at some point and had numerous shares of stock, which at the time the papers were drawn up, had a value of $100,000 worth of gold bullion.

"Oh my god! These papers are dated fifteen years ago. That stock is worth a lot more now. Maybe three or four times that amount." She stumbled back on the bed and sat there staring at the papers. "I don't know how he is so calm about it."

"He has to be. You are only thing keeping him from it. He doesn't want to mess this up. That invention of Mr. Bell's is talked about widely. Your father must have had a very good intuition."

"Then Mr. Peeble had better find some other way to get rich! There is no way I am letting him have that money. Or me!"

"So are you just going to refuse and let it go to your aunt?"

"It's my only option, I guess. I would rather she get it than him, wouldn't you think?"

"That's true. At least he would not get it and you would have means until you marry."

She giggled. "What if I never marry?"

Suzanne smiled, "Oh pretty girl, I don't see how that is going to work out for you."

A knock at the door made them both jump and stare at each other.

"Who's there?"

"It's just me, Mr. Clark. Are you ladies alright? I was worried about you. I think Mr. Peeble is worried you jumped out a window and he'll lose his fiancé'"

Stifling a laugh, "I'm fine, sir. We will be right out. I am almost ready."

Suzanne was already helping her with her laces and pulling the gown over her head. When she was presentable, she stashed the legal papers under her mattress for safe keeping, and they made their way back down stairs.

The three men were all looking in different directions not talking. Mr. Steel's hair was wild on his head apparently from repeated rakes with his hand. The tension was thick enough to cut with a knife.

As they approached, all three men jumped up. Mr. Clark released a very stiff sigh of relief. He grasped his wife's hand and kissed her knuckles giving her an exasperated look that only Everleigh and Suzanne could see.

"My beautiful darling. So glad to have you back," he paused. "Perhaps you could tell us one of your funny stories about when your family tried to raise camels when you were a child. We could use some light-hearted conversation."

Everleigh stole another glance at Malcolm. At Mr. Clark's last three words, the corners of his lips turned a devil-who-cares snarky smile. He pulled out Everleigh's chair for the second time and helped her be seated.

After some thinking, Suzanne started in on her story about a camel chasing her around a field when she was a child and then taking off through the gate at full gallop. Her father and a workman had a time getting it back as their lasso's kept falling on the humps and slipping off.

Everleigh chuckled and looked at Mr. Peeble who was fidgeting with his dinner fork. He was sitting back in his chair as though he had a thousand other things to do and this dinner was keeping him from them.

Dinner was served and for a while, they all ate in awkward silence. When Mr. Peeble put down his fork, he abruptly excused himself and demanded Everleigh come with him.

Her mouth fell open at his complete inconsideration.

"Mr. Peeble, I'm not finished enjoying our host's wonderful meal."

"I think you have had enough. Besides, I will not have a fat wife."

Like the thud of a book hitting the floor, an ache hit her heart. She looked around for any support and the others, even Mr. Steel sat motionless. This was hers to deal with. It was apparent that in that time, what happened in a marriage was no one's business.

Her skin started to sizzle from the neckline of her dress up to her eyes. He might have gotten away with it if he had been talking to only a twenty-year-old, but her 21st century mature self would not have it. She stood turned to face him and felt the unfurling of a dragon inside her before she spoke.

"Mr. Peeble! Your opinion of my appearance is of absolutely no value to me. Beside the fact that I am already too good for you aside, you would do well to brush up on your manners as a gentleman.

Furthermore, I will finish my dinner, if for no other reason than I shall never take orders from you again."

With that she sat down, picked up her fork and took a bite of mashed potatoes. When she looked up, they were all staring at her wide-eyed.

"What? Can't a woman speak her mind? Puh-lease!"

She turned to Malcolm whose face morphed from shear surprise to a satisfied grin.

"Miss Addison, I warn you, I will not be spoken to in such a manner from a woman." She turned and watched him stomp off. She hadn't realized it, but the other diners had all stopped during her scene and were now watching it unfold.

She gave Mr. Steel a side glance and saw him purse his lips and furrow his brow. A renewed flush of steam scorched her face.

How could he think I should bow to the man? Are all the men of this age pigs?

"I think I have lost my appetite now and actually feel a bit ill. If you will excuse me, I think I should go get some air." She stood and the two gentlemen jumped from their seats.

She made her way across the dining room and out the side porch doors.

The air was cooling down to a comfortable soft breeze. She sat on the wicker bench under a trellis wrapped in morning glory vines with the blossoms all swirled closed for the night.

Feeling lonely, she wallowed in the snarl of non-romance she was experiencing with either of these men. If Mr. Peeble would have been in love, it would have been one thing. As it was, he seemed to loathe her.

Then Mr. Steel would wax and wane with affection and aloofness. She couldn't figure him out, but he surely wasn't pursuing her. Whatever his problem was, he had some big hang ups. She rubbed her arms and enjoyed the silky skin of the back of her arms. Maybe being alone really was the best answer. She could just go to her aunts and stay there awhile. Her aunt would be well taken care of. Eventually she could use the lavender soap again and go back.

A board creaked and she looked up. Mr. Peeble leaned against the pole watching her.

"I thought you were going upstairs," she said.

"I will do as I please and not answer to you. You will need to learn your place."

"I know my place. I am free to do as I please as well. You are not my master."

He strode the distance between them in three paces, pulling her up in front of him by her arms.

"I will be soon. Would you rather be penniless, begging for food and a dirty bed? Maybe you could sell yourself for money?" He turned her roughly looking her up and down. "You might get someone to give you a quarter for a roll in the hay."

His vulgar comments cut her to the bone. In the modern time, she had endured comments about being fat and no one wanting her from rude men and women, but now she saw the other side. Being thin and attractive meant being called a whore. There was never any peace. She had always thought the pretty girls must have had it so easy.

"How I manage will certainly be none of your concern!" She shrugged away from him.

"It doesn't matter anyhow. You will be marrying me tomorrow. We will get this settled and then I don't care what you do."

She lifted her chin and eyed him, "And what if I say no?"

He stood dead still sizing her up. She didn't take her eyes off him and watched his expression change from anger to nonchalance.

"You will marry me. It will be for your own good."

Thinking of the papers, she knew she had other options.

"Maybe I'll just live with my aunt. Together we will get along. It's not like I need you or something."

His eyes lowered to barely a squint. Grabbing her arms just below her shoulder again, he squeezed his fingers until they dug in her flesh. She tried to pull away and he shook her.

"Everleigh, I don't think you understand. I will not take no for an answer!"

"Please! Let go of me! You're hurting me!" The pain of his fingers gripping her felt like stab wounds.

"Mr. Peeble, I think you have no right to talk to the lady like that. Not at least until you are legally married. She absolutely has the right to say no to you." Mr. Steel's calm gravelly voice cut the air in barely a whisper yet halted Mr. Peeble into a freeze.

He let go of Everleigh and turned around composing himself as he did. She nearly stumbled from the quick change. Taking the opportunity, she slipped away and stepped behind Mr. Steel, rubbing her bruised arms.

"Mr. Steel, you should really stay out of other people's business."

"Is that so? But tell me how her rights to refuse you are your business?"

Mr. Peeble started and stopped to say something. Seeing he had nothing that would refute Malcolm, he tipped his hat.

"Everleigh, we will finish this conversation another time. Until then…" he stepped inside the dining room doors and disappeared.

Malcolm turned to her, his face downcast and searching.

"My dear, are you alright?"

A tear slid from her eye as she rubbed her arms.

"He hurt you, then. Bast-" he started, "excuse me. He is the most repulsive man I have ever seen."

"But you seemed upset at dinner when I spoke my mind. I thought you were mad that I talked to him like that."

He looked at her with drawn brows, searching her eyes, then realization caused him to smile gently. "No, my dear, it's not you." He caressed her delicate cheek. "It's me, I, it's something I have to deal with."

"Can't you tell me?"

He smiled at her and her heart thudded into over drive. His tender lips drew her eyes to them. She wanted nothing more than for him to take her in his arms and crush her with his kiss.

"It's personal, you understand."

"But, Mr. Steel," she looked at the ground embarrassed, "don't you, don't you want me? I need to know."

Pain crossed his eyes as she looked back up as though he couldn't bear to see her so vulnerable. With sudden purpose, he reached around her and pulled her against him. The warmth of his body melted her like hot wax in the sun. She breathed in his scent, rugged and earthy, and relaxed into his hold. The effect of their closeness affected him as well. His breathing got more rugged and his hand searched her back in a soft rub. His head leaned down so his lips grazed the soft curve of her ear.

"My dear," he whispered, "more than you know. It takes all my strength to be a gentleman next to you."

She raised her hand and caressed his cheek and looked into his eyes. Closing his eyes, he covered her hand with his and nuzzled into her palm. He kissed her fingertips then sucked in a breath and looked into her eyes again. She could see a lifetime of desire rise in his eyes.

"Mr. Steel, Malcolm, I think I don't want you to always be a gentleman around me." She turned her face up and kissed his jaw lightly.

The effect on him was his undoing. His breath hitched as he pulled her body up and against him. He buried his face into her neck struggling to not let go of his resolve and yet his body betrayed him.

"Oh, Everleigh," he choked out hoarsely letting all his breath go giving up. His mouth found hers and her head leaned against the crook of his elbow as he bent over her. Tender lips covered hers searching and hungry. His tongue traced her lips, tickling with a satiny touch before plunging deep into her mouth searching for hers. In a sensuous tango, he kissed her soundly and completely until she felt the dizziness from not breathing overcome her.

"Malcolm," she moaned.

"Yes, my love," his eyes danced with

happiness.

"Malcolm, I need you." Her hands inside his coat, she explored the texture of the firm muscles of his chest covered by his white shirt

"As I need you."

They embraced until her arms ached and then pulled away. His green eyes held her gaze as though a tangible cord between them had been created.

"Walk with me in the gardens behind the Inn," he invited with a slight smile of a scoundrel.

"Do you think it's safe?" she asked peering around him to see through the trellis.

"Probably not," he stole another kiss and smiled, "but you can hold my hand if you are scared."

She giggled and put her hand in his. Her hand was like a child's in his, so small. His skin was hot and rough. She felt like nothing could ever harm her with him there. He led her down the wood steps that led behind the house. The moonlight lit the path of crushed seashells. The scent of roses tickled her nose as they passed several bushes as tall as she was. They came to an opening between two hedges that served as garden walls for an inner terrace. Tall grasses shot up in a spray of spikey leaves that grabbed at her lace sleeves as they passed. She heard water babbling and as they turned past a section of daisies, she saw rocks stacked around a grassy spring that bubbled up out of the ground and tumbled away toward a small pond with cattails and lily pads. An iron bench, nearly hidden by a leafy tree, glowed white in the moonlight. He pulled her with him as he sat down, wrapping a protective arm around her back.

They sat listening to the water and the cooing of a dove nearby. Her heart pounded and jumped inside her chest as she leaned into his side under his arm. He turned to her and lifted her chin, pressing a delicate kiss across her lips that felt like butterflies drinking nectar from her mouth. She traced the length of his muscular neck, feeling goosebumps rise on him from her touch. The heat of his pulse burned the center of her palm as she felt it throb in her hand.

He bowed his head and took her hands in his.

"Everleigh, I have tried, but I cannot deny my feelings for you."

"Tried? Why have you tried to deny it? Is it because of that creep Mr. Peeble?"

He smiled at her description of him.

"I'm not certain what a creep is but it sounds right. No, although I will say it is imprudent to fall in love with another's betrothed."

She snorted, "I am not marrying that guy, no matter what he thinks."

"I am glad to hear you say that. I wouldn't wish that man on any woman. But, no, that is not the reason. My life is," he paused, "um, complicated."

"Whose isn't?"

He smiled at her attempts to make him feel at ease.

"When you find out what I am trying to say, you may think differently. I have something to tell you. After you hear it, I will not hold it against you if you find it too difficult."

"What are you trying to say?" She searched his eyes.

He took a deep breath before beginning, "I am the guardian of my nephew. A little boy."

She sighed a great breath of air, "Is that all? For heaven's sake. Why would you think that would deter me from wanting you?"

Her words affected him and he closed his eyes trying to regain composure. He shifted his position.

He stood suddenly facing away from her with his hands on his hips.

"Malcolm," she stood up and put her hand on his back, "I think it's wonderful you take care of your nephew. That's a lot of responsibility. I didn't realize your aunt and uncle had a child."

He turned to face her taking her hands in his, "And Bethann, Mrs. Monroe, she is his nanny."

Everleigh looked at the spring bubbling happily in the moonlight.

"But why didn't you just tell us earlier about Bethann?"

"I," he paused, "it would raise questions, you see."

"I don't see how. That seems like a typical thing to happen. After all, my aunt is taking me in. How is that any different?"

He stared at her in the moonlight watching her response. He breathed a heavy sigh and she knew there was something more. Surely this was not what he was hiding. It was not worthy of being hidden.

"I just want you to understand that I have obligations that are mine to deal with."

"Oh, don't give it another thought. I can't wait to meet him."

She turned and bent to smell a rose blossom giving him a plain view of her backside. His eyes shot up and he sucked in a breath.

"Yes, er, there is no rush. I do not want him to be involved until, uh, when our relationship is more determined. It might be hard on him, you understand."

Turning back to him, "Oh. Yes, I suppose that makes sense. I'll leave it to you then."

He released a held breath. He reached for her and crushed her to him suddenly moved with passion.

"Darling Everleigh, I do care for you so."

"I feel the same for you." She smiled, filled with joy at his closeness.

"Can I see you tomorrow for dinner?"

"Yes! I would like that very much." Then she remembered Mr. Peeble. "Of course I will need to give Mr. Peeble the heave-ho. He is getting on my nerves."

"I would be happy to run him out on a rail for you. I have a rail that would work." His eyes jumped with mischievous delight.

"That is very nice of you to offer, but I can give him the bad news myself."

He wrapped his hands around her tiny waist and pulled her close, playing with the ribbons of the bodice with his thumbs. Then he bent down and left a trail of hot kisses along her collar bone. His breath felt like hot feathers beating against the wet skin. She shuddered at the touch of his mouth. Taking his face in her hands, she turned his head up and held him, lingering several seconds before she boldly kissed his mouth in reply to the heat that was coursing through her. His arms wrapped double around her torso and pulled her off the ground as his desire took hold. His passion left her breathless. He kissed her until she was nearly faint and she realized she had stopped breathing. The whole garden seemed to buzz with the magic their hearts were creating.

***

Malcolm took his time putting General in his stall. The sweet night air seemed to have followed him all the way from that garden. He could feel her mouth on his, feel her soft fingers on his cheeks. His hands had memorized the contours of her back as it curved to barely nothing before delicately fanning out in a blessed curve of hips. She was going to be the death of him. He had wanted to lay her down on the soft grass next to the brook and make her his right then, but he was too much of a gentleman for that.

His father raised him to protect ladies at all costs even if it meant your death. It was a godly man's duty. Women gave life and therefore it was a man's job to give her his. He would have drowned himself in that pond before he violated her tender beauty. That didn't stop his mind from daydreaming, though.

He pulled the saddle from the horse's back, set it aside, and grabbed the brush. He carefully stroked the soft hair of the horse brushing away the perspiration from the ride. The horse whinnied its pleasure and turned back from the bucket of grain to nuzzle his hand.

"Yeah, ol' boy. A soft hand makes the world go round, does it not?"

The horse resumed munching oats. Malcolm gently smoothed the horse's rump until a glossy sheen emerged. When he'd finished, he hung up the brush and flopped onto a pile of hay in the center of the barn. The sweet husky scent of the hay drifted past his nose. The horse continued to chew the oats as a light cross breeze carried along the floor of the barn. He could smell rain in the air.

He tried to imagine Everleigh meeting Percy. Would she gasp in horror when she knew the truth? Would she understand? He was such a sweet boy. Surely she would be able to look past the circumstances and see the sweetness in him. Worse yet, would she contact the sheriff?

Suddenly he felt so selfish. How could he jeopardize so much over a girl? And with the lawyers on his back, he could quite possibly lose the estate. He couldn't take care of her if he had nowhere to live. He had already liquidated all of his assets in Louisville to pay for Bethann and without the income from the estate, he would have to let her go. Bethann was so good with Percy. He had come so far. He was stupid to let his heart get so tangled in Everleigh's grasp.

**

"Have you heard the news?" asked Suzanne as she strode over to Everleigh having tea and toast on the porch.

"No. What news?"

"Apparently Mr. Steel is about to lose his estate."

"What? Why?" She imagined him with a wagon of all his belongings wandering down a road looking for a home. And now there was a little boy involved.

"Apparently there is some craziness about the title. His uncle's Revolutionary War ancestor acquired the land through a land grant, like so many did. But then he went and changed the title so that if at some point down the line there is no heir, the land is to go back to the government."

Everleigh shook her head in confusion.

"But, but there is an heir. He told me about his nephew."

Suzanne looked at her now, "What? No dear, there is no heir. His aunt and uncle died childless."

"He just told me last night he cares for his nephew."

Suzanne clucked her tongue. "Cecelia had been with child at one time. It was about four, maybe five, years ago. The little doll died at childbirth."

Everleigh sucked in a breath confused.

Suzanne continued, "She grieved so. She wouldn't receive visitors for months. Even after that, they rarely invited anyone over. She seemed changed. I suppose it affected her so badly she never got over it."

"Could this be a nephew of another sibling that he keeps?"

"I don't think so. Besides, we have never seen the child? Surely it would go to school. Did he say how old it was?"

"Young, I think. I'm not sure."

"I suppose he will introduce you soon enough and then we will know."

"I suppose. I told him I was looking forward to meeting the child but he acted like it would be a while."

"Our Mr. Steel is very mysterious."

Everleigh wracked her brain trying to piece together the mismatched puzzle pieces.

Suzanne continued, "I suppose, if there is an heir, that would help save the estate."

"Yes. I imagine he will have it worked out before long."

"Everleigh, what are you going to do about Mr. Peeble? Surely you are not going to marry that vile man."

"Heavens, no! I will have to talk to him today."

"Don't expect him to take it lightly. Not with all that inheritance tied up. But I agree, your only time to choose is now, before the marriage. Afterward, you have no choice at all. I got very lucky with my Edward, he never raises a hand to me, but I know of many other woman who don't fare as well. "

The front door opened and Mr. Peeble stepped out, pulling his cuffs and straightening his jacket.

"Speak of the devil," Everleigh mumbled.

He turned his head then and noticed her sitting with Suzanne.

"Ah, my dear, I was just going to search out the fine justice of the peace."

"If you will excuse me, I think I have some business inside." Suzanne made her getaway.

"Mr. Peeble, why don't you sit with me a minute?"

"All right. For a minute, but not long."

She waited until he was seated and then took a breath.

"Mr. Peeble, I must decline our arrangement. I have no interest in marrying you." She had decided that being perfectly clear was a better route than him misunderstanding.

He looked out at the yard seemingly to take a moment to think of the right words. Then turned to her.

"Miss Addison, I have no concern for what interests you. The arrangement is final. Your father arranged this marriage fifteen years ago and I have waited. I cannot imagine that you would sacrifice your father's wishes and your family fortune over some silly notions of what *interests you*."

This wasn't going to be easy apparently. She continued with what she knew from business. You don't back down and be clear.

"I have told you my decision. I will not marry you."

His jaw slacked and he looked around agitated. She figured he was not used to women being so firm of mind.

"I have papers that state you have no other option." He continued.

"I have seen your papers. It is not a binding agreement on my part. I do have a choice."

At this his eyes narrowed. He jumped from his chair and hissed out his words, "You conniving devil! You went through my room!"

"For matters that pertain to my life, I think I have a right to know."

"You have no rights, woman."

"No. You have no rights over me. Now, please do not come around me again."

She turned her posture away from him to show with her stance that she was through with this discussion.

His hands shook and strands of hair had fallen over his forehead. He turned on his heel and darted inside. She wondered if he would ransack her room. She decided it would be best to tell Mr. Clark.

She went inside and found him at the desk in the parlor.

"Mr. Clark, I have told Mr. Peeble of my

intention to not marry him. He did not take it well. I am worried he may go into my room and bother my things. Could you check on him?"

Mr. Clark studied her for a minute. She could tell he was surprised that a woman that young had had such a conversation and still had her wits about her. He stood up and told her he would check into it.

"I certainly don't want any unpleasantness in the Inn."

Suzanne came in as he was leaving and took her hands.

"Is everything alright, dear?"

"I'm not sure. He took it badly. I just asked Mr. Clark to check on him. I told Mr. Peeble I had seen the papers, so I am sure he is going to look for them now."

"Oh dear! It was smart of you to tell my husband."

They heard a crashing noise upstairs and sound of breaking wood.

"Oh no! Edward!" Suzanne cried.

"I'll run and get the sheriff!" said Everleigh. She darted out the front door.

Two men from the dining room dashed upstairs. The sounds of a fight rang out with the smacking of fists against bones.

Suzanne wrung her hands waiting for it to end. The sheriff burst through the door with his firearm out and took the stairs two at a time. A single gunshot rang out and Suzanne screamed.

Everleigh made it back, apparently unable to keep up with the sheriff. She ran in the parlor and the women wrapped their arms around each other. Suzanne began sobbing.

The upstairs quieted down and they heard the thumping of shoes on steps. The sight of the sheriff holding a handcuffed Mr. Peeble came into view.

"That's her! The thief! She is the one you should arrest!"

"Yeah, yeah," said the sheriff. The men following the sheriff watched them leave and then closed the door before turning back to the dining room.

"Edward!" Suzanne tore off up the stairs. Everleigh followed.

Upstairs, Suzanne stopped short on the landing. The door to Eveleigh's room was splintered and shattered hanging on one hinge. Mr. Clark was examining the damage shaking his head and rubbing a red spot on his jaw. He turned to Suzanne when he noticed her there.

"That man is crazy!" he said.

"Oh, Edward. I heard the gunshot and I was so worried!"

"Oh no, dear. The sheriff was just getting Mr. Peeble's attention. He was crazed." Then Mr. Clark looked up at the ceiling trying to find the hole.

He continued, "Miss Addison, you made a wise choice. That man is unbalanced. Suzanne, why don't you take her down and give her a spot of tea. She looks a little piqued. You do, too, actually. I am going to try to clean up this mess."

"Yes, dear. I'm so proud of the way you handled him! You're such a hero!" She gave her husband a wink and a squeeze. Mr. Clark blushed and smiled modestly.

"The sheriff helped, too," he added.

Suzanne took Everleigh by the arm and the

two of them went downstairs to the back porch. Suzanne told her it would be best to stay away from the front until it all dies down. There would be gawkers and such. Everleigh was glad. She just wanted to hide now. She'd had courage at the time but now her strength was crumbling and she shivered.

"Dear, dear. Now you just sit and take deep breaths. It's all fine now."

She helped Everleigh to a bench and Fluffed pillows around her.

"I'll just tell the cook to make us a tea service and I'll be right back."

Everleigh thought back to her conversation with Mr. Peeble. She thought she hadn't said anything so wild that he should lose his mind. Perhaps the prospect of losing a fortune was more than he could handle.

She breathed a deep breath, relieved he was now in custody. She held her hands together trying to stop the shaking. The sound of a man yelling jerked her head up, fear seizing her.

Lord, did he escape?

As the voice came closer, she recognized it.

Malcolm!

"Everleigh!" he called from inside the Inn.

She jumped and ran inside. He was standing in the foyer trying to decide which way to go.

"I'm here, Malcolm!"

He ran to her and scooped her into his arms.

"Oh, God, thank you. Everleigh. I was in town and I heard the gun shot and then saw the sheriff dragging Mr. Peeble away. I was scared to death for you. Are you alright?"

"I'm fine. Just shook up."

He pulled her away to look her over.

"I guess he didn't care for your decision?"

"You can say that again."

He hugged her to him again. Suzanne appeared and smiled.

"Mr. Steel, would you like to join us for tea on the back porch. I was just trying to calm Everleigh's nerves. But, you might be able to do a better job than tea."

Not taking his eyes off of Everleigh, he nodded. They filed through the hallway and out the door to the back porch. This porch was much smaller and more of a utility porch. A swing hung on the left and a wood garden bench and chairs were on the right. Everleigh and Malcolm sat on the bench. He put his arm around her shoulders as he kept looking at her to reassure himself she was alright. Suzanne set the tea service on a small side table and poured each one a cup. She settled herself into a wood chair.

"Darling," he started, "what happened?" Suzanne's brows shot up at the affectionate nickname.

"I was very clear and didn't mince words. I thought it best not to give him any false hopes. He had legal papers that he told me said I had no choice but to marry him. I'd snuck into his room and found them. He hadn't told me the whole story. I knew my rights and that incensed him. I asked Mr. Clark to check on him and he found him breaking into my room."

Malcolm stiffened and then smiled at her pleased.

"That's very brave for a young woman to stand up to him like that. I'm certain he didn't expect it."

"Apparently not. I will not get my parents' inheritance now. It will go to my aunt. I suppose that's alright. It's not like I'm homeless."

Suzanne chimed in, "You can stay here with us as long as you need to, you know."

She smiled and said, "Thank you. Your friendship means the world to me."

"I need to go check to make sure the lunch menu is settled and if the maids need help. Will you excuse me?"

She sat her tea down on the tray and went back inside.

"My darling, you should have let me talk to him. What if he'd hurt you?" His brows pressed down in concern.

"I'm sure you telling him to shove off would not have made him take it any better," she laughed.

"At least that is done. I need to go to Midway and check on the station and schedules today. Are you up for an outing? I could show you around a little. You could do with getting away from here a little, I'm certain." His right eyebrow perked up mischievously.

She straightened and smiled, "I would love that! When are you leaving?"

"As soon as you are ready," he said with a satisfied grin.

She jumped from his arms and told him she just needed to get her hat and she would be right back. She darted gracefully up the stairs, carefully stepped past the broken door and went to the vanity table. She affixed the summer straw hat with a pin and smiled at herself. The glow of color on her pale cheeks made her feel alive. A handsome sweet man awaited her downstairs. She savored the moment.

Tiptoeing past the broken door and splintered wood again, she made her way back to him. He stood up from the bench in the foyer and took her hands.

"You look lovely," he breathed kissing her behind her ear.

She giggled. Holding out his arm, he escorted her outside and across the road to his carriage. She cast a glance toward the sheriff's office. It appeared to be calm. She was relieved to know Mr. Peeble was locked away and couldn't hurt her. She thought about what a dangerous man he could be to be married to and shivered.

"He can't get you now," Malcolm reassured her sensing her thoughts.

She smiled and he lifted her up into the carriage. Malcolm climbed in behind her and Mr. Sloan lightly snapped the reins. The carriage jumped forward.

"So is your work in Midway?"

"Yes, for the most part. I manage the station and the section gang from Midway to Lexington. I tend to the men, ensure the coal and water supplies are available. If the track needs repair, I send the gang to fix it. The trains stop in Midway to fill up their tinders coming and going from Lexington."

"I see."

"I transferred to this station two years ago when I moved to my Uncle's estate. I worked at the Louisville depot before. Taking care of the men is a big job. They are a good group of guys. Colorful folk. Some get liquored up and get themselves in a predicament and I watch out for them. I could tell you some funny stories. Not just about the men, but also about the things we see along the line. You name it and we have seen it."

She chuckled.

The ride to Midway took over an hour. As they approached town, she remarked, "It seems like a long ride to work and back."

"I usually hop on the baggage car of the Versailles & Midway train rather than carriage. Some nights I sleep at one of the section houses in Midway. It's alright." He got a faraway look in his eyes as he gazed out the side window.

They pulled onto Main Street and the station loomed. Midway was smaller than Versailles. One short main street with a station. The tracks ran through the middle of town with a street and row of shops on each side. People were walking on the boardwalk in front of shops. The town seemed alive with commotion.

"What a cute town!" All the gingerbread details in the architecture made it look like a perfect scene of Americana. She didn't recall ever coming to Midway in her prior business trips so it was hard to compare it to what it would become by 2016.

"Here we are." Malcolm opened the door of the carriage and jumped out, then turned and lifted her down with ease making her feel light as a feather.

"Mr. Sloan, we'll lunch here in Midway, so it will be several hours until we need a ride home. Why don't you enjoy Midway for a while? "

"Very good, sir. I'll visit my sister, then." Mr. Sloan clucked his tongue and led the horses and carriage away.

They made their way into the agent's office in

the depot and she took a seat on a side bench to give him some space while he spoke to the men.

"Mr. Steel," said a man in an apron with glasses. He had a black band around his bicep that made his blue shirt bellow at the top, "The 11:30 to the Asylum is short a hand. We don't have anyone to spare. Any way you could go with it and back?"

Malcolm looked back at Everleigh. "I have a guest with me, Mr. Newsome. I'm not sure it would be a good idea to take a lady on that trip."

She jumped up, "I don't mind to go. I enjoy riding the train."

He strode over to her, "It's not just an ordinary run, darling. It's to make a delivery to the Lunatic Asylum in Lexington."

She noted a slight shiver when he said the name. His mouth turned down in a sour expression. It was plain he detested the place. Something in her memory caught her.

He continued, "They have their own rail line for deliveries. I'm not certain it is safe, much less desirable, for a lady to be there."

Mulling it through her mind, she remembered why it sounded familiar. Her client in 2016, whom she had come to the Bluegrass to consult with, was Bluegrass Career and Technical College. They had relocated to the site of the old Eastern State Hospital. Was this the same place?

"I am rather curious. I'd like to go. What if I stayed in the passenger coach while we are there so you wouldn't have to worry?"

"Mr. Steel, we are in a bit of a pickle. The delivery train will be here shortly and without another hand, we won't be able to make the delivery. We really have no place to house the box car until we have an extra hand tomorrow. And, of course, they are depending on the delivery."

Malcolm sighed seeing he was overruled. "Alright. Send a message to my driver that we will be later than we expected. Here is his sister's address." He jotted down a note and handed it to Mr. Newsome.

"Certainly, sir."

"We should find a bit to eat before we go. It may be awhile before we have a chance once we get going and the cargo hasn't been loaded yet, anyway." He led her out and down the boardwalk to a café at an inn. After being seated and served tea, Everleigh remembered his scowl at hearing the name Lunatic Asylum.

"You didn't have a favorable reaction when your man talked about the Lunatic Asylum? Have you had a bad experience?"

He sighed and thought before he answered.

"The people there are always nice to us. But," he paused, "I worry about the residents there."

"Why? Are they dangerous?"

"Perhaps some are, I suppose, but really I worry *for* them. I can't imagine what kind of life they have there. There is a Children's Asylum nearby and those children grow up to live at the Lunatic Asylum."

"I'm sure they are taken care of."

He looked at her searching for understanding. "Have you heard of Sir Francis Galton?"

"Um, no. I don't think I have."

"He is the cousin of Charles Darwin."

"Oh, I see."

"He has been very active in England passing

eugenics laws."

"Eugenics? What is that?"

He sighed. "He is of the belief that there is a supreme race of people, notably white, Nordic, blue eyed, intelligent people. I have seen his book *Hereditary Genius* where he describes, much like Darwin's theory of evolution, the quality of humanity can be improved with deliberate pairing of couples over several generations much like breeding dogs or horses."

"What? So this man is actually making progress getting legislation to support such inhuman ideas?" So what does this have to do with the Asylum?"

"I'll tell you. His beliefs are worse than just natural selection. He believes we should euthanize anyone who is not worthy The United States has opened an Office of Eugenics in New York to evaluate immigrants. It seems that followers of this line of thinking are making headway in this country. One of the key populations they focus on, besides immigrants who could sully the population, are the feeble-minded."

"Feeble minded? You mean disabled?"

He looked at her curiously, "Dis-abled? I am not familiar with that word."

"It's okay. I get the idea."

"So, one of the latest propaganda papers I have seen is that they want to make it a law that all children or adults who are born deformed, simple minded, or Mongoloid are to be immediately admitted to asylums. It's being debated in several states."

"Required? You mean parents would have no choice?"

"Exactly. Most are anyway. The newborns are immediately turned over at birth because of the shame it can bring on a family. And on top of that, these children would be sterilized and even forbidden from ever marrying."

"That seems extreme."

"Not if you understood the point of view of these proponents. There are people who argue that the deformed are not even human, just an animal. They would actually like to euthanize them. That is what happens in some European countries even now. Europe is ahead of us on this issue."

"How could they just make this a law? Why couldn't families just take care of their own?"

"It's already difficult because many doctors refuse to treat people who suffer from these disorders. The kindest doctors say it is for the best to let nature take its course. Even with doctors who treat them the cost is so high many families cannot afford the care."

"Refuse to treat them? What right do they have to do that? I thought doctors had to take an oath to treat anyone whose life was in danger."

"I know of no such oath. There are many schools of medicine and they all have their own school of thought. Maybe some have this oath but they can certainly choose who they deem worthy to treat. In fact, many doctors are getting on board with the notion of requiring undesirables or immoral women to be sterilized for the good of everyone. All it takes is a statement from a doctor that a woman is unfit for propagation and the authorities can seize her for forced sterilization."

Everleigh's head was swimming. Talk about going back into the dark ages, it was frightening to think of the lack of regulation and personal rights in this time. She had never heard of such atrocities here in America. Apparently her high school history book left that out.

A tickling in her mind about Hitler and his Supreme Race made her wonder if these eugenics laws had influenced him. The timing would be pretty close.

One of the things about herself that she was most proud of was being an advocate for the disabled. As a consultant, she had to spend time learning what life was like if you can't get around well. She understood that without access, a large section of the population was unfairly excluded from many goods and services. She realized for the first time that the work she did was not unlike the western expansion of the railroad. She made it possible for many people to get to doctors and businesses that made their life easier. Maybe she did dream big after all.

She also volunteered for the Special Olympics in the summers. In fact, it was coming up in her time in two weeks. Her favorite job was helping the Olympians at the swimming pool. She would sit at the starting line and call them over when it was their turn. She would say a word or two of encouragement and then when it was over, she was the first to congratulate them for trying hard. The look of pure joy and pride made her heart sing. She knew they had practiced and dreamed of competing and they all, each and every one of them, tried their hardest. Even if they didn't place, they felt like winners.

She wondered if they ever got a chance to feel like a winner in other areas of their life, but on this day, they were not just winners, but Olympians.

He continued, "I don't know if they do it at the Asylum, but I have heard from train workers that have worked for asylums on the east coast that some hospitals withhold care, or worse, to reduce their patient load. One guy I talked to said they had buried hundreds of bodies after an isolated outbreak of consumption. There were no other cases in the town around them. He just couldn't shake that they had been purposefully infected."

"Malcolm, that is horrible! How could they do that?"

"It's not that hard to fathom. Think about it. These vulnerable people, some just children, have no advocate, no family. Just a ward of the state that is required to pay for their room and board. The asylums have a budget they have to meet. And, then you have people like Sir Galton, a scientist, telling governments that the feeble-minded are lesser animals, maybe not even human. Some sort of deranged mistake of nature. Many people believe they are possessed."

"I see. They could even talk themselves into thinking it was the humane thing to do to let them die."

"Exactly. Like I said, I have no idea that it's going on at the Asylum, but I wonder, and it makes me sad."

Everleigh thought about an article she had read about the college now at that location that said there was a cemetery for the old hospital that held thousands and thousands of remains of unidentified patients. A shiver went up her spine.

After lunch they made their way back to the station. The soft summer breeze cut the scorching sun that radiated through the shoulders of her dress. Water Maples waved in the wind showing their leaves' silvery undersides. She shivered as trickles of perspiration ran down the center of her back. She and Malcolm waited on the platform for the train to pull up and the hiss of the steam overshadowed the rustling hiss of the leaves raking against each other.

With a gentle chugging whoosh-whoosh-whoosh, the short train pulled in. It was just an engine, a box car and passenger coach. Malcolm spoke to the office a minute and returned. Taking her to the passenger coach, he settled her in a wooden bench inside and went to speak to the engineer. Before long, he returned and they were on their way. The green landscape blurred by so fast she had to focus on a spot in the distance. Green fields came and went, punctuated by fields of tall corn with yellow sprig flowers blowing on top of each plant. Children ran alongside the train now and then waving their hats. The little girls' hats had long ribbons trailing behind them.

Malcolm offered her a drink of lemonade. Despite the windows being open, the stuffy humid air buffeted her, blowing wisps of loose hair around her ears. The gentle rocking of the car could lull her to sleep if she'd been tired. They had the car to themselves as the brake man was up with the engineer.

Malcolm sat next to her and traced the edge of her collar bone covered by her shirtwaist with his finger. The tickle on her skin gave her goosebumps and she leaned into his hand caressing the back of it with her cheek.

***

He couldn't imagine ever talking to a woman about such things as they had at lunch. She had such a kind heart. He had heard conversations about disfigured or feeble-minded folk that disgusted him. People's callous reactions and revulsion to such a topic was commonplace and made him angry. How could they be so cruel? But yet, she didn't recoil. She was even sympathetic. Everleigh moved him deep in his soul. Certainly she was beautiful, but he had seen many beautiful women. It was the woman under the skin that enchanted him.

He realized right then that he could not let her get away. He wanted her to be his wife. He wanted to love her every day and night of his life. He wasn't sure if she was willing or if she would be once she knew the real truth, but he would rather her turn him down than never try. His heart ached to have her so badly that now the pain of being rejected made no difference. He must try.

She heard his breathing quicken as he reached around to pull her shoulder toward him.

"Everleigh, I must tell you, I'm falling in love with you. You delight my very core."

"Oh, Malcolm, I love you, too. I have never been happier than these past few days."

"I'm not sure how I can offer you my hand in marriage. I may yet lose my uncle's estate." He sighed. "I will promise you, though, you will never go wanting for my love. Everleigh, will you marry me?"
***

Shocked at the sudden proposal, she blushed. Despite her fantasies of him kissing her, she had not allowed herself to think of him as a husband in every way. She had planned to enjoy a little side trip to the past, enjoy some romance, and then return to reality. Neither had she planned on falling in love, but she had. She couldn't help it. Malcolm was every girl's dream. Broad shouldered, smoky-eyed passion all in a tailored suit. He exuded masculine aura like steam rising off wet pavement on a hot day. Now thoughts of sharing his bed floated up in her mind. Heat rose on her cheeks.

What if she just let go of her fears and said yes? Was there a down side? Could she just stay in this time? Would she miss the conveniences of the next century, like air conditioning? She looked into his eyes and saw a lifetime love. She could love him with everything she had and he would return it back ten-fold. She knew the answer deep in her soul.

"Yes. Yes, Malcolm. Yes!"

There! She had said it. She followed her heart and let go of her fears. She wanted him with every fiber of her being.

He smiled like the sun rising on a spring day after a long winter. He leaned in and kissed her with smothering fierceness.

Unable to breath, she finally pulled back and smiled at him coyly.

His face turned serious and he held both her hands.

"I must tell you, though, you need to know something before we announce it. You are free to walk away if you must and I'll never hold it against you."

"What is it, Malcolm?" her brows knitted together in confusion. A tingling anxiety crept up her neck. She knew there was more to his secret.

"When we get back to Versailles, I need you to come to my house for a visit. Then you will understand."

She didn't know what to say. It sounded so mysterious. He looked at her with a faraway hope. Apparently whatever it was, he hoped she could live with it. She wondered what kind of secret the man must be hiding.

***

The train began to slow as it came around the bend. Malcolm stood and looked out the window toward the front of the train, his brown wavy hair blowing in the wind behind him. He looked back at her with a furrowed brow and then smiled softly.

"Everleigh, please stay here and I'll come back after we are unloaded."

She smiled and nodded. As the train squealed to a stop, he was out the back of the coach and disappeared.

She listened to the sounds of the grinding cargo doors being pulled open. Crates scraped the floor of the train car. Men shouted instructions. She looked out the window of the coach. The Asylum was a collection of buildings with the largest in the middle between two wings. The large building was three stories with two wings coming off either side. Numerous outbuildings dotted the green landscape. She noted how serene the lawn looked with benches and walkways.

A scream burst through her quiet reverie and she turned to look at the source. On the second story of one wing, she saw a woman trying to climb out a window screaming at them to help her. It appeared someone inside was trying to pull her back in.

The woman's face was contorted with fear. Was she truly a lunatic, Everleigh thought? What if someone were brought here against their will? Would anyone believe them? Would they ever get out? A shiver ran down her spine.

What if Mr. Peeble had had her committed?

The woman was pulled inside and the window slammed shut. No other noise was heard. She wondered if there were children here. At what age did the Children's Asylum move them? She didn't see any nor did she hear the sounds of anyone playing. She crossed to the other side of the coach and looked out the other window. Acres and acres of lawn stretched out. She could see a reservoir in the distance. The whole scene looked ironically idyllic.

Then she saw a tiny face peering at her around a tree. It was a young man with Down's syndrome. He smiled at her. She wondered what he was doing out there alone. Perhaps he had managed to sneak away from his caregiver. He beckoned her to him with a little motion of his hand.

She looked back toward the other side. They were still unloading the cargo. She decided to see what he wanted and let herself down the metal steps to the rocky rail tracks. Looking both ways to see if anyone was watching, she made her way over to him and knelt down. He looked young, maybe fifteen years old.

He smiled at her and touched her face.

"Pretty lady," he said.

She smiled back at him, "What are you doing out here?"

"Ahhh. I sneak away. They not know."

"Won't you get in trouble?"

He laughed. Then his faced turned down.

"They whip me if they find me." He looked around her quickly.

"Whip you?" She was appalled.

"Yeah," he paused. "I go with you?" He gestured toward the train.

"No, sugar. I'm sorry."

"Ah, it's alright. I know."

He looked around again and then his eyes opened wide.

He continued, "You go now. I hide."

She gave him a concerned look and turned back to the train. She had just made it to the step when she saw a man in a white uniform poking around the corner of the coach. He stopped when he saw her and abruptly changed his expression from annoyed to polite.

"Madam," he bowed his head acknowledging her, "You should stay on the train. For your own safety."

She nodded and climbed back onto the coach platform. She waited until he passed by before looking back toward the young man. She couldn't see him anymore.

He must be good at hiding.

Soon Malcolm climbed aboard and sat next to her on the wood bench. The train lurched backward and left the way it came. The sound of a boyish cry rang out. She jumped to look behind them in the window. The caregiver was hauling the boy by the corner of his shirt toward the building.

She heard, "I be good! I be good!" and her heart wrenched.

The train turned around a corner and she couldn't see anymore. She turned to Malcolm who had been watching, too. His eyes glistened with moisture.

He looked at her like he wanted to say something but stopped himself.

"Do you think they will hurt him? He wasn't hurting anything."

"I don't know. I do know they treat Mongoloids as though they are insane."

He watched her reaction. Her eyebrows shot up and he stiffened.

"They are not insane! That's crazy!" she said.

She saw him swallow hard and bow his head. "You realize most people do think that, that they are insane or monsters?"

She didn't know much about the history of how the disabled were treated prior to the nineteen hundreds. In her lifetime, she had seen disabled children moved from hidden rooms in schools to mainstream classrooms. The Special Olympics advertised smiling faces of Olympians. Bullying of people who were different was a stigma of intolerance.

She knew there were some in society who were truly insane. People who lived in residential treatment facilities and received therapy. Most disabled people, though, dealt with physical or intellectual challenges. Even those with behavioral challenges were able to live in group homes or function on their own after research-based therapy.

She felt a grip on her heart as she realized the ignorance that pervaded in times before hers. Not just this time, but in all of history, how many sweet people had been hidden away, abused, or worse? How many had cried in fear, not understanding, no one comforting them? She could imagine that many had been beaten like animals, possibly to death and no one would have noticed they were gone. Her gut clenched as she grieved for the ones harmed that no one knew about.

She stared absently out the window to hide her grief for all those souls. Trees now blocked her view of the Asylum. She wondered if those that lived there were treated well. If they weren't, would anyone know? Was there any government oversight? She figured not. Chances were, for the most part, no one really knew what went on there. That was a recipe for all manner of human abuses when you had a population that was vulnerable.

Crossing a road just outside the walls of the asylum, she saw a sign posted that read: Lunatic Ball, September 20th.

Good Lord! They really see nothing wrong with calling a fundraiser that!

The ride back to Midway was quiet as they were both lost in their thoughts. Everleigh wondered if somehow she could do something now, in this time, which would hasten the movement toward seeing the disabled as valuable citizens. Maybe it was just a matter of getting through to people to change the culture.

She knew that the eugenics laws would be stifled since they were unheard of in the future, but more needed to be done now to help the disabled of this time. Perhaps, like in her own time, if people were just exposed to them more, they would see they are just people who want to be loved. They were not crazy or dangerous. Maybe if articles were published, like a pre-historic blog of sorts, that talked about the everyday life of the disabled, then people could peek into their world and see for themselves.

Instead of having asylums, maybe schools could be opened where people with mental and physical handicaps could live and receive therapy. One thing is for certain she knew, she could design such a facility that would make it easier for them to get around in. She wondered what impact she would have on the future if she started all this in 1888. Maybe it wouldn't take until the 1980s for them to come out of hiding.

As the train slowed into the Depot at Midway, she pulled out of her thoughts. She looked at Malcolm who had been chewing his lip. Had this trip actually started with him proposing? A blaze of emotion tore through her. What a tender-hearted man he was. She felt humbled that she had made an impression on such a man that he had fallen in love with her. She could feel the heat of the blush creeping up her neck.

Feeling her gaze, he turned to her and all at once his countenance changed. His chest swelled and he flashed a smile that made her heart melt. He pulled her under his arm, folding himself around her. He kissed her forehead and lifted her chin to look in her eyes.

"I love you, Everleigh, with all of my being."

She nearly swooned in the delicious umbrella of his hold.

"I love you, Malcolm."

They departed the train and after he checked on some things with the agent, they found Mr. Sloan waiting patiently for them on the road next to the depot. The afternoon light was fading on their way back to Versailles. Her belly rumbled with hunger.

"Are you up to supper at my estate? If you're too tired, I can drop you off at the inn."

"No. I'm fine. I've been sitting most of the day, so I'm not tired. In fact a good walk might be nice to stretch my legs."

He exhaled and relief filled his face. He called out for Mr. Sloan to take them all the way to his estate. The night air softly wafted through the open windows and the scent of honeysuckle filled the air. Rock walls lined the dirt road and bushy green trees grew along the wall covering the road making a cool, shaded tunnel for them to escape the summer heat. Beyond the rock walls, great open grassy fields extended over gentle rolling hills dotted with graceful horses.

She thought back to May and remembered she had watched the 142nd running of the Kentucky Derby. That meant the 14th Derby had just been run in this time. She glanced up at Malcolm and wondered what he would think if he knew the truth about her. Would he ever believe her?

"So what do you think of the Derby?" she asked.

"What? Oh. I guess it's alright. I don't really have time to keep up with it. It seems to be a sport for the rich. I can't see how it'll last as expensive as it is to raise these horses for nothing but racing."

She giggled.

"Is that funny?" he looked confused.

"No. I'm sorry. It's just that sometimes reasonableness has nothing to do with what lasts."

"I suppose that is true."

They pulled into the drive of his estate. Her pulse quickened. He had been so guarded before about her being in his world. She shot a glance at him. He was looking toward the fields in a resigned, relaxed manner with no concern at all on his face.

At the house, he jumped out and turned to lift her down.

"Welcome to my home, madam," and he offered his arm.

Jones appeared to greet them and Mr. Sloan drove the carriage down a small path around the side of the main house.

Jones, will you let Cook know we will have a guest for dinner.

"Very good, sir."

Malcolm led her inside into a foyer with a great staircase that wound around as it disappeared into the ceiling. He motioned to the left, and through a wide opening, she entered the parlor. Thick rugs covered hardwood floors that gleamed in the light of the oil lamps covered the large room. A red velvet-covered sofa and two chairs sat around the focal point of a great hearth with ceramic tiles around the opening. The tiles had carved scenes in them of people involved in various farm activities. A wide glass case of various curiosities sat along the back wall. She could see large seashells and sponges mounted like scientific specimens and various books and a magnifying glass lay on top.

"Please sit down." He motioned to the couch and pulled a cord and moments later a footman appeared.

"Bring us a tea service and biscuits, please," Malcolm asked.

Without a word the footman disappeared. Malcolm sat in a chair opposite her.

"Can I get you anything else? Would you like to freshen up?"

"Perhaps that would be nice in a minute. Thank you."

"Certainly."

She noticed his leg lightly hammering. He stopped as soon as she looked and ran a hand through his hair.

"The room is lovely. Did your aunt decorate it?"

"What? Oh, yes. I suppose so. I haven't changed anything."

He looked around as though noticing it for the first time.

"Is that them? Your aunt and uncle?" She pointed to a portrait over the mantle.

"Yes. That is Cecelia and Jasper Williams."

"Your aunt has the same smile as you. They seem like they were very nice people."

If it were possible to smile and frown at the same time, Malcolm did.

"Thank you. They were, indeed. They were very loving people."

The footman brought tea and set it on the table and left. Malcolm poured and handed her a cup. He sat staring at the floor with his jaw flexed and just a straight line of lips.

"Malcolm, are you alright?" She had a note of concern in her voice.

He looked up and tried to smile but all he could accomplish was a watery turning up of the corners of his mouth. He got up and sat beside her taking her hand, holding it with both of his.

"Everleigh, there is something you must know. If you choose to marry me, it may be difficult for you."

"How so?"

He looked down and sucked in a breath of air.

"My nephew, I take care of him. My aunt and uncle had hidden him away. When they passed, I knew that for his sake, I must continue what they started."

"Why did they hide him?"

He looked at her with sad eyes but the hope of understanding set his mouth in strength.

"Percy is feeble-minded." He watched her closely to see her reaction.

"Why would you have to hide him, though?"

Hs brows shot up. "Surely things are not so different in Charleston." He paused, "Percy is a Mongoloid. Even in Louisville it is scandalous. Children such as Percy are either allowed to perish at birth or quietly transported to an orphanage for such children. Usually, the story is told that the infant died in childbirth."

Everleigh thought about what Suzanne had told her about Cecelia's childbirth and subsequent lying in. Her gut twisted at the unfairness to parents of this time.

So the child hadn't died. They choose to hide him and keep him.

It all made sense now. His reaction at the asylum. His fear. He was protecting Percy. This wonderful man was willing to sacrifice his own dreams to protect this little boy. Emotion shot through her like coursing lava.

"There are no laws yet, but we were so afraid he would be taken from us. For his sake, we have kept him a secret."

"Oh, Malcolm! I'm so glad they kept him! How awful it must have been for them to feel so alone. And you, you have loved him just as your own."

Tears sprang from his eyes and he looked down to hide his emotions.

"Yes," he said hoarsely, "it was unbearable for them, but they loved this child, as do I. How could I not continue to care for him, even if just for my aunt's sake? The boy shares my blood."

Everleigh's eyes filled with moisture as she imagined being his aunt.

"I have worried so about it. I made a decision to remain single until somehow I could ensure he would be taken care of. But I love you, Everleigh. I love you like you are part of me. I cannot choose between you and him. I need you both. I have feared you would reject him. That you would reject me for having a mark on our family that our family line is damaged."

"Oh, Malcolm!"

"But, as I came to know you, I realized that you are different. You aren't like other women I have met. You have such different sight with regard to people. You have your own mind and aren't like the sheep that follow convention. I can't help but love you even more."

"Can I see him, please?"

He patted her hand and his face lit with quiet joy. He stood and took her hand to pull her up.

"Yes. I would love to introduce my nephew.

Let's go to the nursery."

At the top of the stairs, she could hear giggling. As they neared the nursery door, she heard a little boy quietly say, "I found you, Miz Beff-en!"

"You're a smart boy, Percy! Now let's get you ready for a bath. Would you like to play in the water?" a woman's voice said sweetly.

Malcolm knocked lightly on the door and looked at Everleigh as though looking for signs she had changed her mind.

"It's alright, Malcolm." She hoped to ease his fears.

The door opened a crack and half of a face peeked through the small opening. Her brows jumped as she saw Everleigh and then her eyes darted back to Malcolm.

"It's alright, Bethann."

The woman opened the door slowly and stepped back. Everleigh saw a tiny little boy playing with a corn husk doll on the floor. When the door had fully opened, the child looked up and looked from Malcolm's face to Everleigh's and back. He pushed himself up onto his knees and then stood on stout legs and hurled himself into Malcolm's leg. He hid himself behind Malcolm and peered around him, then looked up for assurance.

"Who's dis, Uncle Mack?" the boy asked him.

"Percy, this is my friend Everleigh. She wants to be your friend, too. Will you say hello?"

"Hello, Miz Evvie," the garbled words came from behind the fabric of Malcolm's trousers.

Everleigh got down on one knee and quietly offered, "So very nice to meet you, Percy. I hope we will be friends for a long time."

He poked his head around and looked at her a minute and then ran to her with his arms out. A wall of solid child crashed into her and put his short arms around her. She laughed at his free display of affection and hugged him back. When he pulled away, patting her shoulder, she looked into his childish eyes, the telltale skin covering the inside corner of his eyes, the flat nose, the lips full and stretched into a smile. His thick round glasses. His pillow of a tongue extended slightly through his parted mouth. She noticed his shorter fingers and limbs. He was surely a Down's baby. Sweet and loving, ready to accept anyone who accepted him. How could anyone have not protected such a sweet person? She wanted so much to give him the love that the young man back at the asylum never got.

"Percy, I hope you know how much you are loved just because you are precious."

"Aw! Miz Evvie, you're nice!" His face lit up with joy and he hugged her again. She rubbed his back as she held him.

Malcolm said, "Alright, Percy. I think I heard Mrs. Bethann say you get to play in the tub now. I need to make sure our guest has something to eat. Maybe we can visit with her more tomorrow."

Percy stepped back and gave a much practiced mannerly bow.

"Gud e'ening, Miz Evvie." He took Bethann's hand and she led him through a door on the side of the nursery, closing it after they went through.

"Everleigh! My heart sings! I love my nephew so much. I never thought anyone else would accept him."

"Malcolm, I am used to being around people

with Down's, I mean Mongoloids." It was hard for her to use the old word.

"Really? In Charleston? Did you volunteer at an asylum? Bethann has studied under a man named Phillipe Pinel from France who has had great success with his 'moral treatment' techniques for Mongoloids."

"Uh, yeah. Sort of. You might say that. I am not familiar with Mr. Pinel, but yes, I believe with therapy, Mongoloids can lead very happy, productive lives."

"You amaze me more and more. Everleigh, I feel like us meeting was a fate arranged by God himself."

She laughed at his choice of words, "I agree! It was certainly a meeting of supernatural proportions."

He pulled her to him and crushed her against his chest. The scent of his skin was intoxicating. Holding her around her waist, he covered her mouth with his lips and kissed her with delicate passion like she might break or disappear if he took her for granted.

"And I will love and keep you forever, if you will have me," he said.

"Oh, yes, Malcolm. I love you."

***

He kissed her again, more fiercely this time as his passion rose. For so long he had restrained himself, denied that part of him that was a caged lion. He was finally free. Everleigh knew about Percy and accepted him, more than that she cared about him. He couldn't imagine there would be a woman like her and now she was here in his arms kissing him back.

Taking her by the hand, he left the nursery and crossed the wide hallway. He had to be alone with her. He opened his bedroom door and pulled her inside, closing it behind them. In the quiet privacy of his bedroom, he stopped and turned to her. Suddenly aware of the intimacy of the situation, he gazed into her eyes looking for any evidence of her rejection and found none.

She reached her hands up his chest and explored with her fingertips. When he felt her delicate touch on his neck, he lost all resolve to be a gentleman and crushed her against the back of the door and with his arms around her waist, lifted her to his height. His lips searched out hers and claimed her with smothering fierceness. The urgency of the long denied passion for both of them erupted in a frenzied, savage dance to consume each other.

He kissed her face and ear until he got to a place on her neck where the scent of flowers from her perfume sent him careening off the edge of sanity. He bit her earlobe and neck with little love bites. She threw her head back, inviting him to do as he pleased and moaned a low growl of delight. That was more than he could stand and he lifted her into his arms and strode to his bed.

In one movement, he laid her on the bed and covered her with his body. This bed was a place where he had spent many lonely nights wishing God would bring him a woman he could love with all of his being. Clasping her hands over her head, he covered her mouth with his. Her tongue licked the inside of his lip and a surge of lust consumed him. She answered his passion with her own and he groaned with desire. He sucked on her tongue and a wall crumbled inside him. A wall that had been built to hide away the beast of his passion.

He plunged deep in her mouth with desire to know every part of her. Her sweet breath buffeted his cheek as he made love to her mouth. He wanted more of her than decency allowed and fought the urge to make her his own right now. He knew she wanted him just as much as her body arched up to press against him. It would have been so easy to let go of his integrity.

"Everleigh, my love," he said with ragged breath against her neck, "I cannot defile you."

He said it more to convince himself than for her. He rolled next to her and stared at the ceiling. The beast inside him growled to be set free but he was the master of his body. His breathing slowed to normal and he turned to look at her. With a knowing smile of delight, her love for him was plain to see. Her hair swept down onto the bed in a glorious mess. The rise and fall of her chest from her passion nearly made him lose his resolve. He wanted her as a husband wants a wife so badly he had to turn his gaze away and stare at the ceiling again.

"We must be married soon. I fear I cannot last a lengthy engagement." Turning toward her again, "Everleigh, I want you terribly."

She smiled and caressed his cheek. "Oh, Malcolm. I want you, too."

Sitting up on his elbow, "Let's go downstairs and eat supper. This is a dangerous place for you to be lounging around with me." He smiled a devilish grin.

Chapter Five

Everleigh awoke to a thunderstorm pelting rain against her window. The wind blew so hard, the rain sounded like pebbles hitting the glass. Her room was dark and gray. She thought back to the previous day with the train ride, the hospital, and meeting Percy. It made sense now, all the times he'd acted strange. No wonder he had fought his feelings. He had worried that bringing another into his family could be so dangerous to Percy. She wondered at how few men would have chosen his path to care for his nephew.

She had never even considered that it would have been a black spot on his pedigree that he may carry the Mongoloid trait and pass it to his children. Seeing how little they understood in this time about genetics, she could understand why marriageable girls would have turned away from him if they had known. Even he may worry that his family is damaged and could pass it on to another child. He obviously had worried what it would mean to her.

She shook her head at the fears. What a dark time to live in even with their dawning of inventions. She sat up and ran her fingers through her hair. Lightening flashed outside the window and she waited for the booming thunder. It came with a crack like boulders rolling down a rocky cliff and rattled the walls. Despite Malcolm's invitation, she didn't see how she would be going to his estate in this weather.

She splashed water on her face and cleaned her teeth. She dressed in a simple white blouse and dark linen skirt, over the corset, of course. She missed shorts and tee shirts if nothing else because it was so much cooler to wear.

Pulling her hair up in a bun, she felt pangs of hunger for breakfast. She put on her shoes and headed out the door.

Pulling the door closed, she stepped toward the stairs. Turning the corner at the landing a hand shot out and covered her mouth while another snaked around her waist. She struggled but the arms were too strong. He drug her back down the hallway. Fearing she was about to be raped, she kicked and twisted. Like a snake pressing in, her movements only increased further tightening of his arms.

He managed to get a door open and hauled her back inside her room, kicking the door closed with his foot. He turned and pulled her onto the bed with him lying behind her.

"My dear, Miss Addison. I don't take kindly to being inconvenienced by a woman. That is certainly not going to be tolerated in our marriage."

Everleigh sucked in a breath. *Mr. Peeble.* She wondered if this guy was a masochistic freak. Adrenaline shot through her veins burning everywhere her blood pumped. She lay very still thinking that maybe he would at least take his hand from her mouth.

"Very good. You are learning fast. This might be easier than I thought." He released his hand over her mouth and turned her face toward him. She was inches from him. Close enough to smell the stale liquor on his breath. Apparently he had managed to be released from the sheriff.

"You are forcing me to take drastic action. Here's how it's going to work. You will come with me now to the justice of the peace. If the one here insists on continuing to not do his job, we will ride to Lexington and find one there. We shall be married, consummate this infernal arrangement and then I don't care what the hell you do as long as you show me respect in public. I promise," he laughed as though the thought of it was ridiculous, "to never lay a hand on you ever again. I find you utterly undesirable and will have to close my eyes to get through the consummation."

She winced at his words. It made no sense. She was attractive. If it had been her old body, it would have made sense. A tear slipped from the corner of her eye as she realized it was not about appearances. Our outward body was merely a mask covering our souls and had nothing to do with who we were on the inside.

"Touching with the tear. Really. If I gave a damn perhaps it would matter, but I don't."

He sat up, still holding her arms against her as he held her waist. He pulled his bag out from under her bed.

He's has been in my room.

He reached into his bag and pulled out the leather cuffs. She struggled to get loose and suddenly heard a crack and felt blinding pain in her back. Like a rock had lodged into her, she felt his fist still tight against her side.

She slumped onto his other arm around her and wheezed trying not to breathe deeply. Her mind started to swim and she felt like she was spinning or the room was spinning or just her head. She realized she was going to pass out. Blackness engulfed her and she felt like she was slipping down a long dark slide.

She felt a tapping on her cheek, then a flicking. She opened her eyes and tried to sit up. The white hot pain in her rib made her cry out.

"Shhh! None of that, my dear."

She looked up at him as he sized her up. She was laying on the floor on a rug. Apparently she had fallen there when she passed out and he didn't bother to pick her up.

"You look a wreck. We can't have that."

He went around behind her and pulled her up with hands under her arms. Her hands were bound by the leather cuffs behind her back. She turned sickly white and felt like she was going to throw up.

"Water?"

"Sure, sure, but first we must get you ready for your wedding day. He roughly sat her on the stool in front of the vanity."

She looked at herself in the mirror. Her bun was hanging loosely over her left ear. He tried to fix it and it looked worse. He rummaged in her trunk until he found a fancy stiff bonnet. He pulled it over her head and tied it under her chin. Lightening flashed outside. Again the sound of an avalanche of rocks assaulted her ears.

"There! Perfect. Now..." he rummaged some more until he found a cloak. He tied it around her shoulders so that it covered her bound hands. "That should do nicely. We are about ready to go."

Everleigh felt a prick of impending doom. She had to get away from him. If he managed to get her away from the Inn, away from Suzanne and Malcolm, who would help her?

"You'll never get away with this," she tried to stall him.

"Why not? I see no reason why we will not be married."

"What makes you think I will go through with a ceremony? Say, 'I do'?"

He leaned on one arm on the vanity and smiled an ugly smile.

"I have been anticipating you being difficult, my dear. So I have taken the liberty to, shall we say, make sure you are compelled to be agreeable."

Creases of confusion split her forehead

Enjoying himself, he chuckled. "Your aunt my dear, she is shall we say, in a perilous situation. Only you can save her, really. She is being detained in Lexington by a gentleman who is given to outbursts of violence."

Her eyes shot open wide. She had never met the lady, but couldn't bear the thought of some woman scared to death and her fate bearing on her. The realization dawned on her that this was why she was not home when they went there. How long had she been kidnapped?

"Oh no, don't fret. As soon as we are in a state of wedded bliss, I'll have funds, your funds," he laughed at himself, "wired and she shall be set free. It's as easy as that."

It was so easy for him to be mean, she thought. Without a sound he slipped a handkerchief around her head, gagging her, and tied it behind her bonnet.

"Now you stay here very quietly, like I know you will to save your dear aunt, and I shall go arrange for our carriage." He slipped out the door with a click of the latch.

She sat there alone wondering what she could

do. If she got away now, she would never find this aunt. She didn't even know what she looked like. She could try to get to the sheriff, but surely Mr. Peeble would see her.

She tried to stand and nearly fainted from the pain in her ribs. There was no way she would be able to make it down the steps. Her mind circled back to what would happen to her aunt if Mr. Peeble never wired the money. No one would even know where to look for her.

She heard footsteps in the hallway. Maybe she could just alert someone to follow them but how would they be able to do that? And he said he would not wire the money until after the marriage was consummated. She shuddered at the thought of that vile man touching her.

The doorknob clicked and he was back, quietly closing the door behind him. He turned.

"Ah, good, you're up I see. Come along then."

She must have looked like she was going to pass out again because he put his arm roughly around her, causing her to wince, and pulled her with him. Halfway down the stairs, after she kept stumbling, he gave up and picked her up into his arms and darted through the front door before anyone saw them go. It was the middle of breakfast and apparently Mr. Clark was in the dining room.

Everleigh thought of Suzanne so close but out of reach. Her head began to swim again from him pressing his arm around her torso and the darkness covered her again.

She woke up laying on the leather seat of the carriage as it swayed and rocked with the horses at full gallop. She tried to sit up and a searing ache of broken bone gripped her. She coughed lightly and tasted blood. She wondered if the rib had punctured a lung. She couldn't take a deep breath without white hot pain burning in her side. She saw him sitting in the other seat of the carriage watching her like you'd watch a weirdo on a subway. The absolute lack of concern for her, for another human being, was startling to her. It made her wonder what he was truly capable of.

She managed to set herself upright and propped into the corner. She winced at the pain.

"Nothing some bandages can't fix. Actually that's all they can do, really. So just get a hold of yourself."

"You're sympathy is heartwarming. Do you treat this Cherise as kindly?

He smirked at her like she was an idiot.

"She behaves. It makes things so much easier. You should try it."

Everleigh wondered what was in it for the girl. Why would she put up with him?

The rain had continued to follow them. Apparently, it had set in for the day. The sucking noises of the horse's hooves in the mud punctuated the static hiss of the downpour. Everleigh wondered how much he'd had to pay the driver to go out in this mess. The justice of the peace must have been unavailable. She was certain they had to be nearly to Lexington by now.

She heard the whistle of a train calling. The chugging of the train's wheels got louder and soon the train sped past them with a blur. She wished she could have signaled them for help, but really, there was no way. If she hadn't been injured, she might have been able to leap from the carriage and try to run away. She wondered if he would get his clothes dirty to come after her, but of course he would, she was the golden goose.

***

Malcolm had promised to have her visit today and Percy had chattered non-stop at breakfast. He never got a chance to meet new people so this was a big deal to him. Despite the hurricane-like Kentucky summer thunderstorm, Malcolm was going to head into town. Hopefully the rain would ease before they made the trip back to the house.

His carriage was pulling into town when he saw Mr. Peeble running out of the inn with Everleigh in his arms. His heart lurched at the sight. It appeared as though she was unconscious. His heartbeat pounded in his ears. The distance was too great to catch up to them before Mr. Peeble's carriage was already heading out the other side of town at full speed. Malcolm followed them.

The pounding rain and booming thunder covered the sound of their pursuit. He was sure Mr. Peeble had no idea he was following them. Unfortunately, Malcolm had brought his smaller carriage made for two people with a roof that extended over them. He didn't want his driver to be perched up in the front of the regular carriage with this lightening. This carriage wasn't made for going long distances and wasn't as fast. He was having trouble keeping up. Outside of town a road had washed out as a creek overflowed and Malcolm's carriage wheels struggled to keep hold and they had to slow down. He cracked the whip to keep the horses moving forward. They tried to turn and go back the other way.

He made it to the side and the horses pulled the carriage up onto the sloppy road. Mr. Peeble's carriage was nowhere in sight, but Malcolm knew where they were headed. This was the road straight into Lexington. He plowed ahead hoping to catch up with them further down the road.

Malcolm stared ahead into the gray downpour hoping to see sight of the carriage. His knuckles gripped the reins so tightly his hands turned pale white. He was powerless to make any headway.

***

The carriage pulled and jolted her. She winced at the pain in her side. Mr. Peeble looked at her with a smug grin. The horses' hooves made a more distinct 'clop clop' sound as the cobblestones of Lexington met them. The bumping and swaying of the carriage calmed. She looked out the window and a line of row houses had formed along the road.

Instead of heading straight into town, the carriage turned onto a side road. They stopped in front of a two-story brick home with a slightly unkempt lawn. This area looked a bit run down. A sign by the front door announced the owner was a lawyer.

"Don't move. I will be right back"

He jumped from the carriage, ducking under the steady shower of rain. She watched him climb the steps from the street and head up the brick path to the front door. Puddles of water exploded away from him as he upset them. A man answered the door and Mr. Peeble disappeared inside. She looked both ways out the windows for a place she could hide if she could get out of the carriage. Just as she started to slide from the bench seat, the door opened and she heard voices. She slid back in place.

He must have ran back to the carriage because his head popped in sight surprising her. She scrunched back into the corner refusing to cooperate. He sighed with annoyance and water dripped a steady stream off his shoulders.

"My dear, surely you would not be the cause of your old aunt's demise. I'm certain she would haunt you. How could you ever be happy again?"

A burning fire crept up in her throat that threatened to strangle her. She hated him.

"It's really quite simple. No need to get bothered. Besides, its making you look frightful." He paused and then concluding that she was going to be difficult, he jumped into the carriage.

"Look," he continued, "The honorable Mr. Babbage is a judge and friend of my family. He won't mind if you are awake or unconscious. It's up to you."

He raised his hand to strike her and she flinched."

"Alright. Alright! Please!"

"Wonderful. I detest unreasonable people."

He took her by the arm and pulled her to the door of the carriage. He jumped down and helped her out which was hard for her to do with her arms behind her back. Taking her by the arm, she felt like she flew to the doorway with her feet barely making contact with the ground. The man was obviously much stronger than she, propelling her through the air with each step. He led her through the opening.

The parlor was dark, even so, looking down she could make out the puddle of water that creeped out from their feet exploring its new surroundings. Dust covered the surfaces of the tables. She wondered what kind of judge this was that he didn't have any help to dust his home. A coughing fit ensued in the hallway signaling she was about the meet the *honorable* judge. How honorable could he be if he agreed to marry a woman to a man against her will? She was shackled, for heaven's sake! She supposed if he was anything like Mr. Peeble, he didn't think highly of the rights of women.

"Ah-hem! Now then, here we go," the round little man said as he came in thumbing through a small leather-bound book.

Mr. Peeble turned to him, turned back at her, and grimaced. He roughly placed his hands on her shoulders and turned her facing forward with him.

"Yes, yes," the judge continued, "very good. Here we go. Now we can dispense with much of this. So," he paused looking her up and down. She assumed he was determining if she was actually female. His eyes slid down her chest and lingered. Turning his head slightly at the curve of her hips, he nodded and licked his lips, until his gaze finished with the hem of her skirt. She swallowed back the nauseating feeling of being visually violated. He smiled briefly and nodded at Mr. Peeble, who smirked even more and crossed his arms.

The thought occurred to her, *here she was. The day she'd always dreamed of, her wedding day.* She pushed the thought aside like it was a sad child on the first day of school realizing that school was not all that fun like the pretend games. This was most certainly real and she had no way to stop it. Soon she would be legally bound to this jerk. From what Suzanne had told her, after that, she had even less rights than before, as she would technically be the property of Mr. Pebble.

"Wait! Your honor!"

Both of the men's heads snapped in her direction.

"My darling, what did we talk about in the carriage," Mr. Peeble warned through his teeth.

She sucked in a breath of strength, "Your honor, I can't marry this man!"

The judge stammered and looked at Mr. Peeble imploringly.

"You most certainly can. Please continue, your honor. Quickly."

The judge cleared his throat and began again, "…Gathered here, in front of witne- I mean, anyway, ah, do you take this man, oh yes, of course," he never even looked at her. "And you take this woman," looking up at Mr. Peeble who nodded perfunctorily, "by the power vested in me, pronounce you man and wife. Done." He slammed the little book closed with a fripping noise like shuffling a deck of cards.

"There we go, Mr. Peeble. I'll expect a deposit in my account before the close of business today or I will not submit the paperwork. Do we have an understanding?" He tilted his chin in and his forehead forward regarding Mr. Peeble with a serious eye. ""For the full amount. This is, ah, a bit irregular and therefore, ah," he glanced over her one more time, "I expect to be compensated for my skin in it."

"Certainly, your honor. Most obliged." Mr. Peeble put out his hand and the judge just looked at it and suddenly shivered. He nodded back and turned to the front door.

"Now, if you will excuse me." He held the door open. "May I be the first to offer you congratulations on your marriage and good day?"

Mr. Peeble grabbed her by the elbow and shoved her in front of him out the door. The sudden twisting of her body sent a sharp stab of pain into her side and she cried out. Neither of the men responded to her pain in any way except that the door slammed behind them with a thud.

Mr. Peeble jerked her along the sidewalk and hastily lifted her back into the carriage. She heard him yell some directions to the driver who had sat in the rain the whole time. By now, the bonnet had come untied and slid down the back of her head. Her hair was a clumped limp mess underneath. Small blond tendrils stuck to the side of her face and she pushed them out of her eyes with her shoulder.

He sat on the other bench looking very preoccupied with his hands together, elbows on knees, fingers up like he was praying. He rested his chin on the points of his fingers and looked out the window as the carriage lurched forward.

Water streamed down the muddy window leaving an ever-changing impressionist scene of blurry row houses. A tear slid from the corner of her eye as panic seized her. Afraid for this unknown aunt, but could she go through with this? Could she allow his cold pale fingers to touch her, to violate her? Despite the age of the body she inhabited, she was no child. She was not a virgin. She knew the mechanics of the act and, since it was her choice, maybe she could endure it to save this woman.

She stole a glance at Mr. Peeble. She realized she could call him Horace now. *Bleh!* Not much better. *What was a nickname for Horace? Ace? Hore?* It was so hard for her to tell what he was thinking. He seemed to have no emotion what so ever. He must have felt her stare because he turned to her and stared back.

Her skin started to crawl under the weight of his stare and she looked away.

"I will need to take your hands out of the shackles. People will stare enough because you look horrible."

He stepped across the space and sat next to her while she turned her back to him to give him access to her hands. She immediately folded her arms around her ribs to protect them.

They turned a corner and stopped in front of a long awning that led to a hotel. She couldn't see the name of it or hardly even see the building itself as the rain came down in sheets. A bellman ran up with an umbrella and held it up while Horace jumped out. He kept walking and the bellman took her hand and helped her out.

"Any bags, sir?"

"No," was all he said over his shoulder as he kept walking. She shook out her dress and wondered if she could make a getaway. Again, she realized he still had her in invisible handcuffs. She couldn't go anywhere as long as this aunt was in danger. He knew it, too, and sauntered on with a smirk. She hated him even more.

The carriage driver snapped the reins and pulled away. She looked back as the carriage turned the corner. It was her only tie to Versailles, to

Malcolm, or to Suzanne. She supposed it was going back to town now that the driver had finished his job.

Turning back on the damp carpet that led to the doors like the long red tongue of a snake, she put one foot in front of the other and determined she would get through this. She would persevere until her aunt, Everleigh's aunt, was safe and then she would file for divorce.

The doorman held the door for her, more of a gentleman than her new husband, and she stepped inside. As she passed through the entry, she caught sight of herself in a tall mirror. She gasped reaching up involuntarily to touch her hair. Like a cat after a bath, she looked a wreck. She wondered what the judge must have thought. Yet, he still looked her up and down like a piece of meat. Pulling off her bonnet, she slicked her hair back off her face and rubbed a smudge of mud off her cheek. Not that she cared what Horace thought, but she didn't want the patrons of the hotel to stare at her. She fixed the bonnet back in place and tied the ribbons in a bow, albeit a very tired one. There was nothing she could do about her skirt and blouse. Wet, muddy, rumpled. She could have fallen off a cliff and they would look better. What's worse is that she had no clothes to change into.

She determined that was as good as it was going to get for now and went into the lobby. As she suspected, the hotel guests were in their finery with perfect hair. At least Horace looked not much better than her. A bellhop motioned for them to follow him and they all stepped up the royal red carpet of the sweeping stair case. Everleigh held the handrail tightly to brace herself from the pain in her side and tried not to cry. She wasn't successful and a tear escaped down her face before she could dash it away.

On the second floor, the bellhop opened a large white painted door with the number eight in gleaming brass in the middle. The men waited for her and after hesitating, she stepped inside. The bellhop held out his hand and Horace looked at him like he must be crazy and pulled the door shut behind him.

The room was gorgeous. She had to admit. From the golden silk curtains to the silver tea service already sitting on the table next to the sofa, this room screamed rich. She was certain even in her own time with the fancy hotels she's stayed in, none had this kind of opulence. The crown molding gracefully curled around the ceiling in giant acanthus leaves. The large fireplace was couched in a white marble mantle and hearth. She saw a door that lead off to a bedroom of the suite. Her heart lurched and her stomach felt like it might turn inside out.

She heard the delicate babbling sound of tea pouring in a cup and turned to see Horace pouring them tea. He set her cup on the far side of the table away from him and took his to sit in a chair. Dark green velvet covered the chairs and the sofa begging you to smooth your hand across it.

"Have some tea. You look slightly unhinged. We must keep up appearances."

Her jawed dropped a bit. How could he possibly care about appearances after everything else today?

"I- I need to wash up." She actually just need to get away from him.

"Yes, good idea. I don't want to get dirty, you know, when…" he trailed off with a look like he had stepped in something. "Why don't you take the tea with you?"

She really couldn't figure him out. At one moment he sort of acted like he cared and the next moment he could break her bones. She crossed the room and took the tea. She did need something to settle her stomach.

Feeling lighter with each step farther away from him, she crossed the bedroom and went into a small powder room that doubled as a closet. A small window that didn't open let in gray light from the stormy day. The hotel had gas light fixtures that made her feel like she was in the Haunted Mansion at Disneyland as the light flickered. She poured the cold water left in the pitcher into the ceramic basin and put a small piece of folded linen in the water. She watched the shadow creep quickly across the linen as it soaked up the water. She carefully took off her bonnet and set it aside. Picking up the linen cloth, she squeezed out the excess and rubbed her face. Her skin tingled as it dried. She looked at herself in the mirror.

So young! Much too young to have to go through this.

She realized how glad she was that the other Everleigh was gone, wherever she was. This would be so traumatic for her. She would be so frightened. She was afraid, there was no denying that. However, it was not the kind of fear a young girl would have. She knew what to expect. She just had to bear it and get through it.

She pulled the loose pins from her hair and looked around for a brush. Nothing. They had no luggage. She certainly had not planned to take a trip. He had flung her, unconscious, into a carriage. Apparently, luggage wasn't on his mind either.

She ran her fingers through her hair as best she could. She was about to put it back up in the pins and then decided that was wasted effort. She wondered how long the consummation would last. Maybe it would be quick. That would be preferable because she was hungry. Unfortunately the thought of lying down with him made her stomach lurch and the hunger turned into nausea.

The gentle rapping on the door made her jump. She figured he would at least give her a minute. A woman's voice made her eyes go wide.

"Mrs. Peeble?"

What? Who? She thought. Then reality caught up with her. *Mrs. Peeble? Make me gag!*

"Oh. Yes?" she answered.

"The desk said you may need a few things, so I brought you some toiletries. May I come in?"

"Yes, please do."

A maid in a black work dress and apron came in with a small woven basket filled with necessities.

"Thank you. That's really nice."

"Your husband said you'd had quite an ordeal losing your trunks in the storm. If you need anything at all, just call the desk. There is a store nearby with ready-made clothes and a seamstress that works very fast."

The maid set out some fresh linen towels, a comb, a brush, two toothbrushes, some baking soda in a jar, some scented water, and a small bar of soap. Then she curtsied and left with her basket closing the door behind her.

Everleigh was so grateful for the toiletries she smiled as she picked them up to examine them. It was like going through items from a museum. The labels had scrolling cursive script. She held the soap to her nose. It smelled like roses. Without thinking, her hand went to the place in her stocking where she had her magic soap hidden.

She entertained the thought of taking a bath right now. She could call the maid to the bring water. In no time at all she could be over a hundred years away. Horace would be long since dead and rotting in a grave. Her heart fell as she realized so would Malcolm.

NO! She couldn't bear that. She had to get through this and get back to him. As tempting as escape was, the aunt would still be in danger and she might never see Malcolm again. She would love to see her mom again, though. She couldn't let herself dwell on what must be happening in the future. Logic told her the future hadn't happened yet, so it should be frozen still.

She brushed out her hair and decided this was it. It was time to get this over with. Steeling her resolve, she looked in the mirror and saw a strength that she had not seen in the reflection before. Her strength. Thirty-five years' worth of making her way in the world, dealing with a demanding supervisor, taking care of herself, learning to guard her heart, showing compassion for those more vulnerable than she was. Everleigh of 1888 had the beauty to free her from her fears and Everleigh of 2016 had the heart and strength to see her through anything.

She appeared in the doorway and held her head up. He looked up at her and, imperceptibly flinched. She could tell her strength surprised him. She was better than him and he knew it. He swallowed his insecurity and stood up.

"My dear wife, let's put a seal on the bargain, shall we."

He stepped closer to her and, for the first time, seemed unsure of what to do, hesitating at kissing her, he just reached for her hand.

"Oh, bother!" he fussed and yanked her into the bedroom.

Pushing her face down over the side of the tall bed, he lifted her skirt.

***

Everleigh sat in the warm water of the small hotel tub and cried. Being a fancier hotel than Suzanne's Inn, the tub was nicer, deeper, with a rolled top but sat flat on the floor. Despite her stoic strength, alone and so far in space and time from anyone she loved, she broke down. Sobs wracked her. Disgust made her skin crawl. She couldn't wash away the dirty feeling of him touching her.

He had promptly left to visit an attorney to see to the inheritance. She hoped he was also doing whatever was needed to free her aunt.

She squeezed her eyes shut wishing the world would go away. Maybe she could slide into the water and slip into some place between life and heaven and hide. The smell of lavender tickled her nose and she opened her eyes. Her magic soap lay on top of her stockings on the chair. The paper was rumpled now from being hidden in her clothes so long. The scent was oddly strong, like it was calling to her.

'Perhaps,' she thought, '*that would be better*.' I could go back to 2016 and forget this nightmare. Everleigh's aunt is safe now. She could go to her mother and curl up next to her on the couch. She

would talk herself into believing none of it really happened. It was just a horrible nightmare.

Malcolm's face filled her mind. She couldn't leave him. She couldn't be without him. Even violated, her body seemed to reach into the distance between them and tether her to him. She could feel him out there, breathing the air that the sky between them shared. Had it only been the night before that they were together. She imagined his arms around her now. She imagined him carrying her broken, naked body out of that hotel and daring anyone to stop him. She knew he could never find her there. No one even knew when or where she had gone.

The loneliness held her and wracking sobs of grief mixed with cries of pain from her ribs. She curled up in a ball in the water, her head just out of the water and closed her eyes and wished for sleep to take her away. Sleep was the only escape.

She cried until consciousness faded and woke in cold water shivering. At first confused, but then the crashing memories of the day tore at her again. She stepped out of the water and pulled a linen towel around her. She glanced at herself in the mirror and gawked. An angry purple bruise the size of a fist graced her porcelain skin under her left breast. Around that a deeper purple emanated about eight inches across that must have been from an internal bleed. She decided that now she needed to see a doctor.

She pulled the linen towel around her and peeked through the door. Horace wasn't there. She did see a plain dark dress across a chair. She wondered if the maid had left it for her knowing she had no other clothes to change in to. She snuck out and grabbed it and snuck back in the powder room. She pulled on her undergarments, leaving the corset as loose as she could and still get the dress around her waist. Scrunching them up into her hand, she pulled her stockings over her feet. Finally she pulled the dress over her head and let it settle around her. It was a bit big for her, thank goodness, and so she didn't have to tighten the corset over the bruise. It was a very 19th century deep V design bodice with a high neck. That was fine with her. She wanted to hide her body from everyone as though it were an abused child she was protecting.

She brushed out her hair and secured it into a tight bun. She had an overwhelming need to have every hair in a tight hold. After putting in the pins, she looked at herself. Dark circles had appeared under her eyes. Her soft blond hair was caught up in such a severe style, she hardly recognized herself. She stood and slipped on her muddy granny boots and laced them.

In the sitting room of the suite, she found a table with a covered silver tray. Champagne sat unopened. She smirked at the absurdity. Apparently the hotel thought they would be celebrating. She pulled the cord to alert the maid and sat at the table.

Lifting the silver cover, a wave of aroma assaulted her. Normally it would have been wonderful. She was torn between feeling nauseous and starving. She decided she needed to eat something to at least stay strong. She lifted some of the beef onto her plate and spooned some cooked carrots next to it. She found that as she nibbled, her appetite grew and she really enjoyed the comforting flavor. In a bread basket she found fluffy rolls dusted with flour and devoured two in a row.

A knock came at the door and she called for them to come in. The maid popped through the door. It was the same young brunette that had brought the toiletries.

"Yes, madam?"

"I need to see a doctor. Is there one near that could see me?"

The maid's forehead furrowed and her mouth turned down. "Certainly. Doctor Baker is around the corner. I'll send for him. Are you alright? Is there anything I can get you?" She looked over the plate seeming satisfied that she'd eaten. "At least you have an appetite, then."

Everleigh's old shame of loving food tried to nip at her but she stamped it out.

"Yes, traveling and," she paused, "and all."

The maid blushed assuming her meaning.

"Oh, excuse me. No. Heavens! Just please have the doctor see me as soon as possible. Thank you." She stammered. What could she say, she wondered? Of course, it would be what most would consider a honeymoon. A horrible honeymoon, nevertheless.

As the maid was leaving, Horace came in. He briefly looked at her and then went to the desk pulling an envelope from his pocket. Sitting at the desk he turned to her.

"All the papers have been filed. The inheritance has been transferred to our account in Charleston. The bank wired us funds to get home. I purchased our tickets for tomorrow's train."

Her head started spinning. "Home? Train? Tomorrow?"

He exhaled slowly. "This is how it will work. You and I will return to Charleston on tomorrow's train. When we get there, I will see to that you are settled in your parent's estate, which now belongs to me, and then I shall be living at your family's beach cottage, which is also mine now." He smirked. "I, frankly, could care less what you do with your time as long as you aren't a bother."

She sat there speechless listening to his little monologue. When he finished, she pulled it all together in her head.

"Ah, no! I'm not going back to Charleston."

He jerked his head back surprised. "Was I not clear this morning?" he said without taking his eyes off her. "I will not have any discussion about it."

"But I need my things in Versailles!" she was trying anything to stall him.

"I'll have them sent by freight."

"I am not going anywhere until I see a doctor. I certainly can't travel until I've healed. If you are going to treat me so roughly, you will have to deal with the consequences of that."

"You're very tiring, Everleigh. And I don't remember you ever being so mouthy. Perhaps breaking a few bones was heavy handed. I'll have to find more acceptable ways of training you to be a good wife. Perhaps a good rod."

She was so utterly shocked at the implication of his words that she honestly couldn't breathe.

Who did he think he was?

"Come, come, Everleigh. Don't be so shocked. Truly you act like your mother never told you anything about domestic life. It is perfectly within my right to beat my wife if it will help her."

She had never in her life imagined having such a bizarre conversation with a man. Was this really normal married life in the 19th century? Did men really lord themselves over their wives and families like they were cattle having trouble finding the gate to the barn yard?

She shook off the fog that threatened to take her breath away.

"My aunt," she started.

"--is perfectly fine and on her way home as we speak," he completed her sentence.

She felt a wash of dizziness and the room spun for just a minute. She held onto the edge of the table. The food in her stomach lurched.

"I don't feel well."

He stood up and came closer. You do look pale. Perhaps I *should* call the doctor now."

"I already did. Would you help me to the couch?"

He took her by the arm and held her steady while she crossed to the velvet couch and laid her head back.

"You'd better put your feet up." He picked up her feet and set them on the couch so she could lay back.

She tried to focus on his face but the more she tried, the more the room spun, so she closed her eyes.

"Maybe a cold compress will help. Good grief. What's wrong with you now?"

He disappeared into the bedroom and she heard him swishing a hand towel in the bath water. Then she felt it on her forehead. She wondered why no time seemed to go by between those two events.

"Everleigh! Wake up!" Someone was yelling

at her. She felt water on her cheek and then a slap that stung like the prickles of a thousand needles.

Her eyes fluttered and she saw him over her with a stern look on his face. She tried to talk but couldn't. She felt numb and cold all over. Her arms and legs felt like stones too heavy to pick up. Another slap stung the other side of her face as her head jerked the other way. She felt disjointed from her body, though.

A man's voice, not Horace, began talking, yelling. She felt her body being picked up and she crumpled against a strong chest and then darkness. Darkness and peace. She just wanted to fade into the sleep and let go. She was weightless, floating in the darkness and all the voices were a million miles away.

***

With her eyes closed, she saw the light in the room flash like lightening. She thought it must still be storming. It kept going though. The light not so much flashed as fluttered against her eyelids. No sound came, no thunder, no pelting on the window. Curious, she fought back the fog and pulled herself out of the sea of darkness she had welled up from.

She blinked and sucked in air. Turning toward the movement of light, she saw the sun shining through the dark green leaves of the maple tree outside her window. She was not in the hotel room. The walls were white and plain. The bed was small and a white sheet covered her up to her shoulders. A tall thin woman stood at a table next to the bed writing on a paper. Her hair was pulled up in a pretty auburn bun and her big brown eyes batted long black eyelashes. The woman turned and looked down at her with scrutinizing eyes.

Then, suddenly smiling, she said, "Good afternoon, lady bird! Welcome back!"

"What happened? Where am I?"

"Sugar, you passed out from an internal hemorrhage two days ago and you were brought here, the Protestant Infirmary. Now don't you fret. I can see you are a fine lady and you have a private room instead of being in the common ward. You're too far from home to make the trip and recover there."

She thought about all that a minute. "The last thing I remember was being slapped." She pulled her hand to her face to feel.

"Uh huh. Your *husband* is being detained." The nurse waited to see how she took that news. When she didn't say anything, the nurse continued.

"You had some significant internal injuries. Three broken ribs and one punctured a lung. Honestly, no one can figure out how you managed as well as you did."

Everleigh followed the nurse with her eyes. Apparently the nurse thought she was afraid of her husband because she leaned in and said, "Oh honey, it's alright. He can't get you here."

"On what charges is he being held?"

The nurse paused, "I'm not sure it's my place to tell."

"It's my place to know. Please tell me."

The nurse sucked in a breath and snuck a peek toward the door.

"From what I heard, when the doctor got there, they heard your husband yelling at you and slapping you. They came right in, afraid for you.

When they got you here and examined you to see why you were unconscious, they found your injuries and reported them to the sheriff as signs of abuse. Your husband has been detained with charges of criminal wife abuse."

"Oh," was all she said. This was better than she had hoped. She wouldn't have to do anything.

"It's for the best, really. It would just get worse, you know?"

"Oh, I'm not upset. He kidnapped me and forced me to marry him to get my inheritance. He said he was holding my aunt hostage. I couldn't let him hurt her."

The nurse gasped and brought her hand in front of her mouth. "Oh my word! And here I thought you'd be mad at the sheriff. Believe me, I have seen women brush off some pretty bad treatment saying they loved him or they deserved it. It's sad, really." The nurse paused to assess her again.

"Here. Have something to drink." The nurse handed her a cup of water. "I need to get you some broth now that you are awake. Also, be careful moving around. You have some stitches in your side."

"Stitches?" Her eyes sprang open wide. The thought of a 19th century doctor cutting her open scared her to death. She wondered if he washed his hands or any of the instruments.

The nurse smiled sweetly. She had a beautiful big smile that even shined through her eyes. "Ah, honey, you are fine now. Your wound is healing nicely. You were hemorrhaging and the doctor had to stop it. You had lost so much blood and it was pooling in your chest. Dr. Baker is really very talented. You'll feel better in no time now."

Everleigh grimaced. "Does he wash his hands? Did they wash the instruments? I hate to ask, but I worry about cleanliness."

"Oh, shoot honey. Dr. Baker is just the same. I have never seen anything like him. He teaches all of us nurses how to care for patients using clean techniques."

"So the wound looks alright? No redness or drainage?" She sipped some water waiting for the nurse to answer

"Oh my, you certainly do worry more than most. But don't you worry, darlin'. You are healing fine. I just changed your dressing a few hours ago."

Everleigh felt her own forehead for signs of a fever.

The nurse laughed at her, "And no, you have had no fever!"

Everleigh blushed with embarrassment and took another sip of water. The nurse patted her leg and left. With the room quiet, her thoughts turned back to her present situation.

So he is in jail. Bet he's mad!

She needed to see if her aunt was alright. With it being two days, surely her aunt would have made her way home by now. She wondered how she could send a message. She suddenly felt very isolated and stuck.

The nurse brought her some warm chicken broth.

"Nurse, I need to get a message to my aunt and my friend in Versailles. Is there a way to do that?"

"Sure, honey, just write down a message and we can wire it."

"Oh, that is great. Thank you!"

The nurse left again and she picked up a sheet of paper and pen that looked like an antique calligraphy pen on the bed side table. There was also a small jar of ink. She dipped the tip in the ink and scribbled out a note to Suzanne. She figured that was the best idea. Suzanne would know what to do. She wondered if Malcolm was worried. By now they all had to wonder what happened to her. She still really had no idea how long the doctor would make her stay there.

She didn't know much about recovery times in the 19th century but she figured it was much longer than modern medicine found to be necessary. She finished the note and laid it on the table. She felt around her middle to figure out how extensive the bandage was. It actually wound all the way around her. She figured they probably didn't have adhesive tape either. The luxuries of the future floated through her mind.

Her mind drifted to Malcolm. She missed him terribly. The memory of him kissing her, holding her in his arms made her stomach clench and a zing of joy caught her breath. The feeling made her ache for him. She frowned as the feeling got mixed up with the memory of Horace and him violating her. Her head was a mess. She tried to block all thoughts and hum in her head. The thoughts still came. It seemed the harder she tried to clear her mind, the more stuck the thoughts became. She felt like screaming in her mind where no one would hear but it would block her thoughts.

She needed a therapist. In 2016 she would have just seen a therapist and dealt with this trauma.

She was certain there were no therapists in 1888 that had any idea what to do with her, at least if she didn't want electric shock therapy or a lobotomy.

***

He buried his head in his hands and tried to hold back the rage before it consumed him and everything around him. The warm breeze flitted at his brown waves. It was already approaching 86 degrees and it wasn't even midday. Suzanne brought him some tea and sat down next to Edward. He glanced at the tea and grimaced at the steam wafting from it.

All three of them leaned back in their seats with defeat.

"Alright," Edward started, "where did you last see their carriage?"

"Right before Slickaway. The creek was flooding and my carriage got stuck. It took a bit to get it out of the creek without turning over. By the time I got on high ground, they were nowhere to be seen."

"She couldn't have just disappeared," Suzanne pleaded with no one in particular. "It's been three days. They had to stay somewhere. Did you check the hotels?"

"Yes, I checked several."

"Did you check the justice of the peace?" Edward asked.

""Yes." His jaw tightened and he turned his body away from them. He was tired of their endless questions. He had gone up and down every reputable street in Lexington. Of course there could have been a hotel he missed. The town was too big to hit every one of them alone. Images of that scum Peeble terrorizing her slid through his head. He could feel his blood pressure mounting as each minute passed.

Suzanne sighed and her mouth turned down. "What about the police? We should contact them. After all, he did kidnap her."

Malcolm straightened and looked at her with a new resolve.

"Yes. I agree. Its time to bring in the authorities. I will talk to the sheriff here and see if he can wire the Lexington Bureau. With this amount of time, though, they could be half way to Charleston by now. Maybe they should alert Charleston, too."

The memory of her limp graceful body as Peeble roughly shoved her in the carriage replayed in his head. Peeble didn't care about her at all. He would be capable of anything. She was just a means to an end to him. What if he managed to marry her and then killed her?

His heart crumpled and contracted. He could feel her out there somewhere. Whatever the tether was that he felt at Mammoth Cave, it still gripped him.

Everleigh, I'll find you.

A soft wind blew and the scent of lavender tickled his nose. He closed his eyes thankful for the gentle caress of the wind. He exhaled and, for a moment, let go of the tension in his shoulders. With his mind finally calm, an image emerged in his mind. A white room. Shadows of leaves dancing on the wall in the bright light of day. A small bed. And her. Her delicate body, her serene face etched with grief. Lonely and hurt.

He shot up to his feet with his eyes wide. Suzanne and Edward startled and nearly dropped their tea cups.

"By God, man! What is it?" Edward inquired.

Malcolm stood there a second more before he spoke.

"I saw her. I saw her in my mind." He jerked his head in all directions checking to make sure something wasn't out of the ordinary.

Suzanne stood up and put her hand on his arm.

"Mr. Steel, please. Surely you must be tired."

He stared her in the eye, but wasn't looking at her. "No, Mrs. Clark. It was as clear as anything. I could smell the lavender on the breeze and then I saw her in a room. A white room. She was in a bed. She looked, she looked, -- oh God, help her! She is hurt. We have to check the hospital. I never checked the hospital!"

He dashed off the porch and left her standing with her hand still in the air where it was on his arm.

"Lavender?" she turned and looked at Edward. "There is no lavender growing here. I never could get it to grow for me." She sighed. "Poor man, he is losing his mind."

Malcolm ran all the way to the post office to have the clerk wire the hospital in Lexington asking if they had her as a patient. He knew it would be a while before he got an answer back, so he then ran to the sheriff's office and reported Everleigh as missing and that she was last seen with Horace Peeble in a carriage headed toward Lexington.

He figured in the time it took to visit the sheriff's office, there probably had not been a response yet but he checked anyway.

"No," said the clerk. Malcolm sighed in frustration. If he left to ride to Lexington, he would miss the response. If they said no, there was no one by that name, he would be on a fool's errand. All he could do was wait for the telegram to come back with its news and then go from there. He headed back to the Inn.

A carriage was parked at the end of the walk and a driver was helping a woman out of the carriage. She was dressed in an intricately detailed white linen dress with lace and white embroidery setting off the deep V in the front from her waste to the high neckline and small bustle in the back. Her elegant salt and pepper hair was styled and pinned with several small curls framing her face and small brimmed hat was secured at a jaunty impossible angle on the back of her head. As she straightened and smoothed her skirt, her gaze shifted to his approaching footsteps and she looked up and smiled.

"Ah, Mr. Steel!" She reached her hands out for him to greet her.

"Miss Heartwell!" His eyes crinkled in joy to see her but as he kissed the back of her hand, his heart thudded in pain. He would have to tell her about her niece being missing.

"Mr. Steel, I am so, so glad to see you. Can we go sit and talk? I have some distressing news if you don't already know."

Now he was confused. How could she know? His brows knit together and his mouth parted slightly.

"Of course! Yes." He held out his arm for her and she smiled a dazzling flirtatious smile at him. He felt awkward at his body betraying him as he blushed at the charming beauty on his arm. Part of him basked in the sweet comfort of a presence that was so close to Everleigh's. They did not look alike in coloring, but it was as though their souls had been cut from the same fabric. He wondered what Everleigh's mother must have been like if her sister was this beautiful.

When they reached the porch, the door swung wide to welcome them. Suzanne escorted them into the parlor and went to get more tea and biscuits.

Everleigh's aunt wasted no time and said, "Dear Malcolm. Please tell me Everleigh is here safe somewhere." She looked toward the stairs as though expecting to see her come down.

He grimaced and looked down. That told her all she needed to know.

"That's what I was afraid of. I have been held against my will for two weeks in Lexington. A very surly man had me locked in a room and threatened horrible things if I tried to get away. Namely, he kept saying that Everleigh would be hurt."

"How awful, Miss Heartwell!" He looked her over for signs of abuse."

"I assure you, I am quite alright now. Other than being captive, I was taken care of. But then two days ago, the man put me in a carriage which brought me straight to my home without stopping, despite my protests to take me to the police station."

"Do you know who the captor was?"

"Honestly, I am not even sure where in Lexington I was being held. He covered my head coming and going and tied my hands. I am sure he was a hired man. He had no interest in me at all. He always covered his face when he talked to me."

"I think you are right."

"Yes, but I have wracked my brain trying to figure out what on earth this was about. I thought Everleigh was in Charleston. In fact, I was planning to send a letter to have her come visit me for a while.

Then when I got home, my butler told me she had come to see me. I was about to come to town to look here at the Inn, but found that my driver and carriage apparently never made it back from Lexington. I have been stranded until one of my men could get another one. I will need to visit the sheriff shortly and report all this. I do hope my driver is alright."

Malcolm listened as she quickly laid all this news out. Then he sighed and shook his head. Peeble had gone to great lengths to orchestrate this nightmare.

"Miss Heartwell, we believe Everleigh has been kidnapped by a man named Horace Peeble. I saw him put her in a carriage three days ago and head toward Lexington. She was unconscious."

She gasped and shook her head.

"Please tell me this isn't true."

He paused to give her time to accept it. "I'm sorry but it is. I have been searching Lexington trying to find her."

"Have you notified the police there?"

He sighed. "No. I should have. There was some thought that she went willingly. There was a note left in her room here that said not to look for her. We knew the police wouldn't waste their time if they thought she went of her own free will."

"Oh heavens! We have to find her. Why would this Mr. Peeble do this?"

"Apparently her father had made an agreement for an arranged marriage some years ago with him."

"What? Why was he here? Why was she here?"

Malcolm realized she didn't know anything

about her sister and brother-in-law. This was going to be a very difficult conversation. He excused himself and went to get Suzanne for a lady's help. They came back and Suzanne sat next to her.

"My dear, we have some unfortunate news…"

***

Miss Heartwell sat on the front porch looking out at nothing in particular. She had taken the news better than Malcolm would have expected. Miss Heartwell must be a strong woman, he thought. He stood in the parlor watching her through the window. He wanted to get back to the clerk to see if there was any news. Now that Everleigh's aunt had calmed down and was taking a minute to get her head around all this, he might be able to check. If there was news, it would be helpful for everyone to know.

Suzanne stuck her head around the corner and asked if he needed anything.

"No, thank you. I was just going to check and see if a wire came."

"Yes. That is a good idea."

"Alright then, I will be back soon."

He stepped out the front door and made his way to the post office. He couldn't shake the image of Everleigh in the white room with the waving shadows of leaves.

At the clerk's counter, "Have you gotten any telegrams for me?"

"Yep. One just came through. Here you go." The clerk handed the slip of paper to him.

It read:

We do not have a patient by the name you

referred to. Sorry. –Protestant Infirmary

Malcolm was crushed. He thought for certain she had to be in a hospital. Maybe Suzanne was right, but it surely seemed real. He trudged back to the Inn stumped and glad he hadn't set off for the hospital.

He stepped on to the porch and a boy darted past him and into the foyer. The screen door slammed with a clack as he went. Moments later he darted back out and ran down the road. Suzanne burst through the door looking for him.

"Oh! Malcolm! Miss Heartwell! I got a telegram from her!"

"What? What does it say?" Malcolm riveted on her.

"It says, 'Suzanne, I am at the Protestant Infirmary. Please tell Malcolm I need you both.'

Malcolm scratched his head and frowned.

"What's wrong, Mr. Steel?" Miss Heartwell asked.

He handed her the telegram from the Infirmary. "That came for me just now."

She showed it to Suzanne who said, "That makes no sense." She compared the two telegrams.

He stiffened and took a deep breath. "It would since I was looking for Everleigh Addison, not Everleigh Peeble." He nearly choked on the last word.

Suzanne and Miss Heartwell gasped.

He turned away from them. The crushing emotions threatened to overtake him. A surge of anger mixed with a surge sadness.

She is married to that son of a ...

All at the same time he wanted to kill Horace Peeble, punch a hole in the wall and fall on his knees and cry out with a broken heart. The lump in his throat was about to choke him. He curled his fists and pumped them several times.

He couldn't stop the vision of Peeble taking her to bed, touching her, kissing her neck. His face turned red and swelled as he clenched his jaw.

"Mr. Steel, it says 'I need you both.' She needs you."

He turned around with a jerk, "You know what this means, don't you? She is married to Peeble. I cannot interfere with another man's marriage. She is lost to me now."

"Mr. Steel! Surely you cannot turn your back on her. She is at the Infirmary. She is asking for our help. Married or not, I will not turn away from her. If the man forced her to marry him under duress, the marriage can be annulled." Everleigh's aunt became nearly hysterical hissing the words. She started looking around her for her bag and putting her hand to her mouth and looking at Suzanne. "We must go immediately. Where is my carriage? We can take my carriage."

Malcolm watched the woman nearly stumble down the steps in her shocked haste. Part of him was ready to race her to the carriage and part of him had crashed through to the pits of hell with disappointment.

Forced? Annulled?

The words tumbled in his head. The thoughts prattled like race horses in his mind. Her note said don't follow her. She wanted this marriage. An annulment can be filed if a marriage had not been consummated.

Oh God, help me! Consummated.

Revulsion shot a wave of nausea through his gut. He was going to be sick.

Had that bastard *consummated* the marriage? Is that why she was in the infirmary? The desire to rip Peeble limb for limb superseded all other thoughts. He heard Suzanne tell Miss Heartwell to wait that she had to tell Edward and get a bag of things. Her voice sounded far away.

He gripped the wood railing of the porch to steady himself. He didn't need any *things*. The carriage would slow him down. One thought led to another and he found himself swinging up into the saddle of his tall, crazy horse, the General, which loved nothing better than to run for all the wind.

"HAW!" he cried and pulled on the reins. With a nudging of his feet, the horse needed very little prodding to let loose to try to break a speed record. Five hundred pounds of sleek brown, solid muscle shot down the dusty road. Emory Heartwell watched him ride away with a cloud of dust obscuring him the farther away he got and she smiled to herself.

"I knew he was the right man," she whispered to herself.

***

Everleigh watched the waving shadows on the wall across from the window. The light breeze ruffled the leaves outside and the breeze tickled her arms. She had never felt so alone. Her broken body ached. Her heart felt as sore as her side. Her mind kept a steady rerun of events at the hotel. Despite the serenity of the hospital room, every part of her heart, mind and soul roiled with anger and grief. A tear slid down her cheek.

A small part of herself tried to fight it. She

told herself she could beat this. She was stronger than this. She was no little girl. But, the demons whispering in her ears where relentless. One tiny part of her mind held the tether to Malcolm and waited for him. She could see him in her mind. He was coming. She knew it. Like vibrations down a taunt electric cable, she could feel him coming toward her.

She didn't see her come in. A woman stood at the foot of her bed. The woman was tall with long blond hair pulled up on the sides and curled into barrels behind her ears under a large hat with cream crepe folds. She was pretty with a pouty full mouth in a permanent pucker. She had on a cream and light blue dress. The light blue bodice formed the deep V with welting to accentuate the seams drawing the eye down from her shoulder, over her full breasts and down to a point between her hips under cream pleats spraying out and down.

She smiled slightly and had an easy to trust expression.

"Who are you?" Everleigh asked.

The woman waited as though refusing to take orders from her even if it was just answering a polite question. Despite her charming pouty smile, Everleigh could see a multitude of thoughts crossing the woman's mind and it made her wary.

"I am Cherise Watkins." She waited without blinking to see if the name was recognized.

Everleigh stopped breathing. Horace's mistress.

She continued, "I see you are familiar then. Good. That makes things a little easier." Oddly, she smiled and tilted her head slightly. Everleigh wondered what this woman was up to and it probably wasn't good.

"Why are you here?" Everleigh asked firmly. Of all the parts of her swirling in her head, the business woman stepped forward. The one who didn't put up with any crap.

Cherise didn't move a muscle but Everleigh heard her suck in a quiet breath. Apparently she had assumed she was dealing with a dumb little girl.

"I have come to get you and take you home. We need to leave."

She stared at Cherise in disbelief and even chuckled. "I am not going anywhere. Have you not seen what that monster did to me?"

She gestured with her hands over her torso.

Cherise stepped forward and pulled the sheet off. As she was putting her right arm under Everleigh's shoulders, she pulled her knees off the bed to pull her to a sitting position.

"We are just going to get you up and out of here. You are not staying here anymore. We have to leave."

She kept insisting that, Everleigh thought. She had this pleasant friendly demeanor but she also had something else going on in her head. It was like talking to a person with split personality but you could only see one of the personalities.

"Whoa whoa whoa." She tried to push Cherise away as she winced and gripped her side with her other hand. "What is the rush anyway?"

Cherise put her hands on her tiny waist and for the first time showed any change in expression. She blew a hard breath and puckered her mouth even more. Collecting herself, she looked Everleigh in the eye and very clearly spoke her next words.

"You are going to stand up and come with me," she smiled a surprisingly genuine-looking smile and continued, "or I will make you wish you had. Are we clear here?"

This woman was a piece of work. She had the face and control to get what she wanted. Everleigh was certain that men were putty in her hands. She was not that young. She looked to be about thirty by the fine lines around eyes and mouth.

The woman sighed again and shook her head, "Look, I don't have time for you to contemplate your next move. We have to get out of here now." She reached around Everleigh, putting her right arm around her and positioning her hand right over the wound on her right side. Abruptly pulling Everleigh into her, Everleigh cried out. The hot searing pain from the wound and the deep soreness from the broken bones was still very fresh. The pain hit a crescendo and darkness closed in around her. Dizziness washed over her and she went limp.

"Good grief!" Cherise groaned.

She let Everleigh slump over on the bed and darted out of the room. She came back quickly with a wheel chair. Going around behind Everleigh, she put her arms around her and pulled her over into the chair. Her head fell backwards and Cherise shoved it forward. Everleigh slumped over her arm held by the arm rest.

Cherise pushed the chair to the door and peeked out, looking both directions. Then she made a dash down the hallway and turned to go out the back door. No one saw them as they whizzed past. Out on the empty back porch, Cherise whispered into the carriage sitting there.

"Come on! Help me. She is passed out."

Horace Peeble looked out the door of the carriage and frowned.

"Come on! Get her in the carriage!" Cherise fussed when he didn't move fast enough.

He jumped out and pulled Everleigh up into his arms and set her on the floor of the carriage. Cherise climbed in and pulled her by her arms out of the way. Horace jumped up onto the driver's seat and clucked his tongue as he snapped the reins. The carriage jolted into action and they left the wheel chair sitting on the porch.

The bumping and jolting about stirred her and she twisted her mouth in pain. Her white hospital gown was twisted around her. She tried to sit up and every movement was like a knife cutting her side. She tried to brace herself with her arm and her gown clung to a warm wetness. She pulled her hand away and looked at the crimson smear that covered her palm. She looked up at Cherise who was watching her.

"Don't get that on my dress." Cherise said flatly.

Everleigh wondered how anyone could be that lacking in concern for another person. After all, she should be thanking her now that she would be living the life of luxury because of her father's inheritance.

The carriage bounced along until Everleigh heard the sound of trains rattling on tracks. She pulled herself slowly up onto the bench seat to see out. They were at the station. She didn't see how they could sneak a woman in a white bloodstained nightgown on to a train in broad day light without causing a scene. In fact, she could scream and help would come. That would be great, she thought.

Cherise was looking out the window, too. Her puckered full lips curled at the corners to make a satisfied permanent smile. The woman was truly an ironic icon. She looked so sweet, like someone Everleigh would have as a friend, but yet she clearly had the lack of concern for others that you would see in a sociopath.

Cherise turned her attention to a black satchel at her feet. She opened it and pulled out a rolled up wad of fabric strips.

"Turn around and put your hands behind your back."

"What?"

"Just do it or I'll find some other way to get this done. He says it would be preferable for you to make it to Charleston alive, but I am not opposed to a tragic accident on the way. Both ways, Horry gets the money and I'm good."

"Tragic accident?" She was stunned. She really hadn't expected Cherise and Horace to be murderers. Apparently they really would go to any length to get at the money. She was in their way like a rock in the road. She turned backwards and put her hands behind her.

"What kind of a nickname is Horry? Good grief!"

Cherise said nothing and bound her wrists roughly and then pulled a black cloak from her bag. She wrapped it around Everleigh and tied it at the neck. Then she sat back down on the other seat and looked at her nails. Finding a hang nail, she bit at the side of her finger.

The carriage stopped and the sound of

Horace's feet hitting the cobblestones made a thud. He came around to the door, opened it and looked inside. He actually grinned. He seemed pleased with himself. It made sense. His plan was working. How he got out of jail was a mystery. She wondered if Miss Puckers broke him out.

"Come on." Cherise prodded her.

She stood and tried to figure out how she was going to get out without the use of her arms. She stooped and sat and waited for him to lift her out. He sat her on her feet on the ground and then offered his hand to Cherise as she stepped down the steps like royalty. She noticed Cherise's shoes were exquisitely decorated with silk and pearls with a very dainty fashionable heel. She wondered if Cherise had already been shopping with her money.

Everleigh was waiting for the right time to attract attention. Horace had parked the carriage too far from the station. They were a long way from the platform. They walked along with trains passing beside them. The platform was on the other side of the rail yard and they started to cross the tracks. They came to a train that was stopped and passed around the last car.

"Let's file along here and cross farther up," Horace said. "Ladies, first!" he smiled at Everleigh. She didn't see but he winked at Cherise and she winked back.

Everleigh stepped around the back of the caboose and made her way toward the station. Cherise followed behind her.

Horace leaned in to Cherise's ear and whispered to her, "I've changed my mind. When the next train on the tracks to our left comes by, shove her in front of it." She nodded, still sporting the pouty upturned smile that made you believe she was good as gold.

Everleigh heard the grinding of the engine getting closer. She stayed as close to the train on the right as she could. The tracks were far enough apart, but the trains towered over them. She glanced over her shoulder to see it was closing in. The massive black steam engine's "Chuh, Chuh, Chuh" was loud in her ear. She didn't hear Horace tell Cherise, "Now."

Cherise grabbed her by the shoulders and heaved Everleigh with all her might toward the track. Everleigh screamed and pulled her shoulder away from her right hand, kicking out with her left foot as she lost balance spinning into the air.

For just a moment, she was suspended in the air as she flew toward the track. Twisting around to the right, unable to move her hands to break her fall, the cape fanned out like a bird taking flight. She caught sight of two things as she spun around: Cherise had been knocked off balance and was falling backward, twisting to the left but toward the track, and Horace stood there with his mouth in a half-spoken yell, straining to reach Cherise but too late. His hands outstretched grasping the air.

She and Cherise hit the tracks at nearly the same time, lying across the metal rail. Eveleigh's head rested on the far rail and Cherise's head was between the rails, not quite as far across. The vibration of the oncoming track hummed against her skull as it rested on the metal. Her hands were pinned under her. The thudding of the wheels was like a galloping horse and she wondered if it would be the last thing she heard. She closed her eyes and waited for the darkness to take her, hoping it would be too fast to feel anything.

She felt a jerk that pulled her from her very core and then a freeing flying sensation. Her very soul must have been let loose. The darkness closed in again as the pain in her ribs ripped through her. Pain. She thought there would be no pain after death.

***

Malcolm's horse was like a dragon without wings. It flew barely touching the ground. The huffing and snorting was the only sound Malcolm heard over the whistle of air in his ears. The horse's eyes were wild with freedom. The trip that should take two hours took less than one. He kept seeing her face in the bed with dark circles under her eyes. Thoughts of Peeble hurting her, molesting her, caused him to goad the horse to run even faster. Adrenaline coursed through him like fire.

He got to town and raced through streets like a wild man on horseback. People jumped out of the way as they heard the racing thuds of the horse's hooves. Finally up ahead, he saw the two-story home that had been converted into an infirmary. It had been white washed over brick. A large maple tree stood to one side on the front yard casting its waving shadows across the windows. He knew this was the creator of the shadows he saw in his mind.

Malcolm swung down in front of the infirmary and was inside the foyer in three steps. He was about to head to the left to start looking for her when his gut stopped him. He stopped and turned his head to the right. The hallway turned to the back on that side of the building.

The invisible cord that held them cut through the air like a fallen electric line. He barreled down the hallway, around the corner and out the back door. There sat an empty wheel chair. No one was there. The wheel chair had a smear of bright red blood on the arm rest. He ran his finger over it and the wind blowing across it spread goosebumps up his arm. He heard a creaking wheel and looked to see a carriage rolling away on the next block. The driver didn't look like a hired driver. He was wearing the coat of a gentleman.

Peeble!

Malcolm's instincts drove him now. He leapt from the porch and ran around the house. He swung onto his horse who was still breathing hard and prodded him into action again. The horse rose up on its hind legs and whinnied a screeching call, then bolted down the road following Malcolm's instruction with the reins. He lost sight of which direction they went and doubled back around looking down each side street. People on the street stopped and looked as he went past in a blaze of thunder. The General was no ordinary horse. He commanded respect and awe.

Finally, he saw the carriage turning off a side road and followed in pursuit until a cart loaded with hay blocked the path. Malcolm pulled the horse around it looking for a way to get past and finally decided to just go down a nearby alley. The alley took them to a street that didn't cross with the one the carriage was on. Frustration mounted in Malcolm as he grimaced in anger.

All he could think about was getting to the carriage. If he lost track of her again, it might take days to find her or worse. He had a sinking feeling about it this time. As though the walls were closing in on him, he could feel the cord being stretched between them. If it snapped, if the laws of time, physics and life drove a wedge that couldn't be overcome, he would lose her forever. His heart was pounding so hard, the whooshing waves of his pulse filled his ears.

Finally on a connecting street, he could see the train station ahead. He knew that had to be their destination. He didn't see the carriage but he knew she had to be close by. Riding alongside the tracks, a train was pulling in to his left. The great engine towered over him even on horseback. The General redoubled his speed as though the engine dared him in a race. Malcolm searched the platform in the distance with his eyes and didn't see her.

His vision caught a sight that drew him in. A black cloak, fanned out like the petals of a black velvet petunia was floating suspended with Everleigh's serene face in the middle. The cloak twisted around her and she landed across the tracks, the tracks of the train pulling in next to him.

Adrenalin shot through him like a coursing fire and he kicked the horse into high gear.

"Go, General! Go!"

As though coming around the last stretch for the Derby, his horse was ready for the win. The 'Chuh Chuh Chuh of the engine was its opponent and this horse only knew how to come in first. Long powerful strides propelled them ahead by a length.

Malcolm held the saddle horn with his left hand and leaned as far to the right of the horse as he could without falling or getting caught in the horse's legs. Hooking his left foot over the saddle he stretched and reached and in the split second that they passed Everleigh, he snatched her up by the twisted cloak encircling her. Her body limply shot into the air following the trajectory of her chest upward.

"Whoa, whoa, whoa, fella!" he slowed the horse. The train sped past them blocking his view of anyone on the other side. He slid off the saddle and lowered Everleigh safely onto the dusty ground. Crashing down beside her, grabbed her onto his lap cradling her head. He could see the red soaked hospital gown around her and his heart caught in his throat.

"Everleigh! Eveleigh!" he gently shook her shoulder. "Everleigh, please. Stay with me. I love you. Oh, God! Help us! Everleigh!" Tears coursed down his cheeks and fell on hers.

She squinted and grimaced. The sunlight bathed around them but in his shade, she opened her eyes and smiled.

"Malcolm. If this is heaven, I believe it."

Screams from the platform tore his eyes away. The adrenalin in his veins still painfully washing to the farthest parts of his hands and feet, he looked back to the tracks. The trains had passed and what was left made him suck in his breath. The body of a woman, sliced in two, lay across the tracks. He hadn't seen anyone but Everleigh, so focused as he was to save her. Peeble was laying on the ground next to the track with his arms outstretched. Rail workers were converging around the pair and others were running toward him and Everleigh. From the look of the scene, it appeared Peeble had pushed both ladies in front of the train.

He looked back at Everleigh. Her breathing

was shallow and quick, but she looked up into his eyes.

"You'll be alright. Help is coming."

She nodded and said, "Kiss me."

Very gently, he lifted her and covered her lips with his. Closing his eyes, he could feel the energy of a thousand suns explode in his heart.

***

Everleigh tried to block the pain in her torso. She was certain that a truck could have run over her and it would not have felt any worse.

"My hands."

He turned her toward his body and cut her hands loose with a knife in his boot. She saw the anger surge in his face as he bared his teeth.

"If I get my hands on Peeble..."

"Malcolm, just hold me. I'm so glad you're here."

She focused on Malcolm's face, drinking in his presence. Just moments before she was sure her life was over. There seemed no way to survive. The train was barreling down on her and she couldn't move. Now, by a miracle, she lay cradled in the arms of the most wonderful man she could imagine. The sunlight was behind him lighting up the dark waves of his hair. She just needed to hold on to life and soon all would be okay. She could feel herself slipping into the darkness of her mind.

"Stay with me, Everleigh. Do you hear me?"

She nodded and tried to smile. She wasn't sure if her lips actually moved.

"I feel so weak, so heavy."

"I know, love."

A carriage rode up to them and a man with a black bag jumped down.

"I'm Dr. Baker," he absently told Malcolm as he started to look her over. "My God. It's my patient from the Infirmary. What is she doing here?"

He looked up at Malcolm as though he had taken her.

"She had been kidnapped by Horace Peeble and a lady he knows. She was about to be run over by the train when I pulled her off the tracks."

"It's astonishing!" He looked back toward the crowd surrounding the late Cherise.

"The lady didn't make it." Malcolm turned the corners of his mouth down in a grim expression.

Turning back to Everleigh, "I need to get her back to the Infirmary right away. Can you come with me? You can help me stop any more bleeding."

"Of course!"

Malcolm lifted her gently into his arms and carried her to the wagon. He laid her down on a stretcher. Then, he went to get General and tied him to the back of the wagon to follow them. Dr. Baker wrapped a wide piece of linen around her torso to stop the bleeding and support her ribs.

"If you will keep talking to her, that would help."

"Certainly!"

Dr. Baker opened his bag and pulled out a stethoscope. He listened to her heart and examined her.

The carriage jolted forward and they all rocked with the wagon. Malcolm took her hand in his and kissed her fingers.

"Everleigh, I have been so worried. We all

have. When Suzanne got your telegram, I came right away."

"Oh, Malcolm. I worried you thought I went with him willingly. He kidnapped me."

"I know, love. I'm just so glad I got there in time. If I'd lost you, I couldn't live."

"It has only been thoughts of you that have kept me sane. Malcolm, he--"

"Don't!" he cut her off. "Don't speak of it. You are safe now."

She felt so guilty. How could he understand? As hard as it was, she had to tell him.

"I must tell you," she paused, "he forced me to marry him."

"I know. I figured that out. It could not possibly have been a legal marriage. We will have it annulled if we have to. Whatever the case, it was not valid. Don't worry, love."

She knew he didn't understand. The marriage *had* been consummated. How could she tell him that? Maybe she wouldn't have to. Maybe she could say nothing about it and the memory would just go away. She knew better than that, though. It tore at her like a dog nipping at her heels.

They pulled up to the Infirmary and two orderlies ran out to help. As they carried her inside, Dr. Baker turned to him, "You will have to wait. I need to tend to her."

Leaving Malcolm on the porch, the doctor turned and darted inside.

***

Feeling totally helpless, he sat on a chair. Surely she would live, he thought. She had to.

Without her, he could not imagine living. How could he go back to his life before and carry on. It was so difficult letting go of his fears and letting her in his heart. There would never be anyone like her again. They say it's better to have loved and lost than never to have loved, but that was a lie. He held his head in his hands and prayed for God to let her live.

***

The next morning, she woke up in her room at the infirmary with the nurse fussing with her bandage.

"Good morning, sunshine! Glad to see you back. You left a little too soon before."

Everleigh smiled.

"Doc stitched you all back up. You will feel weak and dizzy for a couple of days from the blood loss, but you should be fine." The nurse smiled at her.

"I don't know your name."

"I'm Annie, baby. I'll go get you something to eat. You have some visitors who have been driving me crazy, so maybe you can talk some sense into them." She giggled and left the room.

In the hallway, she heard Annie tell them one visitor at a time for now. Malcolm stepped in and she sucked in a breath. He looked as gorgeous as ever, even with the furrowed brow of concern. He sat next to her on the bed and held her hand.

"My love, do you hurt?"

"No. They must have given me something. I'm a little sleepy but I don't feel anything."

"Good. They said you will be alright. I have been praying for you around the clock."

She pulled his hand to her mouth and kissed his palm.

"I love you," she said.

He smiled and she felt a zing as her insides flip flopped.

"I love you madly." He leaned in and gently kissed her cheek. "Suzanne and your aunt are here."

"My aunt? She's alright?"

"Yes. She is a remarkable woman."

"Well good. I'm glad." She looked at Malcolm, "Everything I did, I want you to know, I did it to save her."

He looked at her with pain in his eyes. "Love, you have been through a horrible ordeal. None of it is your fault. I hold nothing against you. When you want to talk about it, I will listen, but know, there is nothing you could tell me that would make me love you any less."

She sighed in relief. She wasn't sure she would ever be able to tell him everything that happened. Hearing his words helped, though.

"I will send in your aunt. She has been beside herself to speak to you."

He left and a tall, elegant woman glided into her room. She stood at the end of the bed and beamed.

"Aunt Emory! I am so, so glad to see you're alright," she said.

"Thank you, your ladyship, I know what you did for me and I hate it that you went through that, but I thank you."

Your ladyship?

The phrase caught her and she froze. Her eyes widened. Aunt Emory, watching her closely, nodded and smiled.

"Aunt Emory?" she tilted her head

questioningly.

The handsome woman perched on the bed beside her and caressed her hair back.

"Yes, honey. It's me."

"But how?"

Her mother smiled. "I got the soap from this woman in France. She looked at me and said she knew just what I needed for you, Eveleigh. Her eyes looked through me like she was looking across the horizon. She handed me two bars of lavender soap and told me to use one first and I would understand."

"So you, you had already come here. You had been here?"

"Yes. I really liked it here. It was fun getting to play reenactment for real. But then I met Malcolm and I knew he was yours, stuck here in this time without you. You both didn't know how much you needed each other. So I went back and gave you the other bar. Remember what I said?"

Everleigh thought a minute, "You said, no matter what the year, you'll always be there for me."

"And here I am!"

"Oh, Mom! I missed you so much!"

"I've worried ever since I got back here. I didn't know who you would be. I knew you would have a different body than your 2016 self, just like I did. Then I got kidnapped and wondered if I would ever see you. When I finally got back home, the butler told me my niece had come to see me from Charleston, I knew that had to be you. Apparently we have been caught up in the same person's snare."

"Yeah, that Mr. Peeble. Good grief."

"He is in jail. He will be for a very long time. He may never get out. They are charging him with

Cherise's death and attempted murder for you, assault, extortion, along with various other charges like escaping from jail, stealing a carriage, and so on."

"Wow."

"And papers have been filed to annul your marriage since it wasn't legal in the first place."

"Ugh." A wave of shame and disgust filled her. She dropped her head back on her pillow and looked at the ceiling.

"Baby, I know you went through with it because of the threat to me, actually to a woman you didn't even know. I know your heart and you would do anything to protect another from harm. It's the only thing that makes sense when you put all the pieces together."

She nodded, "If I'd known it was you," she trailed off with her face crumpling into a grimace.

"Oh! Oh, there, there, now. I am just fine."

Everleigh hugged her. Tears slipped free and streamed down onto her mother's shoulder.

Her mother continued, "I am worried about you though. You have been through too much." She paused and gave her a pained smile, "Did he *hurt* you, honey?"

Everleigh leaned back and took her mom's hands. She didn't want to make her sad. She didn't want her mother to think of her in the context of what he did. She sighed and looked into her mother's eyes. The one thing she did need was to get past the pain of it, though, and no one would be able to love her through it like her mother. Gratitude for the events that led them together here in this time melted her heart.

"Yes. He did," she admitted. She bit her lip and let that sit in the air adding nothing more.

Her mother sat very still, not betraying any emotion that had to be running through her head. Everleigh saw her mother's brows crease together slightly and her jaw clenched. Finally she took a deep breath.

"Then we will get through it together. Your heart is my heart and we will heal through it in each other's arms. When you are ready, I will listen and you will not be alone. Okay?"

She nodded and cried. Sobs broke through and her mother held her and rubbed her back.

"Cry it out, baby. He stole something from you that is precious. You did nothing wrong."

When she felt at peace, she wiped her eyes with a handkerchief and looked up.

"Will you just look at you? What are you, like 20?" said her mother.

Everleigh laughed, "Yeah! And with a rockin' bod! Before this mess," she gestured at her side, "I was having a blast. Oh! Hey! Malcolm proposed!"

"Everleigh! Oh my goodness!" she said excitedly and then tilting her head down and looking up at her through her lashes, "Is he not a total hottie?" Then she fanned herself like she was swooning.

"Mom!" They both laughed.

"I knew you two were meant to be together."

There was a knock at the door and Everleigh called for them to come in. Suzanne and Malcolm came marching in with a tray that had a plate covered with a silver dome and little finial on top.

"Food to make you heal quickly!" said Suzanne laying the tray on Everleigh's lap.

"We didn't care for the selection being cooked in the kitchen so we walked over to a restaurant across the street.

She pulled off the lid and the plate was piled high with crispy fried chicken, mashed potatoes and green beans. The aroma wafted over her face and she breathed in the delicious steam. She looked around her and had everything she needed. Her mother, her good friend, and a man that was surely created just for her to love.

Chapter Six

The Infirmary would not release her for two more weeks. Finally, Everleigh was resting on the sofa of her Aunt Emory's house, as far as the world knew. She had put away the corset until the stitches completely healed and wore a loose day dress. She was able to get around slowly. Her mother came in with a tray of tea and biscuits and set it on the table next to the red velvet sofa. She poured them a cup and handed Everleigh hers.

"Everleigh, when you feel up to it, we need to call a seamstress to come and discuss your wedding gown."

"Oh! That will be fun. It's awesome that gowns in this time are all tailor made. No bridal stores!"

"And, they don't have to be white. It could be any color or fabric you want."

"White is fine. I'm so glad you are here to see me get married!" She paused, "Do you ever wonder what happened to the real Everleigh or Aunt Emory?"

"I have thought about it. I wonder if they actually died and we were placed in their body at that exact moment. With no antibiotics or safety codes, this is a dangerous time. Most people don't live past sixty years old."

"I suppose. Maybe Everleigh died of what her parents had but she caught it later."

"The woman in France would think it was magic that brought us here, but I believe it was God. He can do anything! I do think the woman in France that gave me the soap saw all this unfold in her mind like a prophet."

A knock at the door paused their conversation and they sipped their tea waiting for the butler to come in.

Everleigh thought about how nice it was to have domestic help. This was much better than in 2016 when they did everything themselves. Of course, having Mr. Addison's fortune was helpful, too. She was now ridiculously rich and that stock in the telephone was just going to keep going up.

The butler announced that Mr. Steel had arrived and they looked up. Everleigh's heart wound into a thudding hammer as her gaze followed up from his shoes, up the cream trousers, the suit coat, and to his tan face with green eyes watching her take him in. A slight curl of his lips showed that he was enjoying being the object of her obvious affection.

"Good day, ladies."

"Mr. Steel! How nice to see you. Sit and have some tea," Emory said.

"Thank you. I will." He sat next to Everleigh while Emory poured him a cup.

He took Everleigh's hand in his and kissed her knuckles. Her heart leapt. She wanted to caress his face but decided that was too much for a lady to do in this time period in the parlor in front of her mother.

"So to what do we owe the pleasure of your visit?" asked Emory who was watching the two of them ogle each other and smiled.

"I was hoping to take Everleigh for a carriage ride if she feels up to it." He glanced at her looking for a response.

Everleigh's face lit up and his followed suit.

"I think you have your answer," Emory said. "I'll ring for Betsy to pack a luncheon basket to take with you." She pulled the cord to call the maid and relayed the request.

Soon Everleigh and Malcolm were bouncing gently in the back of his carriage down the dusty road lined with maple and oak trees on both sides. The shade of the leaves making a canopy to hide them as they traveled. The breeze was at least 10 degrees cooler in the shade than out in the open. Malcolm held her hand with one hand and had his arm around her with the other.

"It beautiful," she whispered. "The rolling green hills and blue sky. The rolls of harvested hay. It looks like a perfect landscape painting."

"Yes. I do like living here. Louisville is a beautiful city, but it is so peaceful here. Do you think you will like living here? After living in Charleston?"

She turned to him and looked into his eyes, "Where ever you are is home to me, now or forever."

"That's good," he smiled a pleased curl of lips. "That is part of what I wanted to talk to you about. Remember I told you about the title issue with my estate?"

"Yes. About the heir. But what about Percy?"

"I am having my lawyer check on it. There are some issues because there is no record of Percy's birth. No one even knows he existed. I'm not even sure if the government will recognize him as able to receive the estate due to his condition."

"Oh. Good grief."

"If we are not able to straighten it out, Percy and I, and the help, will have to leave the estate. In fact, everything on the estate including farm equipment will go back to the government."

"Oh no! Can't I just buy it from them?"

He sighed. "That is very kind of you, but no. I will not get by on your money. It's yours. Even though leaving would be devastating on many levels because I have no assets. I sold everything to create a fund to take care of Percy. That is how I have Bethann. She is not just an ordinary nanny. She is educated and studied at an institute affiliated with a Dr. Downs in England."

Everleigh couldn't help but smile.

Dr. Downs. Whom the syndrome would be named after some 80 years from now.

"But, darling, I can't have you and Percy flung into the streets. My inheritance is more than adequate to help us resettle even if it has to be a different estate.

He looked away and sighed. Turning back to her, "That is so kind of you but that is your security. I will not take it."

She grimaced. Frustration tore at her.

He is so stubborn!

She could fix it, but she could see how it would rob him of his need to provide for them.

He continued, "If the lawyer can't find a way to legally retain the estate and its assets, I will be in no position to marry you." His face pulled back in a pained smile as he waited for her reaction.

"But, but, what about Percy? What will happen to him if you lose everything?"

He dropped his head in his hands defeated.

"I will have to place him in an orphanage. I won't be able to provide for him. Maybe in time I will be able to, but I am not sure if I will be able to get him back." He pursed his lips, "Of course, Bethann won't be able to wait that long. We may lose her services."

A fury welled up in her. This was so unfair. Not only to her and Malcolm, but it would be such a devastating blow to Percy. So many changes in his life and none for the better. She couldn't bear to let this happen if she could help it.

She thought about what she could do. She was pretty adept at interpreting statutes and civil rights laws from her work. She had read state and federal regs for sport just to brush up. She had handled workplace accommodations, handicap access in public places and even testified in Congress. She could find her way around complex issues.

Of course she couldn't explain any of this to Malcolm, but she was going to figure out how to resolve this. Surely, Percy's Revolutionary War ancestor hadn't intended to throw his fragile great, grandson out to an orphanage.

She squeezed Malcolm's arm, "I am certain this will work out. I haven't the slightest worry."

The carriage slowed and Malcolm hopped down the steps. He turned to lift her out and gently set her on her feet. She looked around at the scenery. Trees shaded a creek that quietly rushed over a flat stone ledge and fell to a lower stone creating a short water fall. The bank was a grassy slope the rolled up to a meadow. The driver of the carriage handed Malcolm the luncheon basket and a blanket and then hopped up to the driver's seat. He tapped the reins and clucked his tongue and the carriage meandered around the grove of trees to give them some space.

Malcolm spread the blanket on the grass and invited her to join him.

"Are you hungry, beautiful lady?" His eyes narrowed and held hers.

She giggled, "I believe a little refreshment might revive me."

Holding his hand to steady her, she slowly sat and then reclined on one elbow. He joined her with the basket by their heads. He reached in and pulled out a clay jug of tea and poured it into two cups. She sipped the lukewarm tea and smiled. Perspiration made the long white linen skirt of her dress stick to her legs.

Tea. I've never drank so much tea in my life. What I wouldn't give for a Coke! An ice cold Coke!

She tried to remember when Coke was invented. She thought she had read in a flight magazine that it was sometime near 1890. Maybe it wouldn't be long before it made its way to Versailles.

"What are you thinking?" he asked.

She smiled. There was no way she was going to tell what she was thinking.

"I was just thinking of how thirsty I was."

"Ah! Yes, it is a warm day. The shade will cool you soon."

"Do you come here often?"

"Sometimes. It's a good place to think. It makes for a good run for the General."

She looked at the light filtering through the leaves highlighting his hair. She reached out and ran her fingers through the long brown waves. He closed his eyes at the pleasure of her touch. Taking her hand he kissed the inside of her palm. His warm breath felt like feathers on her skin.

She breathed in and closed her eyes then. She could stay in this moment forever. She rolled back and stared up through the canopy of leaves. They gently swayed with the wind above them and rustled against each other with a 'whishing' sound.

"Everleigh, I didn't expect to fall in love. I tried so hard to steel myself from those emotions. But you seem to reach me in a way that I have no way to hide from. It's overwhelming. Many times I have felt like we were connected in some way. "

She turned her head to look in his eyes.

"Do you think other people in love feel this way?" he asked.

"I don't know. I thought I was in love once, but now I see that it can't compare. I think, Malcolm, that we have something very special. I think it's something that is greater than the laws of the universe even."

He smiled. "So you feel it, too, the cord that connects us?"

"Yes." She looked at his pale pink lips and felt her body rush with heat.

He knelt down and covered his mouth with hers. She wanted to be so close to him that she was a part of him. Not just physically, but if she could somehow slip into the space his soul occupied, she would.

His tongue gently caressed her lips until a surge of passion unleashed as he probed every part of her mouth. His tongue danced with hers as his right arm encircled her pulling her closer while his left arm cradled her head. Her hands explored his hard muscled chest and torso. He was a wall of solid warm muscle and she felt so safe in the cocoon of his embrace. She wanted to give all of herself to him and to know every part of him. She reached up and held his head on either side, weaving her fingers into his silky waves.

With her eyes closed, she saw a dizzying kaleidoscope of color and explosion as the energy of his passion increased. He kissed down her cheek and behind her ear, suddenly stopping to inhale the scent of her skin. The cool draw of air against the humidity touching her neck made her moan out loud. In response, he plunged his mouth onto her neck and kissed and licked and gently bit her silky porcelain skin.

She felt as though she would positively come undone.

"Oh, Malcolm," she groaned.

Breathing hard, he paused with his face in the swoop of her hair. "My darling, I look forward to loving you thoroughly for the rest of our lives."

He rolled back onto the blanket and stared back at her. They lay side by side on their backs holding hands. She'd felt so safe in his embrace. Trusting him completely, she decided that the best way to heal from her scarred heart was to let Malcolm show her again and again how to love again.

A thought came to her mind as she stared into his eyes.

Percy cannot be hidden away.

"Malcolm, I understand your fear that Percy would be taken from you. However, the eugenics supporters gain momentum from people's ignorance. I truly believe that if ordinary people knew someone like Percy, knew how sweet he is, they would have a hard time believing he was less than human."

"Everleigh, I don't know."

"I know. It's scary. As you said, there is no law right now. So he *is* safe. They cannot take him away from you. The biggest obstacle I see is people's fear of the unknown. If the people of this town knew him, they would protect him."

"People can be vicious, Everleigh."

"What if we created a school for others like Percy. Bethann could do her therapy with them. If we involved the community, they would develop compassion for the students. Perhaps the students could even be taught jobs to be productive and useful."

"A school? I wouldn't know where to begin."

"I do. And if we can get supporters, we can use the school as evidence that the eugenics laws are wrong. We can keep those laws out of Kentucky. I will testify in Frankfort before the state legislators if I have to."

"You are that compelled about this?"

"Yes. Between you and me and Bethann, we could do a great deal. Wouldn't you have considered letting Percy come to a school like that if you knew he would be safe?"

"Well, yes. I suppose. If I knew it would be good for him."

"Exactly! And you would pay the school to care for him and advocate for his rights, wouldn't you?"

"When you put it like that, yes."

"We could make a difference. Our passion for these vulnerable individuals could help not only Percy, but many, many more like him. They are out there, hidden in homes or not even born yet."

"God, help me. You are an angel. I love you, Everleigh Addison."

***

"I need to go to town. Do you want to go?" Everleigh asked her mother.

"Oh, that would be nice. I will visit Suzanne. What do you need to do in town?"

"I need to ask some questions. Malcolm is in a legal dispute over his estate."

"Alrighty, then. If anyone can hunt down an answer, it's you!"

The carriage dropped her mother off at the Inn and went on to the lawyer's office with Everleigh. Walking in to the office, the clerk looked up. He was a young man with small glasses who had been studying some parchments.

"Can I help you, ma'am?"

"Yes," she stepped up to the desk. "Is the lawyer in?"

"No. He is away at the moment. What's the nature of your visit?"

"I wanted to ask him some questions regarding estate law."

He looked her up and down. Apparently women didn't ask questions like that, she surmised.

"Uh huh," he finally said.

"Look, if you have a set of law books, could I look at them a minute? I won't bother you."

His eyes opened a little wider.

"Now, missy, I'm sure if you came back in a couple of hours Mr. Skeller would be happy to help you."

Her face fell flat. She looked at him through half closed lids of contempt. She felt a bubbling rise of bile in her throat.

"Mr…, what did you say your name was?"

"Sampson, Mr. Sampson."

"Right, Mr. Sampson," she drew out the mister. Do you think I would harm the law books if I looked at them?"

"Uh, no. No, of course not."

"Then I would just ask that you humor a silly girl that wanted to see your magnificent library. I bet you know so many things that those big books say." She smiled and batted her eyelashes.

He started giggling and scratched the back of his neck.

This is too easy.

"Oh my," he started, "Yes, I have had to look up several things. But, honey, I don't think you would understand it." He said it sweetly as though he actually felt bad for her and was trying to prevent her from getting upset.

"Oh. Yes. I see what you mean. I just want to look at them to be amazed. Would that be alright? I promise I won't bother you or keep you from your work. That looks so important."

She smiled again and shifted her posture, pushing her shoulders back and demurely putting her hands behind her back. He seemed to be considering it but wasn't sure. She bit her bottom lip and blinked several times.

"Oh, all right! But if the front door opens, you need to come right on out here and don't say a word about it, you understand?"

"Oh, certainly Mr. Sampson." She nodded quickly.

I should get an award for that performance.

He opened Mr. Skeller's office door and motioned for her to go in. Leaving the door open, he went back to his desk and, looking around a minute, got back to his work.

Since this was not a matter of actual real estate law but rather contract law, she needed to find an example of a case in which a descendant had questionable lineage. She also wondered what rights a feeble-minded person had in regard to property ownership.

Heck, if he was royal no one would question his rights as an heir.

She found a legal dictionary and flipped to 'heir'. She saw that 'an heir of the body' definition is why Malcolm could not inherit the estate. It has to go to a blood relative, not just a person related by marriage.

Scrambling through titles on a shelf she found a book of Uniform State Laws. Pulling the book from the shelf, she flipped through it. A section on property caught her eye. She turned and leaned against a table and skimmed the subheadings. 'Rules Against Perpetuity' caught her eye.

Perpetuity? Like perpetual?

She read in this section that in wills that leave property, the property must be received within twenty-one years. She thought about it, tapping her finger on the book.

"The first heir received the estate after Crazy Grandpa died. They lived their life on the estate and died." She tried to get her head around it. "The will transferred as Crazy Grandpa wanted because it passed to the next owner within 21 years. After that, because of the Rule of Perpetuity, the will was finished."

She tried to figure out what happens next to the estate.

"Oh, my gosh! That's it. There is no hold on the title. The estate passes to the next of kin no matter if they are a blood relative or not."

She shoved the book back in its place on the shelf just as the little bell on the door jingled. She sucked in a breath.

"Mr. Sampson, do I have any messages?" A deep gravelly voice boomed.

"Uh, uh, no, sir."

"Sampson, why are you mumbling?"

"It's just- Wait! Don't go in there!"

"And why would I not go in my office, Sampson?"

She strode through the office door smoothing her skirt, "Oh, thank you Mr. Sampson."

Mr. Skeller stiffened when he saw her, "Madam! What are you doing in my office?" his eyes shot up as he waited for her explanation.

"Oh, I'm terribly sorry. Mr. Sampson was kind enough to allow me a private place to mend my skirt. It got caught on a nail and tore in a most improper place. So I ducked in your fine office and your good clerk was very hospitable. I'll have to tell everyone I know what fine gentlemen you are."

With that she stepped past him with a wink to Mr. Sampson and sashayed right out the door. She heard Mr. Skeller tell Sampson 'Good work, boy," before she closed the door. She marveled at how much a women could get away with because most men thought they had the mind of a little bird.

She crossed the road and made her way down the wooden boardwalk toward the Inn. Horses, carriages and wagons passed her. She was impressed with what a hopping town this was. She would have thought it would be about 10 families and general store. The downtown was not too much smaller than it was in 2016. It seemed like most of Versailles had not changed much in 128 years. She had passed several new subdivisions and stores near them in the taxi, but the feel of the town had remained. The modern Versailles had maintained a feeling of timelessness.

She turned on to the sidewalk that led up to the porch and saw Suzanne and her mother chatting and laughing. Her mother seemed happy here. She was glad for her. For so many years her mother had been alone after her father's death when she was just eight years old. Her mother had raised her and always been there for her. Still, she knew her mother missed sharing a life with a mate. Looking at her now, she saw how beautiful her mother was. The body she had now of Aunt Emory was just as beautiful as her mother's in 2016, graceful and elegant. Maybe she could find a good man in this time.

They saw her coming and waved her over smiling.

"Oh, my dear, we have been having a ball planning your wedding. I hope you don't mind!" said her mother.

"I'm sure your ideas are wonderful. Let's hear it!"

"Suzanne said you could marry here in the garden in the back and we'll have a dinner in the dining room. What do you think?"

She beamed. "I think it would be beautiful! We won't have a very big turnout since there isn't much family on either side. Suzanne and Mr. Clark are all the friends we have here."

"Then it will be perfect! The garden is cozy and the dining room will meet our needs." Suzanne smiled at her reassuringly.

"I couldn't be happier. I have everyone in the world that I need." She winked at her mother.

Her mother smiled but Everleigh could see a crestfallen faraway look in her eyes.

"Aunt Emory, it's alright. My father may not be able to give me away, but I know he is watching from heaven and thank heavens I have you since my mother can't be here. You remind me so much of her anyway."

Suzanne made a sad sound, "Oh, Everleigh. What a tragedy."

"No, no, Suzanne. It will be beautiful. Love has a way of untangling hearts in time."

Her mother squeezed her hand and gently turned up the corners of her mouth.

"You three have your heads together. What are you cooking up?"

His smooth voice caressed her ear and a zing of delight coursed down her spine. She turned to see him leaning against the porch with his arms crossed. She could have melted right into her chair as his gaze never wavered from her.

Suzanne stood up and crossed the porch, "We are planning your wedding, Mr. Steel. So far, all we need you to do is show up." She said it matter-of-factly, winking at him as she sauntered past the screen door of the foyer.

He smiled delighted and chuckled, "That's wonderful. Honestly, I don't care how it happens as long as I get to keep Miss Addison."

Everleigh blushed.

"So I just have to show up, huh?" he asked with all seriousness.

Aunt Emory chuckled. "Of course, young man! Suzanne said every eligible girl in this county will be fuming. We will need you to keep them from accosting Everleigh!"

"They never had a chance. I was waiting for the right one."

Everleigh stood up and crossed to him.

"Malcolm, I need to speak to you about something. Can we take a walk?" She turned back to her mother, "Do you mind, Aunt Emory?"

"No, not at all. When you get back, let's have supper with Suzanne and her husband."

"That sounds nice."

Malcolm held out his arm and she hooked her hand over his forearm. He led her down the steps of the porch and around the side to the garden. They strolled to the place they had sat before. A dragonfly swooped and circled around them before landing on a lily pad in the water of the little pond.

When they settled on the bench he turned to her, "What is it, my love?"

She thought about how to say this without revealing how she found out.

"Malcolm, you said that the title to your estate had a caveat for passing through inheritance."

"Yes. That is what the lawyer told me."

"The lawyer told you?"

"Yes, he showed me papers that said since there was no heir after my aunt and uncle died, that the estate went back to the government. It's true. I have seen the will with my own eyes."

She thought for a moment.

Why would a lawyer say that to him? Surely they would know that will was no longer enforceable.

"Why do you ask?"

"You see," she paused, "When I was in Charleston, I heard my father talking to a lawyer once about wills and estates. The lawyer there told him there is a thing called Rules of Perpetuity."

"Oh, I have not heard of these rules."

"Yes, apparently, when a property is the subject of a will or inheritance, the person receiving it must receive it within twenty-one years or it gets disbursed as if there was no will."

He looked at her and squinted his eyes, "So how does this affect my estate? I'm certain it passed to the next ancestor within twenty-one years of his death."

"Exactly. The will was executed. It was done."

"You mean after that, it no longer affected future generations?"

"Exactly! The estate just naturally passed to the next heir as it would normally."

He rested his chin on his knuckles with his elbow on his knee as he looked out over the garden. After a moment he turned to her and smiled.

"You are amazing! This is wonderful! This means the estate would either go to Percy or if not, then me. Percy and I are all that is left of our family."

"So really you have a choice. You could acknowledge Percy as the rightful heir, but that would mean bringing him out of hiding. Or, you could claim that you are the rightful heir and it would pass to you. You would care for Percy so he would still get the benefit for his lifetime."

He grimaced at the choices.

"I know you might not feel right having the estate in your name, but think about it, if his parents had put him in an asylum, you would be the heir anyway."

"It's a great deal to think about, but either way, it's better than losing it."

"I really think the lawyer is trying to swindle you. Which lawyer was it?"

"Mr. Skeller. He said he was appointed by the government."

She was not surprised. He nearly blew a fuse when he saw her in his office. She wondered if he was worried that she saw something he didn't want anyone to see.

"It might not hurt to have another lawyer, one who represents you, to take a look at this."

"That is a great idea! I know a fine man in Midway that I trust. I'll visit him tomorrow."

***

Everleigh sat outside at a patio table with a sketchbook. She was no architect, but she had sketched out plans for a school and dormitory. She hoped to convince Malcolm to dedicate a portion of his estate to this school. She was certain that she and Bethann could handle the duties at first until they needed more staff. Perhaps Bethann knew of others who had been taught like her that they could hire.

Of course they would have Percy as a student, but they would need to seek out others. She wondered if it was possible for any at the Asylum to come. Perhaps not. Maybe it was too late for them. On the other hand, maybe they could adopt children from the Children's Asylum. She decided that for now, they would focus on Down's kids since that was Bethann's area of expertise.

As she sketched, she added a therapy room for exercising, a recreational room for games and fine motor skills, and an outdoor playground. She wondered if there were any outdoor playgrounds in this time. She had not seen any like there were in 2016. She hadn't seen any city parks with playgrounds or even playgrounds at schools. She knew it wouldn't be too hard to build a playground to exercise gross motor skills. Besides, these kids need to have fun. She also added a kitchen to the design so that food could be prepared on site.

Lastly, she needed a place where the public could be invited. Community involvement was a must for increasing awareness. She sketched a Community Center were events could be scheduled. She would have to make it a place where groups could meet or she could plan events that would attract the community to come there. Maybe picnics or festivals. Maybe she could invite speakers to come and invite the community to come for free.

Her plan was two-fold: to have a place for Down's kids to live and thrive in a loving environment and to increase public awareness of people with disabilities. Since there were no eugenics laws in place yet, perhaps they could turn the tide for Kentucky. She could write a monthly newsletter and send it to the state representatives.

"Everleigh, may I join you?" her mother asked.

"Oh, yes, Momma."

"What are you doing?"

"I am designing the Williams Home School for Mongoloids. It is named in honor of Percy's parents."

"That is wonderful! Oh, Everleigh! When I hatched the plan to get you and Malcolm in the same century, I had no idea that so much more would come of it."

"I guess that's just how God is. He gives us so much more than we could ever dream of."

"And with the Addison's fortune, you have all the financial resources you will need."

"Yes. I am going to ask Malcolm if we can build it on his property, but I plan to finance it with my own money. I just wish there was a way to get the boy I saw at the Asylum."

"Well money talks. Couldn't you make a donation?"

"Of course, I could. I just don't know if they would be willing to let us have custody of him."

"You never know until you ask. Why don't you go speak to them?"

"It might be better if I do that after I have the school up and running with staff and all."

"That's true. I think it's a great idea, though."

Everleigh thought about the boy at the Asylum and wondered if his family still kept tabs on him. From what Malcolm had said, most babies were handed over and forgotten.

"I need to speak to an architect to design these plans."

"Plans for what, my love?" Malcolm came out onto the patio with the butler.

"Mr. Malcolm Steel, madam," said the butler.

"Malcolm! Just who I needed to talk to first!" said Everleigh.

"Well, I will leave you two love birds to your plans," Emory said and went inside.

"Sit down, Malcolm. I want to show you this." He sat down and she continued, "Its some sketches I drew for the Williams Home School for Mongoloids."

He looked at her curiously, "You are serious about this?"

"Oh, yes. I can see it in my mind. I really feel strongly about it."

He looked over her sketches while she pointed out the details.

"Malcolm, I was hoping we could build it on your estate. Would that be possible? That way it would be close to us and Percy would feel safe there."

He thought for a minute, "Of course, I have plenty of land. I see no reason why not."

"And I am using my money to finance it. It will have the best facilities and finest construction. I want it to be very safe and accessible. Bethann, if she wants to, can be the director. With her expertise, we can have a state of the art facility. I was hoping she might know of others that were taught under Dr. Downs that might be willing to come and work there."

"Everleigh, this is a big responsibility. We would be responsible for the health and welfare of the residents."

"Yes. I understand. I think we can do this. I have a great deal of knowledge in this area and the financial means. If we can hire people like Bethann, we can make a difference to some individuals that live there. More importantly, we can change the way society sees Mongoloids and maybe affect change in politics. Will you help me?"

"He laughed, "You know I will. Where will you find residents?"

"I am thinking we can adopt children from the Asylum for Children and then in time, maybe instead of people dropping off infants at an orphanage, they would send them to our school."

"I see."

"Malcolm, do you think we could get custody or guardianship of the boy at the Lunatic Asylum? I don't even know his name, but he doesn't belong there."

"I'm not sure. Maybe the lawyer would know."

She could see it in her mind, the building, the children, and laughter from the windows. She looked at Malcolm and knew that together they could do anything. They could make a difference to Percy and so many more. She thought about how her life before in 2016 was useful, but now she could do so much more.

"Everleigh, you amaze me. Never in a million years would I dream of finding a woman like you."

He enveloped her with his arms and gently held her, minding her injury. She felt like her heart was soaring. Her life was no longer the hollow, feeble movements of a lost heart. Her love for him eclipsed all of her insecurities and her future as an advocate gave her an unshakable confidence.

***

The seamstress pinned and turned her as she stood on the small wood stool. She had on a long corset that had cinched her waist to a size that she could actually get her finger tips to overlap. She worried about her internal organs. Over that, the seamstress had tied on the metal bustle forms, one hung over her back side and one hung low in an arc behind her like half a hoop skirt but pinched on the sides. Next she hung a cotton corset cover to protect the dress. Finally she tied on layers of petticoats that hung straight but had lace at the bottom. The bodice was finished and the seamstress held it up, open in the back for her to slip her arms into the tight lace sleeves with a small ruffle of lace at the wrist. The silk bodice was perfectly tailored to lay flat around her sides and had vertical gathered silk across her bust. Delicate lace then covered her all the way to her neck where a standing collar rose another inch with a soft lace ruffle that tickled her chin when she looked down.

She felt slightly stifled in the bodice with the corset and hoped she wouldn't pass out from not being able to take a deep breath. Once the seamstress buttoned the hundred or so buttons up the back, she began pinning panels of fabric to her bodice for the skirt. It seemed to Everleigh that the woman had unrolled bolts and bolts of glowing white silk, sown them together side by side and was now pinning about fifty yards of draped silk around her. It was like she had on hundreds of layered aprons from her waist to the black pointy toes of her shoes.

The seamstress looked it over darting from side to side and then pulled out two large triangular pieces of fabric where she had sown rows and rows of lace ruffles from the point at the top to the wide base at the bottom. Tiny pearls had been sown to it that caught the light like little candles. Cords of clusters of pearls hung over the top of the layers of lace. A large lace ruffle edged it all the way around. She pinned these to the sides of the skirt so that the aprons of silk disappeared underneath it.

"This gown is amazing! I feel like a royal princess!"

The seamstress smiled and kept working her magic, obviously pleased with the acknowledgement.

"It must have taken you hours, day and night, to sew on the pearls."

She nodded and her fingers flew. She finally stood and appraised the skirt so far. Then she pulled out of another bag a long swath of what had to be another twenty yards of silk. Gathering it into folds, she pinned it over the bustle in the back and along the edge of the lace ruffle she had just finished. It had wide scallops of lace and silk with seeds of pearls in the lace along the edge that would drag on the floor as her train.

Pleased with the result, the seamstress then pulled out a roll of sheer silk gauze with a lace and pearl gather at the top. She shook it out and pinned it to the crown of Everleigh's head. It nearly fell all the way to the floor.

Standing back appraising her work, the seamstress finally asked, "What do you think?"

Everleigh gushed, "It's the most beautiful gown I have ever seen. Thank you!"

Her mother stood with her mouth parted in a gawking stare, taking in the sight from head to toe, "Everleigh, you look like an angel from heaven. I am not sure which glows more, you or the gown."

"The silk, it does catch the light nicely, no?" The seamstress had a slight French accent which made her seem so authentic for fashion design to Everleigh.

"Of course, it is the nicest quality you can find. I don't work with cheap fabric." She sniffed and wrinkled her nose as though the thought of cheap fabric made her ill.

"I absolutely love it! It couldn't be more perfect."

"Alright then. Let me put in some stitches to hold it in place and then I will take it home to finish it. It will take another, let me see," she tapped her finger to her mouth, "three or four days, I think, to piece it together and get it back."

After the seamstress finished, packed it carefully away and left, Everleigh put her day dress back on with her mother's help and they had lunch outside under a tall oak tree. A table was set with a tablecloth and china as though they were in the dining room. Malcolm arrived while they were outside and the butler led him out to their picnic in the shade.

"Malcolm, come and join us. Have you eaten? Barnes, please have another place set for Mr. Steel."

"Oh, don't go to any bother. I had lunch before I left home, thank you. Perhaps just a glass of lemonade."

Taking their hands one at a time, he kissed them in greeting. He joined them at a seat the butler brought out.

"I came to share some news. The lawyer I spoke with in Midway was very helpful. He thinks he can get to the bottom of it quickly. You were right, Everleigh. The restriction on the deed from the will was lifted after the first heir received it. After that, the estate passed as it would have. Now it will be placed in my name. Percy has a trust fund established to ensure his care no matter what happens to me. If

Percy outlives us, the deed changes to a life estate for Percy so that he can stay there for his lifetime."

"Oh, Malcolm, that is wonderful!" she said. "And that reminds me, I meant to ask you, has Percy been examined for his heart? He may need surgery. It's very common for Mongoloids, to need a surgery to extend their life."

"Oh, no. I didn't know that. It's very hard to get a doctor to agree to treat him. Oftentimes they refuse."

She shook her head. "We will find a doctor if we have to go all the way to London."

He smiled, "Now that I am confident that I can provide for you and Percy, we just need to set a date for our nuptials."

Everleigh nearly squealed but caught herself.

Her mother smiled delighted, "I would think we could pull our plans together for next Saturday. A week from today."

"The sooner, the better." He took Everleigh's hand and kissed it again watching her through smoldering eyes.

"You two! Heavens! You'll be impossible to be around." Then she sighed and added, "But I am so happy for both of you."

Everleigh giggled.

"Are you going to take a honeymoon?" her mother asked.

Malcolm made a growling groan and kissed the rest of the way up Eveleigh's arm.

"Yes, I am planning to take my bride to a wonderful place called Cumberland Falls. It's a massive waterfall and on some nights, a great moonbow glows over the falls. We can take the train to Williamsburg and stay in a section house for the railroad. Then travel by horseback to the water fall with a guide. I think it would be the perfect place to become acquainted as husband and wife."

Everleigh blushed a deep glowing red as a zing of passion hit the visceral depth of her core.

"That sounds like such a romantic adventure, Malcolm!" said her mother.

***

The week passed quickly. Everleigh dreamed of her new life and had never been so content. She had a seamstress come to create a new wardrobe for her. Malcolm's estate was preparing to receive its new occupant as the staff polished and scrubbed. The staff felt a tremendous joy for Malcolm. They'd loved him dearly and now he would have his own happiness. Percy rocked and swayed in his own little dance when he heard the news. Malcolm told him he would have a mother now to love him as much as he did. The little boy beamed a huge smile and hugged him.

"Can I call you da-dee? Bethann showed me a book with a picture and the boy called the man da-dee. Bethann told me what a da-dee is."

Malcolm hugged the little boy tightly. "Yes, Percy. I would be proud if you called me daddy."

"I love you, da-dee."

***

Everleigh was reviewing her plans for the school at a desk in her mother's home when Malcolm stopped by. The butler let him in and he rushed to embrace her, kissing her slowly and tenderly.

"Malcolm, what a pleasure to see you!" she breathed.

"My love, my thoughts of you as my wife have made me exceedingly impatient. I cannot wait to show you the depths of my emotion."

She giggled and blushed slightly, "Malcolm! I'm glad I make you happy."

She gave him a quick peck on the lips again. He smiled and his smoldering gaze made her blush deeper. She turned and pulled him to the couch.

"Now did you come here to just stare at me or is there something else?" she smiled coyly.

Regaining his composure, "Yes. I wanted to tell you, I spoke to my lawyer about your idea and the boy at the Lunatic Asylum. He said he could help us with both accounts. As for the boy, we could seek guardianship from the state. The problem, of course, is we don't know who he is and it may be hard to find that out. We can't just go there and walk the halls looking for him."

Her brows furrowed with two wavy horizontal lines as she tried to figure out what to do.

He continued, "At this point it may look odd that we want to bring home a person we know nothing about."

"I can see that," she paused. "What if we told them we were opening the School and wanted to review a patient to see if they would benefit from the therapies?"

He scratched the back of his neck mulling it over, "That seems reasonable."

"We can try, at least."

"Alright then, let's go. I have time now if you do."

"I do!"

Cook packed them a basket of food and they headed out in her carriage. After a little more than an hour, they were turning into the gates of the Lunatic Asylum. The serene lawn with shady oak and maple trees made it look more like a resort to her.

The three-story main building appeared quiet like a very large personal residence. They approached the door and knocked with the large brass knocker. An orderly opened the door and greeted them. He eyed them both up and down. She wondered if he was trying to figure out if one of them was being committed.

"Can I help you," he asked.

"Yes," Malcolm answered, "We would like to speak to someone about one of your patients.

"I see. Please come in." He ushered them into a small parlor. "I will see if the Superintendent is available."

He left them alone briefly and returned motioning for them to follow.

"Mr. Morgan will see you in his office."

"Thank you," Malcolm said.

They entered a plain office with a desk and windows filling the room with the afternoon light. Mr. Morgan rose and shook Malcolm's hand and nodded to Everleigh.

"How can I help you today?" he asked.

Malcolm looked at Everleigh and she nodded. He began, "Mr. Morgan, thank you for seeing us. My soon-to-be bride and I are planning to open a school for Mongoloids in Versailles. We have access to trained staff that learned under Dr. Down's in England."

"I see. That sounds like quite an undertaking. Do you have experience with these patients?"

"Yes," he looked at Everleigh again before answering, "I have cared for my young nephew for a few years who is a Mongoloid."

Mr. Morgan eyed Malcolm, no doubt wondering why the child had not been surrendered to the Children's Asylum.

"Well then, you understand the challenges of caring for the insane."

Malcolm nearly choked on his answer, "Yes."

"What can I do for you, then?"

"Mr. Morgan, I work for the railroad and on a recent delivery, we saw a young man who was a Mongoloid. He was probably in his teens. We were hoping to be able to evaluate him to see if our school's therapies would benefit him."

Mr. Morgan looked from Malcolm to Everleigh before answering. "Mr.—uh, Steel, is that right?"

Malcolm nodded.

"Mr. Steel, we take the care of our residents very seriously. I cannot allow them to become the objects of experiments which have no basis in fact."

Everleigh's mind was busting to speak, "Mr. Morgan, Dr. Downs has proven therapies that have helped Mongoloids achieve a level of ability to be useful and fulfilled. They are not just experiments. Malcolm's nephew is only four, yet he does not act *insane* in any way."

"Be that as it may," he started to say.

"Does the young man of whom we speak have family we could consult?"

Mr. Morgan shifted in his chair, "No. He was orphaned. I am responsible for his well-being."

"What if we brought Mrs. Monroe to speak to you?"

"I don't think that—," he started to say.

Everleigh was becoming irritated but kept her cool. The thought occurred to her, *Money talks.*

"Mr. Morgan, I am certain you have a great deal of expenses providing this wonderful serene home for your residents. It's really beautiful here. You have done such a great job."

He smiled waiting.

"Would it be possible for me to make a contribution to the Asylum to help you further your work? Perhaps you are facing a crowding issue and new dormitory would help."

She let her proposal float in the air. Mr. Morgan looked at her with new interest.

"Am I to assume you would have the means to make such a contribution?"

"Yes, sir. I am quite capable of funding a new building project for the Asylum."

"I see. That would be exceedingly generous. Yes, we are experiencing rapid growth." He sighed. "I'm certain that something could be arranged." Then he quickly added, "Of course, we would need to monitor young Matthew's health and progress at your school to be certain he was getting the best care possible."

"Of course. In fact we would love to work together to share ideas for the best care for all Mongoloids. I'm certain you have other residents like Matthew."

He paused before speaking as though weighing the risks and benefits, "Alright then. I think we have an agreement. Wait here while I ask the orderly to bring Matthew to meet you."

He left the room and Everleigh smiled at Malcolm.

"Money talks."

"What?"

"It's a saying where I come from."

"That's quite a donation!"

"It's alright. In fact, it's great. It gives us leverage to open the communication with the Asylum. It starts a partnership that gives us a way to influence their care of Mongoloids."

His pleased smirk told her he was impressed with her negotiation skills. Mr. Morgan returned with a file in his hand.

"Alright, while we are waiting, I have some documents you will need to sign. Then we will need to be certain your contribution to the Asylum is wired. If all goes well, Matthew should be ready to accompany you by tomorrow afternoon."

Everleigh was delighted. They gave Mr. Morgan the information he needed and before long there was a knock at the door.

"Come in," said Mr. Morgan.

The door opened and the young man stepped through. His mouth was turned down and his eyes were wide. Everleigh realized he was afraid and must think he is in trouble.

Then he looked at her and the frown of fear melted slowly as recognition hit him.

"Pretty lady," he said.

"Hello Matthew."

"I go with you?" His wide eyes questioned her as his mouth fell slack.

"Yes, Matthew. Would you like to live with us? We are starting a school that will help you and you can live there."

His grin now stretched from ear to ear. He looked at Mr. Morgan and the frown dropped in anticipation of his answer.

"Yes, Matthew. It's alright. Mr. Steel and his new wife will be taking care of you."

The beaming expression returned and he raised his arms for a hug waiting to see if she was alright with it. She strode toward him and embraced him. He breathed a great sigh of relief.

Pulling back he took her hand in his as he said, "Thank you, pretty lady. Thank you." He kissed the back of her hand and his face lit with joy.

After talking to Matthew about his life, they left to send the telegram to wire the money to the Asylum so that it would be available first thing in the morning. The sun was low on the horizon when they started the trip back to Versailles.

The next morning, Malcolm came to pick her up and they returned to the Asylum.

"Are you ready?" he asked as she stepped toward his carriage.

She leaned in to kiss his cheek and replied, "Let's go bring Matthew home."

***

The morning light streamed through the windows in bright sparkling beams. Everleigh opened her eyes and rolled over. She yawned and stretched and smiled. She and her mother had stayed at the Inn to avoid having to travel that morning.

Today is my wedding day!

Suzanne and her mother burst into the room as though an alarm had gone off to alert them she was awake. They carried baskets of toiletries to work on her. She felt better than a kid at Christmas.

A maid with a tray of food followed them and set it over her lap as she scooted up on the pillow.

"Good morning, beautiful bride!" said her mother.

"Eat up so we can get to work! Sally, start bringing up buckets of hot water for the tub," said Suzanne. Finding a bar of soap with Everleigh's stockings, she sniffed it. "Oh, this lavender soap is nice. Maybe you should use it instead."

Both Everleigh and her mother shouted, "No!" at the same time. Her mother snatched it away.

"Oh, alright then. You don't have to be so grabby about it."

She bathed and towel dried. She'd washed her hair the day before to give it time to dry. Her mother brushed and brushed it until it shined like the glowing sun.

They helped her with her stockings, shoes, bloomers, corset and corset cover. The petticoats, bustle hoops, and finally the gown was gently lowered over her head and buttoned. Suzanne took over doing her hair by pulling it up into a twist with small braids and tiny curls around her face pinned with tiny pins with pearls attached. The pearls looked like they floated around her head.

Her mother dusted talc powder on her face to take away any shine and pinched her cheeks for color. Suzanne had a tiny jar of crushed berries to lightly stain her lips. Finally they held open a pair of white gloves for her to slip her hands into.

The two women stood back and admired her. Tears formed in her mother's eyes and threatened to spill.

"Oh, Everleigh! You are such a beautiful bride!" Suzanne whispered.

Her mother brushed a soft kiss on her cheek and whispered, "I'm so glad to be here with you today."

Everleigh nodded and tried not to cry herself.

"Alright, we are going to go check on the groom and the garden. You stay here and don't move."

She laughed, "Alright, alright!"

They closed the door behind them and her mind reeled. She couldn't believe this was really happening. She thought back to just a month ago when she arrived. So much had happened. She had changed. She thought of the woman in 2016 getting in a bathtub in the Inn. She had been so lonely and empty. She hated her body and felt powerless to change.

It took more than gaining a twenty year old hot body to change her. While that helped her refocus, she found a person inside her that was brave and strong, willing to sacrifice herself to save others. She had great respect for herself and she loved the skin she was in.

***

Malcolm stood waiting at the carriage with his driver. Matthew stepped out of the front door hesitantly. He had adjusted well the last few days. Bethann had begun to work with him by helping him learn to comb his own hair and wash himself.

Malcolm hired a butler to help him dress and tend to his needs. The butler was a patient man that had taken care of his father as palsy had diminished him. He was used to having to assist with daily living needs. Matthew had not been taught how to conduct himself other than how to avoid making his caregiver mad at him. While he was a gentle young man, no one had taken the time to teach him any manners or courtesy. The Asylum assumed he was a lunatic and beyond help.

With Bethann's help, he had already learned to sit and not interrupt conversation and to say please and thank you. He looked to her for help when he didn't know what to say or do. Anyone could see he was trying so hard to learn.

As he quietly made his way to Malcolm, each step grew more purposeful with confidence. Malcolm smiled at him and held out his hands.

"Matthew, look at you! You are quite a gentleman in your suit."

"Mr. Parker helped me."

"I'm so glad you are a part of our family. Are you nervous about coming to the wedding?"

Matthew hung his head, "What if I scare somebody? At the Asylum, they says I look like a freak and scare ladies if they see's me."

Malcolm put his hand on his shoulder, "Matthew, listen to me. Do you think Mrs. Bethann or Miss Adderly are scared of you?"

Matthew slowly raised his head and looked into Malcolm's eyes. "No, sir. They's not scared. They smile at me and they are nice to me."

"See? What the people at the Asylum said to you is not true. You are not a freak. You are a kind, gentle young man. As people get to know you, they will see in you what we do. I believe that."

Matthew's lips slightly turned up and he nodded. Malcolm watched him climb into the carriage and marveled at his bravery. It would have been so much easier for him to hide at home, but Matthew had a courageous heart. He was also surrounded by people who loved him as the young man God made him to be.

Percy came out the front door holding Bethann's hand and toddled over to the carriage. Malcolm smiled a wide delighted smile at the boy. His brown knickers and coat made him look like a little doll. He wore a little brown hat and brown knee socks and shoes. The socks had to be turned down halfway down his calf because his legs were short. His little round glasses distorted his eyes making them look much bigger than they were, giving him a wide-eyed look of joy. His exuberant smile crowned the whole outfit.

"Look at you little man!" Malcolm picked the little boy up and squeezed him. "I love you, Percy."

"I love you, too, Da-dee." He giggled.

"Now, you must understand that you are such a special little man that some people may not be used to seeing such a cute fella. They may stare or whisper. Just smile at them and know that people who know you think you are precious. The others just haven't been able to know you yet."

"Al-white, Da-dee." He fiddled with Malcolm's lapel.

Malcolm kissed him again and lifted him into the carriage.

"Bethann," he whispered, if anything happens, if anyone makes a scene, I want you to whisk Percy and Matthew away, do you understand? I will not let them be subject to anyone's scorn."

"Certainly, Mr. Steel. I understand. They will have to get through me if they try anything."

He smiled at her threat and lifted her into the carriage. A wagon behind them with the house staff followed to see the wedding. They had told Malcolm they would not miss it.

Malcolm cast a worried look over the boys in the carriage. This was the first time either of them had been out in public. They both fidgeted nervously and looked around waiting. Everleigh insisted they be present at the wedding, not just to witness the event, but also to begin the process of exposing the townspeople to them. The more people saw them, the less fearful they would be. At least that's what Everleigh had told him. It was hard for him to believe but she seemed so certain that the people's mere exposure to them would slowly change the way they were perceived. He hoped she was right. She told him to expect stares and even gasping, but in time, the people would see that Percy and Matthew were nothing to be afraid of.

The carriage and wagon made the journey to downtown in good time and they assembled in the garden at the Inn. Some of the staff from Aunt Emory's were seated, too. A minister stood near an arbor that had ribbons and flowers entwined around it. Suzanne and her sister had spent the afternoon decorating. Mr. Clark chatted with the minister and directed staff to set out chairs or help guests. The shade of the tall trees around the garden cooled the air. Roses and lilies seemed to have bloomed on every plant to celebrate the day. Gladiolas and honeysuckle blossoms colored the walls of the small enchanted escape and scented the air with an intoxicating fragrance.

Suzanne swept in from the back and whispered in her husband's ear. He nodded and looked around for Malcolm. Malcolm came down the path just then holding Percy's hand.

"Is that the boy?" Suzanne asked Edward.

"I suppose so. Cute little fella, isn't he." Edward smiled softly.

"Yes. I'm not sure what I expected, but he does seem like a little doll. Look at him smile. Poor Cecelia. She bore that burden all alone. I wish I could have helped her."

"And look. The young man behind them. That must be the boy they took in."

"Darling, do you think it's safe? What if he—you know, becomes disturbed?"

"I suppose we will just have to trust Mr. Steel that he can handle him if that happens."

Malcolm stopped in front of the Clarks and held his head high, "Mr. and Mrs. Clark, I would like to introduce my nephew Percy and Matthew. Matthew is living with us now and will be a student at our school."

Percy bowed his practiced greeting. His smile and joyful eyes could melt the coldest heart. Matthew looked at Bethann who nodded.

"Nice to meet you," he spoke slowly and nodded at the Clarks.

Suzanne looked surprised as though she didn't expect them to be able to speak. Catching herself in her awkwardness, she blurted, "Oh! How wonderful that you could be here. It's such a pleasure to make your acquaintance."

Malcolm sighed in relief, "Thank you, Mrs. Clark. Your kindness is appreciated."

Suzanne nodded, "Of course, Mr. Steel. Forgive me. Your family—and friends, are always welcome at the Inn. Any time."

Mr. Clark patted his wife's hand. "Is Miss Adderly ready?"

"Oh yes. Everything is just beautiful. Isn't the garden lovely? I've never seen it so full of life."

"Yes, my darling. Of course, compared to you, it pales." He kissed her hand.

She giggled, "Oh my, you rogue!"

Malcolm helped his staff find seats and took Bethann, Percy and Mathew to the front to seats set aside for them.

"Mr. Steel," a man called to him from a seat behind them.

"Oh, Mr. Goodman! So glad you could come!"

Mr. Goodman was a tall man with a commanding countenance. His black hair shimmered with silver around his temples. He jumped to his feet and a dazzling flash of teeth greeted Malcolm.

"The way you gushed about this gorgeous bride, I had to see her for myself."

"I see! Should I be worried you'll steal her heart away before the wedding is over?"

Mr. Goodman chuckled, "Never fear, young man. My heart belongs to another. Besides, I wanted to give you these papers." He handed him a packet of parchment tied with a thin red ribbon.

"The documents have been filed and the deed is secured as you wished. Mr. Skeller, on the other hand, is being investigated. It is clear he was intentionally attempting to defraud you."

"I am in your debt, sir. Thank you so very much. Please send me your bill and I shall pay you handsomely."

"Oh! No, no. It's a wedding gift. Your bride, you said her name is Everleigh, right?"

"Yes. Do you know her?"

"I used to know an Everleigh, in Charleston, you see." He looked away up into the trees.

"I see. Who was she? My Everleigh is from Charleston. Perhaps this is the same girl."

"Oh, she was just a little girl I once knew. A very special little girl. So I did this for her, in her memory."

"Ah. I'm terribly sorry for your loss."

"What lives in our heart is never lost."

Malcolm nodded, "I'm so glad you could be here. It means a great deal to me."

Aunt Emory came down the aisle looking for Suzanne to see how long until she should bring Everleigh downstairs. She turned to look behind her and, not looking where she was going, bumped into Mr. Goodman.

"Oh, I'm so sorry. I really should look where I'm going." She turned and looked up into his eyes and stopped with her mouth open. "Oh. Hello handsome. Are you a friend of Mr. Steel?"

"I'm an associate of his." He looked at her carefully, "You seem familiar in some way, but I don't think I have ever met you."

"Oh," said Malcolm, "Miss Heartwell, this is my attorney, Mr. Goodman. Mr. Goodman, this is Everleigh's aunt."

Mr. Goodman took her hand and kissed it, pausing before releasing her. Standing back up, he looked at her curiously and asked, "By chance, would you have ever met a man by the name of," he cleared his throat, "Daniel. Daniel Anderson? An attorney?"

Holding his breath, he didn't move until she spoke. She sucked in her breath and all the color from her face turned ashen.

"D- Daniel Anderson," she stuttered. "Yes. Yes, I *used* to know a man by that name. It's been a very long time, though. Years, and years." She clutched her handkerchief to her mouth and stared.

"I, uh, I used to know him, also," he stammered without taking his eyes off hers.

Breathing in gasping starts, "How? How could you possibly have known him? Did you know his wife, Charlotte Anderson, then?" She waited with wide eyes.

He closed his eyes, stood very still and then opened them again. Taking a deep breath, he took her hand again. His face flushed and a grin spread across his face.

"Madam, could we talk for a minute, privately? In the parlor?" He glanced at Malcolm as though he didn't want anyone to hear their conversation.

"Yes. Yes I think we should," she mumbled barely audibly.

Malcolm nodded as Mr. Goodman gestured with an apologetic face. Excusing himself, the two of them made their way inside.

Alone in the parlor, he turned to her, pausing in an awkward silence when neither seemed to know just how to start.

Finally he took the plunge and asked, "How is this possible? Is it you, Charlotte?" Hope filled his face.

She smiled with every muscle in her face and tears brewed, then spilled over her lower eyelid and down her cheeks.

"Daniel? Daniel? Is it you?" she cried.

"Yes! I don't know how. It makes no sense. A few months ago." He started talking in disjointed thoughts. "I remember the accident. I knew I would never survive. I saw the truck coming right at me and there was no way to get out of its way. I heard a horrific crunch and then everything went black and I woke up here, in 1888, in this body." He gestured at himself and looked at his hands as if he'd never seen them before.

"What? Did you say a few months ago? Daniel! It's been twenty-seven years. Everleigh is-- she is thirty-five, except, now she is twenty. It's complicated."

"Thirty-five! What? That's impossible." He wobbled a bit and lowered himself in a chair to get his bearings. "Oh, Charlotte. You raised her all alone." He grimaced and smiled at the same time. "I'm so sorry to leave you. I didn't want to."

"Oh, you silly! It's not like you had a choice." She took the chair next to him and he grasped her hands in his.

"I wracked my brain trying to figure a way to get back to you but, short of a time machine, there was no way."

"It's so odd. It's like we were all drawn here together."

"And how did you all get here? Did you," he stuttered at the thought, "did you die, too?" He braced himself with a grimace waiting for her answer.

"No! A woman. A very special woman in France, who apparently had a gift to see more than normal people can, gave me a bar of soap that, well, brought us here. Sounds crazy, I know. Honestly, I think the soap was just a key to follow God's will all along. We are in different bodies, but we are still us. Only God could have brought us all together here." She swept her hand out in the air.

Overcome with emotion, he pulled her to him and kissed her. She held his face with her hands and tears of joy fell. He feverishly kissed her cheeks and forehead and then gazed in her eyes.

"Oh, Daniel, I missed you so much for so long. You don't look like my Daniel, but I can recognize your touch, your soul."

"I've missed you, too. I love you, Charlotte. It's a miracle! It doesn't matter what body you are in. You are the love of my life. You always will be."

She smiled, "What's more, you will get to see our daughter wed to the love of her life. Apparently 1888 is a good place to find a husband!"

***

Malcolm looked over the guest gathered in the garden and joy filled his soul. In the short span of a few weeks, his life had gone from lonely and reclusive to bursting with love. Matthew and Percy sat in their seats quietly taking in the multitude of new things to see and hear.

Malcolm wondered how they were not overwhelmed or afraid. Young Matthew had been locked away all his life with very little to stimulate his mind. Percy had been tutored but had never left the safety of the estate and rarely even ventured downstairs.

Malcolm's eyes scanned the guests and saw only smiles and happy conversation. No one pointed at the boys or singled them out. The love the guests had for this new family resonated in a safe bubble around the whole garden. He realized that was what Everleigh meant. When people know you, they love you despite your imperfections. The only way to beat the fear of being different or imperfect was to increase the number of people who knew them.

It wouldn't be easy and it surely would not always be like this moment, but they had a safe place to start from. They would venture out into the Versailles community and then all of Kentucky. One heart at a time, they would change the lives of those who are hiding like he and Percy were.

***

Suzanne's sister Faith played a wedding march on a small flute. The light reedy music floated on the air as Malcolm stood waiting for Everleigh. She appeared in the doorway like a real life garden fairy ensconced in a shapely cloud of silk and lace. Her blond hair swooped up on her head and tiny curls framed her face. Her rosebud mouth curled up when her eyes fell on Malcolm. All the guests faded from her sight as she felt the covering of his love wrap around her. The invisible cord that had pulled her across a century to his presence tightened, propelling her forward down the aisle, closing the gap of time and space until his hand clasped firmly around hers.

She barely heard the words spoken by the minister. Their responses to pledging their lives and love seemed like a dream conversation as a vortex of energy swept them into an ethereal heaven. Captivated by his gaze, Everleigh heard the words, *I now pronounce you man and wife.* Malcolm pulled her in toward him, encircled her with his protective arms, and kissed her tenderly. She had gone through time and space and survived criminal violence, but now, at last, her dreams had come true.

~The End

If you enjoyed this book, please leave a review on Amazon and Goodreads. Reviews help other readers discover great books through personal recommendations and by boosting books higher in search results.

If you would like to read more from this author, look for Carolyn Bond's book *Between Time* on Amazon. You can also follow her on her web page at www.carolynbondwriter.com.

23051663R60143

Made in the USA
Columbia, SC
07 August 2018